NIGHT, FORGOTTEN

NIGHT, FORGOTTEN

MEGHAN JOYCE TOZER

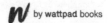 by wattpad books

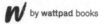 by **wattpad** books

An imprint of Wattpad WEBTOON Book Group

Content Warning: sexual violence, trauma, postpartum depression,
medical malpractice, post-traumatic stress disorder

Published in Canada by Wattpad WEBTOON Book Group, a division of Wattpad Corp.

36 Wellington Street E., Suite 200, Toronto, ON M5E 1C7 Canada

www.wattpad.com

First W by Wattpad Books edition: November 2022

ISBN 978-1-99025-942-5 (Trade Paper original)

ISBN 978-1-99025-943-2 (eBook edition)

Library and Archives Canada Cataloguing in Publication information
is available upon request.

Printed and bound in Canada

1 3 5 7 9 10 8 6 4 2

Cover design by Greg Tabor

Images © belovodchenko, © alvarez via iStock, © nblx via Shutterstock

Typesetting by Greg Tabor

Author photo by Ryan Bates

For Amie and Jonathan.

NOW

CHAPTER 1

I watch my body giving birth from the outside. The obstetrician's hands reach into the cavern of my torso, which is pinned open like a science project.

My husband, Owen, sits on a low stool next to my head. He stares at my closed eyelids. With his wavy blond hair trapped beneath a creased hospital cap and sweat soaking into the neckline of his hastily donned scrubs, Owen looks like a character in a soap opera. Paler, though. In fact, he's much paler than usual. His jaw is visibly tense.

I want to hold his face in my hands and thank him for still being awake beside me, after everything that's happened. But my hands won't move.

A blue curtain hangs perpendicular to the horror show of my open abdomen. It's meant to shield Owen's eyes, mercifully, from this new angle of my senseless body in case he looks away from my face. He doesn't.

From above, though, I see everything. I try to scream. *Wake me up! Put my body back together!*

They must have given me the good drugs because despite my efforts, nothing happens. No one in the room reacts to me.

In addition to Owen on the stool and the surgeon, whom I don't recognize, four or five youngish people in scrubs— medical students, probably—gather in the corner near the door. One of them keeps twisting his shoulders away from the operating table in brief, nauseated jerks. Several assistants deliver tools or directions, type at computers sitting on rolling desks, and yank ream after ream of paper from humming monitors. Two nurses with pinched foreheads flank the doctor, who cups the baby above my open body. The baby is purple. Silent.

A hush falls over the operating room and smothers the passage of time. Everyone pools their breath for the sake of the new life among us, collectively inhaling and holding . . . holding . . . until we can be sure the baby has gotten the air it needs.

Finally, a whine escapes from its impossibly tiny body. The doctor hands the baby—a slimy fledgling person—to one of the waiting nurses to be cleaned, measured, incubated.

Owen's head snaps up. His gaze darts from my face to that of my son.

As he watches the baby, I recognize the emotion in his eyes. Anger.

• • •

By the time I come back into my body, the anger has retreated from Owen's face. He wilts now, hunched forward over his knees with his chin in his hands. The scrubs are gone; he's in the same faded Guster T-shirt and jeans he was wearing when we left the house. The fluorescent glare of a single rectangular light among a grid of Styrofoam ceiling tiles darkens the lines around his frown. It feels like we've been in the hospital for more than a lifetime.

We're seated across from each other on sanitized upholstery in a poorly ventilated, aggressively beige hospital waiting room. I assume we're next in line to be discharged. I wish they'd hurry the process along; now that I'm no longer pregnant, I'm anxious to be back home with Owen and our sweet mutt, Daisy. And the baby.

The waiting room's only other occupant, a young woman in a pink fluid-stained sweat suit, sleeps upright on the plastic bench against the opposite wall. From the angular slant of her legs, I can tell someone has propped her there. Her wheelchair, wedged behind the door to the hallway, will be inaccessible when she wakes up. Whoever pushed it out of the way might have intended to be helpful, but they've effectively stranded her.

If I can kick her wheelchair over so that it's within her arm's reach, she won't panic when she wakes up. She won't have to call someone for help. Numb from the persistent effect of postsurgical painkillers, I lunge forward. Making it over to the wheelchair feels like wading through viscous, sucking mud, but I manage to nudge it. Close enough.

The wheelchair squeaks as it rolls, and Owen flinches. We haven't had a moment alone to collect ourselves since we rushed to Dr. Syed's office earlier today. On the drive over, Owen predicted that Dr. Syed might prescribe bed rest for the third trimester. I'd half listened, convinced the fetus was dying inside of me. Neither of us expected to become parents today.

"Hey," I whisper.

At the same time, a door swings open on the other side of the waiting room and an unfamiliar nurse appears. The young woman in the pink sweat suit stirs. She blinks, locates her wheelchair, and looks up at the nurse with raised eyebrows.

"Porter?" the nurse calls.

Owen jumps to his feet and drags his hands down his face, as if to wipe off the exhaustion. The sign above the door says NICU. We haven't been waiting to be discharged from the hospital at all. We've been waiting outside the St. Elizabeth's neonatal intensive care unit to meet the baby.

The nurse leads us into an antechamber with a sink, where she provides us with surgical masks and instructs us to wash our hands. Then she pushes open another door into a large, dimly lit space that bustles with controlled urgency.

"Come with me," she says, and we follow her to a bassinet in the far corner. To reach it, we must weave among a dozen swaddled bodies on elevated tables, attached to IV stands. Their grunts and gasps are barely audible over the whirring and humming of life-giving machines.

Another couple huddles over a bassinet against the window. They alternate between sniffling into wadded tissues and speaking in hushed voices to the oblivious, unconscious creature below them.

We stop in front of the bassinet over which someone has scrawled on a whiteboard, THOMAS PORTER. He must be one of the smallest babies in here. I was only twenty-seven weeks and three days pregnant when we arrived at the hospital. His entire two-and-a-half-pound body is about the size of Owen's hand.

Countless cords and tubes protrude from beneath the muslin blanket in which he's swaddled, and his gray face is nearly obscured by the oxygen tube taped across it. Someone's smeared a clear, antibiotic goo across his eyelids, which are sealed in a shapeless dream. His fingers flutter in little fists that curl and uncurl, grasping at nothing. It doesn't look like he should be alive.

He reminds me of a finch that died, years ago, on the steps to the entrance of my parents' house. A barely feathered lump, trembling on the bricks beside the welcome mat. My parents had sent a driver to the Bemont School in Deerfield, where I'd already been living for six months, to bring me home to Needham for the weekend. A rare occasion, and only because it was my tenth birthday. The finch, newly hatched, must have fallen from a cup of twigs nestled behind the holly wreath on the front door. I leaned down to scoop it up with my hands, to rescue it, but stopped myself. Mother birds, I'd read somewhere, would reject their babies once a human had touched them.

While I hesitated, the heavy front door swung inward, jostling the nest without dislodging it, and my father's cognac-colored penny loafers stepped down onto the welcome mat. With one worn-in leather sole he scraped the bird's body across the bricks and into the hedges.

"You made good time," he said, as if nothing had died beneath his foot. "Mom's picking up a gift for you on her way back from campus. Happy birthday, kiddo."

My mother had arrived hours later, empty-handed. She'd joined us for cake, though, that birthday.

I don't want to think about my parents today. Today is a different child's birthday. My child. And my child, blessedly, will have Owen for a father.

"There, there, little miracle," the nurse whispers to Thomas. She finishes detaching the wires from his body and tucks them, for the moment, into his swaddling blanket. "This sturdy little boy is doing really well so far," she tells us in the same tone, as if Owen and I are also infants in need of soothing. "If he keeps progressing, we'll aim to have you take him home on his due date"—she references her clipboard—"Friday, September thirteenth."

"Friday the thirteenth." Owen snorts. "Perfect."

It's only June. I'd expected to be allowed to go home with the baby as soon as I'd recovered. But there are still three months of in-between time. A full twelve weeks before we can bring Thomas home and start life as a family. Together. The news fills me with relief and dread simultaneously. I imagine myself a prisoner who's been marched to the gallows only to learn my sentence has been postponed before it must, inevitably, be carried out.

The baby mews in his sleep, as if to scold me for the morbid thought. I'm not a prisoner; I'm his mother, and he needs to be held. He needs to know he's safe. For some reason, though, I can't bring myself to touch him.

"Hi, baby," I say. The voice that emerges from my mouth startles me. It's not the rich, comforting strain I intend. Instead, it sounds so shrill and unsure that I'm relieved Thomas is deep in slumber and hasn't stirred. Owen says nothing but I sense his disappointment in me. I'm a mother now; I'm supposed to know how to sound like one.

I'll try again. I imagine my voice as a blanket, wrapping its protection around the baby's body. Swaddling him in its maternal timbre, in the way it feels to be cherished, snug and warm. That way, he'll have some memory to fortify him, in case I'm unable to love him later.

"You're my baby," I say. Better, but not right. Maybe it will start to sound like the truth after enough repetition.

Thomas's eyes snap open: two dark, mysterious wells. He blinks rapidly, confronting me in the NICU's gauzy dimness. He recognizes me.

I reach for Owen but my fingers foolishly rake the air where I hoped to find his hand waiting. He's no longer standing beside me.

He must have stepped out to give me and the baby some privacy, or maybe to call his mom, or to get a snack from the vending machine. I don't blame him. I wouldn't know what to say anyway. Owen will be struggling with this for a long time.

After all, Thomas is not his son.

THEN

CHAPTER 2

I CROSSED OUR frozen backyard in the dark, moving as quickly as I could in my clumsy winter boots. The first holiday party to which Owen and I were invited, hosted by our neighbors, the Dolans, had started half an hour earlier. I willed my eyes to adjust to the night as I approached the ancient footpath that carved through the half acre of old-growth forest separating the Dolans' stucco-and-glass mansion from our eighteenth-century farmhouse. The entrance to the footpath was nearly obscured by overgrown hobblebushes, but soon the path broadened onto a clearing and wound past the Dolans' storage shed.

I tucked an escaped curl back under my knit cap, and the icy hair crunched between my fingers. Part of me wished I'd stayed at home with Owen. When I'd stepped out of the shower that evening, the sound of coughing and moaning had led me downstairs and into the powder room. My husband was curled up on the tile floor, pressing the bridge of his nose between his thumb and forefinger.

"You feel okay, babe?" I'd asked, noticing flecks of half-digested food spattered around the edge of the toilet bowl.

"Yeah, I just—" Owen leaned forward and massaged his lower belly. "No. I guess I don't feel—I'm not okay."

"What did you eat today?" The back of his neck was far too warm beneath my palm, and he shivered at my touch.

"It must have been the lasagna."

"Liza's goddamn practice lasagna." Liza Dolan had spent the week trying out new recipes for her party. This was a familiar routine. When it came to the performing arts, Liza was spectacularly talented; she'd been a professional ballerina in New York and now she choreographed for the prestigious Jacob's Pillow Dance Festival in nearby Becket. Unfortunately, following even the most basic recipe was beyond her skill set. She referred to the culinary process as an "experiment," and we often found ourselves the unwilling recipients of her practice attempts. That morning, she'd brought over a casserole dish of meat lasagna that had, to her credit, *appeared* edible.

"The meat must've been off." Owen whimpered. "Are *you* feeling okay?"

"I feel fine," I said, remembering the fresh salad I'd

cobbled together for lunch before leaving for work that morning. I'd been on-site at the old Bidwell House when Liza stopped by with the lasagna on her way to yoga. The staff at the Bidwell House Museum were reimagining their outdoor gardens, and I was the designer in charge of making the public tour universally accessible. The project was almost complete, as I'd reassured Liza multiple times over the past couple of months, each time I'd turned down one of her invitations to go hiking or cross-country skiing. In addition to teaching dance and yoga, one of her favorite ways to fill her time was exploring the Berkshires' abundant wilderness and learning about the region's history. She knew the names of all the local wildflowers and the spookiest details of all the local ghost stories. When work was less hectic, I usually enjoyed tagging along on her adventures, even in the frigid winter months.

I'd heated up a slice of the practice lasagna when I got home, but the docent had called with a new idea for incorporating audio cues for blind patrons, and I'd forgotten the plate in the microwave. By the time I'd gotten off the phone, the slice of lasagna had hardened into a crusty pile. I'd tossed it down the garbage disposal.

"See?" Owen moaned. "You didn't eat it, and you're not throwing up."

"I hope she didn't use the same ingredients for the party tonight."

"Shit. The party." Owen never skipped social events. He was no more extroverted than I was, but when he made a commitment, he kept it. "Will you hate me if I bail?"

"Of course I won't hate you," I said. "It's not your fault you ate the practice lasagna. Do you want me to stay home, too, to take care of you?"

He dismissed the idea with a weak cough. "We can't *both* bail on the Dolans. Liza will never forgive us."

"I need to smooth things over with her anyway," I said. "But I don't really want to leave you here alone."

"I'm not going to die," he said. "Just help me upstairs, would you?"

By the time I'd tucked Owen into bed with his iPad and a cold compress, there was no time to style my unruly hair, which was still wet from the shower. In the bathroom, I used my left hand to yank the curls into a pile on top of my head and with my right, I rummaged around blindly for a hair tie in the top drawer of the vanity. A sharp pain sliced up the side of my hand.

"What the—" I yelped, backing away from the drawer. There was no reaction from the bedroom. Owen must have put in his earbuds.

A hairline of blood appeared on the surface of the skin, not deep enough to require stitches. I applied a bandage and looked into the drawer to see what had cut my hand. Among the array of barrettes and jewelry lay a pair of heavy gold earrings, shaped like sparrows in midflight, on long delicate chains. Each bird was about the diameter of a quarter, with feathers that came to razor-sharp points.

Liza would get a kick out of seeing me wear them to her party. She'd gifted them to me not long after Owen and I had moved here to Lee. In addition to the earrings, I pulled on a gold-flecked black sweater and a short black skirt with pleats, carefully grabbed a hair tie from the open drawer, and secured my curls into a bun. I wedged a pair of black pumps into my purse to put on once I arrived at the party. I'd never be crazy enough to traverse the woods between our house and the Dolans' in heels. Especially not in the dark.

"How do I look?" I posed in the doorway to the bathroom.

Owen looked up from the iPad and removed one earbud. "Beautiful," he said sincerely. "If I didn't feel like shit, I'd say forget the party all together and start trying for a baby right now."

Even with food poisoning, my husband was as baby-crazy as ever. "Too bad you feel like shit," I said.

"Yeah, yeah. Feels like I'm done vomiting, for now, at least. Tell Liza and Marcus I'm sorry for flaking out."

"I'll see you in a few hours," I said. "Call me if you need me to bring you anything. Or if you just need me to come home for *anything at all . . .*"

"Go!" He chuckled. "You're going to be cold out there with bare legs, though."

I'd grabbed a pair of clean stockings from the laundry basket by the door and pulled them on under my skirt. Then I'd crossed the room to where Owen was burying himself under the covers and kissed him on the forehead.

My cell phone's flashlight illuminated the snow-clumped trail that connected our backyard to the Dolans'. The night was brittle, with no wind. The forest on either side of me looked cohesive but solitary; a line of soldiers in the immediate aftermath of an explosion that had thinned their ranks. One of my favorite pro bono clients, early in my career, was an Iraq veteran about my age. He'd stepped on a roadside IED, an improvised explosive device, resulting in several casualties. I'd volunteered to redesign his split-level ranch to accommodate his new amputations. He never told me the details of what happened, but the trees looked how I imagined the surviving members of his unit must have looked after he'd stepped on that IED. They stood shell-shocked, as if they, too, might collapse to the earth among the sticks and other pieces of their comrades.

Something poked into my left side, below my bottom rib. The high heel on one of the pumps I'd stashed in my purse. As I shifted my purse to adjust the offending heel's position, my boot slipped on a patch of ice. I stumbled, dropping my cell phone and plunging myself into sudden, frigid darkness. My breath froze in my chest for one horrible moment before I noticed the dull glow of my phone's flashlight beneath a pile of dead leaves. Steadying myself, I picked up my phone and examined it. The screen was wet but apparently not damaged. I adjusted the brightness on the phone's flashlight and, continuing at a more prudent pace, soon emerged from the woods.

As I approached the stone patio extending along the back of the Dolans' house, the illuminated scene beyond the windows of the family room came into view. In the center of the room towered a grand Fraser fir, its needles obscured beneath copious layers of ornaments, ribbons, and tinsel. A couple I didn't recognize in hideously gaudy Christmas sweaters chatted next to an unmanned turntable in front of the tree. A group of men clutching beer cans bopped their heads self-consciously to the faint strains of "All I Want for Christmas Is You," which seeped through the sealed floor-to-ceiling patio doors into the night outside. They'd be crew members from Marcus Dolan's landscaping company.

Marcus stood out even among the group of broad-shouldered men, his gargantuan frame wedged into a crisp red gingham shirt. He looked neat but incongruous, as if someone had carefully upholstered stadium bleachers. The only other face I recognized among the men was that of his little brother, Eddie, who was about a head shorter and thirty pounds lighter than Marcus. Along with nearly everyone else in the room, they were watching Liza.

Liza twirled alone in the middle of the room, a sparkling whirlwind of confidence. Her lithe body was draped in a sequined sheath dress over opaque black tights and her dark, cropped hair, usually secured behind her ears with a headband, was arranged in loose curls that barely grazed her neck. She pantomimed mussing the curls, bending forward then flipping them back, in a stylized dance move. Silly but graceful as always. Completely in her element.

Liza was midpirouette when she spotted me through the sliding doors that opened onto their patio.

"Julie!" She jumped out of the spin and made a theatrical effort to drag open one of the doors. A din of music and voices poured out into the night.

"I made it," I said with a shiver. "It's freezing out here."

"Come in, come in! I'll take your coat."

I stepped out of my boots and onto the velvet-pile carpet. Liza waited with extended arms for my down parka, which I handed over to her after tucking my knit cap and scarf into one of the pockets. The heated air, filled with strangers' conversations, warmed the back of my bare neck as I hastily rearranged the bun on top of my head.

"You wore the earrings!" Liza tucked my parka under one arm and touched the edge of my left ear, giving me a chill. To my relief, she didn't seem upset with me at all. "They're beautiful on you," she whispered.

"I love them." I stood still while she admired the enormous golden sparrows hanging from my earlobes. "Remember when you got me these?"

"Of course! It was that first time we went to the Sedgwick House," she said. "I told them what a talented designer you were, and I was right! They *had* to hire you."

"Speaking of work," I said, "sorry I've been so busy with the Bidwell House lately."

"I get it," she said. "No off-season for you."

As a seasonal choreographer, Liza worked nonstop during the summers, but her lifestyle relaxed considerably when Jacob's Pillow all but shut down during the winter.

"The Bidwell House and its gravel garden paths are taking over my life," I said. "I think I've almost figured out how to make them accessible, though. Now we just need to camouflage the speakers for the audio tour."

"Tourists in wheelchairs are so lucky to have you," Liza said vaguely, having lost interest in the conversation. "Come on, we'll put your coat with the others."

"Let me change into my shoes first." I reached into my purse to retrieve my pumps.

"What happened here?" Liza grabbed my wrist in concern.

"It was the earrings!" I laughed.

"Those little wings are *weapons*, huh?" She brought the edge of my hand to her lips and kissed the bandage, leaving a bright-red mark. "Don't worry about shoes," she said. "You can't dance in heels anyway."

"I'll leave them with the coats, then." Letting the pumps fall back into my purse, I hoisted the strap back onto my shoulder and followed her across the kitchen.

"Where's Owen?" Liza peeked over my shoulder as if he might have snuck in behind me undetected.

"Home sick in bed," I said. "You're not serving that lasagna tonight, are you?"

Liza gestured toward the opulent catered spread as we passed it in our stockinged feet. "We decided to order food instead. Why, how was it?"

"I didn't get a chance to try it."

If she wasn't going to serve the bad lasagna at the party, there was no reason to explain that her "experiment" had poisoned my husband. No reason to hurt her feelings.

"Marcus wanted to clear space in the family room for a dance floor," Liza continued, "which ended up taking forever, so there was no time to cook."

"Oh? It was *Marcus* who wanted to clear space for a dance floor?"

"Make fun of me if you want." Liza grinned with self-awareness. "Everyone loves to dance."

"You mean everyone loves to watch *you* dance."

"Do they?"

We'd reached the butler's pantry, and she flicked on the lights. Marcus's best friend from when they'd lived in New York was leaning against the wet bar, holding a bottle of Jack Daniels in one hand and a half-empty tumbler in the other. I'd met him once, briefly, during the Dolans' Super Bowl party a couple of years back. His name was bizarre, almost a joke, something I should have remembered but couldn't. He wore a tight black cotton V-neck with jeans, and he'd tucked his dark locks into a bun just as high and messy as my own. He raised the tumbler and took a gulp.

"Why were you standing here in the dark?" Liza demanded.

"Hello, there, dear Liza," he drawled in a singsong voice, without answering her question. His eyes sparkled with a mix of mischief and something else.

"Donny Rocket," she said, biting her lip. "Julie, Donny's here from New York for the rest of the month, through New Year's."

"I'm between projects," Donny Rocket said by way of explanation.

He was trying to make a career as a singer-songwriter in the city, I remembered now, with limited success. Before moving out here, Marcus had worked in video production in the city, and he sometimes helped Donny out by recording his performances and editing them into music videos for

YouTube. Donny had stayed with the Dolans before, the last time he'd found himself "between projects."

"Nice to see you again, Donny," I said.

"Where's your husband?" he asked.

I tilted my head in the general direction of mine and Owen's house. "Home in bed."

"With who?" he asked.

"No, I mean, he's sick," I stammered. "He's not—"

"Alone?" He was smirking. Entertaining himself.

"Don't be stupid, Donny," Liza snapped. She reached up to grab two wineglasses from the pantry shelf, elevating onto her tiptoes, as if balancing at a ballet barre. The hem of her dress skimmed the muscular backs of her thighs. "How does a glass of Cab sound, Julie?"

"Don't *you* be stupid," Donny said before I could answer. "It was a joke." He was watching Liza's every move.

Ignoring him, Liza grabbed one of the plentiful bottles of wine from the counter and expertly opened it. The butler's pantry had grown too warm around me, a crowded convection oven.

"Cab sounds great," I said. "Thanks."

After another moment, Donny mumbled, "Nice to see you again, Julie," pounded the rest of his whiskey, and strode into the foyer, away from the party. It felt as if someone had opened a window.

"What was *that*?" I whispered when he was out of earshot.

"Donny?" Liza waved her free hand. "He's harmless."

"Harmless?"

She shrugged. "You know what I mean."

I didn't know what she meant. Harmless struck me as an unsettling way to describe a person currently staying in your house, especially someone your husband considered his best friend. But I accepted the full glass of Cabernet Sauvignon she offered me without question. One of the things I genuinely appreciated about my relationship with Liza was our willingness to let the other have her own secrets.

Liza closed her eyes and took a deep whiff of her wine. She exhaled, then held up her glass for me to clink. "Cheers!"

As I returned the gesture, my phone buzzed loudly in my purse, startling me. I slammed my glass down on the counter too quickly, almost spilling the wine.

"Sorry." I retrieved my phone from my purse and checked the screen.

"What's wrong with him, anyway?" Liza asked.

"Probably just drunk," I said, "but that was border-line inappropriate, right? He acts like he's into you or something."

"Wait, what?" Liza's eyebrows knit together in confusion. "*Who* acts like he's into me?"

"Donny." Too late, I realized my mistake.

"I was asking about Owen." The smile had dropped from her face. "That's who texted you, right?"

"Right. He's got some kind of stomach bug," I lied, flustered. "He was so bummed to have to miss the party tonight. Hopefully it will pass by the morning, and he'll be good as new."

Liza leaned back against the counter and crossed one

stockinged ankle in front of the other. "You think Donny acts like he's into me?"

The hand holding her wineglass moved in tiny, rhythmic circles, churning the red liquid inside.

I wished I could shove his name back inside my mouth. To stall, I took a sip of wine. Its tannins gripped the back of my tongue and settled there before I swallowed.

"You know Donny," I finally said, as if I, too, knew Donny. "He flirts with everyone. That's his personality, right?" He had never flirted with *me*, and we both knew it.

Liza's wine came dangerously close to splashing over the edge of her glass. Her wrist stopped moving and for a moment, it looked as if she was going to say something. Instead, she shook her head and took another sip.

"Ladies and gentlemen!" Donny's voice rang out from the family room as the music shifted. I recognized the familiar cadence of Adam Levine insisting that girls like me did, in fact, run around with guys like him.

"Speaking of Donny." Liza raised one sly eyebrow. "Sounds like he's set up at the turntable. Let's go dance."

She reached behind me to turn off the light in the butler's pantry, then ushered me into the family room. I followed her and the sound of Maroon 5 back to the party, where Donny was dancing behind the turntable by the overdecorated Fraser fir.

"I'm so *over* this song!" Liza shrieked as she pranced ahead of me toward Donny. "Play something Christmassy, *please*."

When she'd gotten halfway across the family room,

Marcus lurched forward and put his body in her path. "Leave Donny alone," he said, scooping her up and tossing her over his shoulder.

Liza scowled, playful. By the time Marcus plopped her down on the leather sectional couch, she was kicking her feet in tempo to the music. Before the next chorus, Donny dropped the needle again to let loose a jarringly percussive techno jam I didn't recognize, complete with festive jingle bell sound effects.

"This yours?"

The distinct odor of a menthol cough drop stung my nostrils, and I knew it was Eddie before I turned around. With one hand, he gripped an open can of Bud Light and with the other, he held the nearly empty glass of wine Liza had poured for me in the pantry. He was underdressed in a Red Sox hoodie, faded jeans, and unlaced work boots, probably attending his brother's party out of obligation.

"Whoops!" I took the glass from him and sipped it. "I thought I'd finished this off. Thanks, Eddie." I felt more relaxed immediately.

Along with Marcus and Liza, Eddie had been one of the first neighbors I'd met the day Owen and I had moved to Lee, a week before our wedding. We hadn't bothered to hire movers, and by lunchtime we'd been exhausted from loading the contents of our individual apartments onto the moving truck and driving across Massachusetts. Owen had gone downtown to pick up sandwiches, and I'd glanced out the kitchen window to discover the three Dolans standing on our dilapidated back porch.

"We're your new neighbors!" Liza had called, waving enthusiastically.

I'd invited them inside. There was no other option.

"Are you guys going to fix up the house at all?" Eddie eyed the crown molding, which was chipped and broken off in some places. "Or is it . . . fuckin' protected, on a register?"

"It was built in the 1770s," I said, taken aback by his casual profanity, "but it's not fancy enough to be protected on a register, so we can renovate."

The whole *point* was to make renovations; that was the reason we'd purchased this centuries-old farmhouse in the westernmost part of the state, nearly a three-hour drive from Boston. I loved the idea of infusing energy back into an old house. It was the perfect spot for me and Owen to start our new life together.

The mention of renovations piqued Eddie's interest. "What are you guys going to do, fuckin' flip it?"

"No, we're not interested in flipping our house," I said.

Flipping a house implied a careless, even callous, disregard for the families who'd called it home before us. My passion as a designer had always been to honor a space's history, to pay homage to the different people who'd inhabited it in decades, even centuries past. I believed human experiences were forever connected to the locations where they'd taken place; as people died and different families moved in, new stories layered on top of the old like sedimentary rock. Over time, a rich and varied landscape emerged. It was my job to recognize and respect it.

"We're going to bring it back to life," I said.

"So you're 'flipping' it, but not flippant*ly*," Liza offered with a smile.

"What's your budget?" Eddie pressed. "You guys going all out? Sky's the fuckin' limit?" He used the word *fuckin'* to fill the space between his thoughts, I realized, the way other members of our generation would interject the word *like*. Still, his tone was cynical, tinged with accusation.

When they'd died unexpectedly, my parents had left me the entire Merritt family estate. And, despite the charitable donations I had set up to funnel the inheritance toward people who needed it, there was no denying that Owen and I were financially very comfortable. He'd already landed interviews at a few nearby accounting firms, but even if neither of us found a source of income right away, we'd still have much more money to put toward home renovations than many other young couples our age. Eddie couldn't have known that by looking at me, though.

"We're pretty flexible," I said.

"Flexible?" Eddie repeated in a way that made it clear he knew who my family was. He must have done some internet research, come across my maiden name.

"I'm a universal designer," I said. "I've just finished up a contract in Boston, so I'll be able to take as much time as I need to work on all the updates."

I was eager to point out that I was the kind of person who enjoyed DIY home improvement projects. I might have come from money, but I could get my hands dirty. Later, Eddie told me he'd initially assumed universal design involved astrophysics or aerospace, not accessibility for the disabled.

In the four years since we'd moved here, I'd established myself as the Berkshires' preeminent universal designer, and now my own house was nearly finished, due as much to Eddie's connections in the region as to my careful designs. Since he'd grown up in Lee and never left, Eddie was comfortable negotiating with all the local suppliers and craftspeople. For every obstacle that arose during my home renovation, he always "knew a guy" who could help me make it work. Most recently, when I'd refinished the quirky split staircase that led independently from both the kitchen and the front entryway to the second story landing, one of Eddie's connections had provided white beadboard for the risers. That staircase had always been my favorite design element of the house, and now it was perfect.

"How are those risers working out?" Eddie asked. The way he pronounced it, the word sounded like "rye-zuz."

"The whole staircase looks perfect," I said. "Thank you again."

"Need a refill?" Marcus passed by carrying a serving tray of other partygoers' empty glasses. He snatched the wine stem from my hand and added my glass to the collection before I could answer.

"Look at the level of service in this joint!" someone slurred, raising their beer can in wobbly appreciation.

"A couple of swanky martinis, and . . . you want some more of the open red, Julie?" Marcus shouted from the butler's pantry.

"Sure, thanks," I called back. "By the way," I said to Eddie, "Owen wanted me to talk to you about materials for the third bedroom. The nursery, I guess, eventually."

"Where is he, anyway?" Eddie moved his menthol cough drop into the pocket of his cheek, scanning the room for Owen.

"Home sick."

"With what?"

Marcus reemerged from the butler's pantry without the tray and yanked open the refrigerator. He retrieved a jar of olives and pointed it at another guest, one of the guys from his landscaping crew. "Can't have martinis without olives, bro."

"Whatever it is, it's unpleasant," I said. "He didn't want to come over and spread it around."

"What do you guys have in mind for the nursery?" Eddie asked.

"Seeing as I'm not even pregnant yet, probably gender-neutral paint to start . . ."

Eddie jutted his chin in the direction of the foyer's grand staircase. "Marcus has some paint chips upstairs in his office," he said. "Remind me to show you later."

"Thanks," I said, with difficulty. My tongue felt thick. It was taking up too much space in my mouth.

"You okay, there, Julie?"

I began to answer but my voice faltered. "I'm feeling . . ."

What was I feeling? And what was that noise? Donny must have made a mistake over at the turntable, mashed up songs with mismatched rhythms. Anyway, the question from Eddie was something about renovating the third bedroom, the nursery. He was asking about the paint color. Wasn't he? I wanted to speak but I couldn't.

Once again, the music changed.

I didn't recognize the song. I didn't recognize anything at all.

CHAPTER 3

First, the roar of rushing water. It filled my ears to the brim, seeped out and over and all around me. Shocked me awake. My head felt stuffed with mothballs, and I struggled to pry open my eyelids.

Through swollen slits, with a few strenuous blinks, I saw that my exposed thighs and the tops of my knees were streaked with ugly red lines. The lower half of my body was submerged in a deep tub of lukewarm water. Everything hurt.

I twisted onto my side and pressed my palms against the edge of the tub, trying to hoist myself up. The motion triggered a sharp pain inside my pelvis. I collapsed back into the water.

"You probably shouldn't try to move," said a man's voice

right behind my ear. I wrenched my neck toward it and another type of pain crashed through my skull.

Where am I? Why am I in a bath?

The answers didn't matter. I wasn't alone and I needed to get out of there. This man must have hurt me. He'd hurt me and now he was going to kill me.

If I could sit up and swing my legs underneath me, then rise onto my knees, maybe I could crawl over the edge of the tub. My legs, though, trembled pathetically, uselessly. It felt as if they'd been crushed beneath something powerful, and then reattached slightly incorrectly.

"Please—" I pleaded.

A massive hand came down on top of mine, gripping it against the edge of the tub, and my voice broke off in my throat.

"Julie!"

Marcus. His breath smelled like the sticky floor of a college fraternity. He sat on the lid of the toilet seat, at the head of the tub, breathing heavily.

I was relieved to recognize him. If Marcus was here, that meant I was probably close to home. My kidneys, most likely, had not been harvested and stored in a cooler for sale on the black market. The relief I felt, though, was closely followed by confusion. If I'd been kidnapped by a stranger, at least the plotline would be recognizable from *Dateline* episodes my mother-in-law often forwarded to me and thirty other recipients with paranoid subject lines like "Better to be safe than sorry."

But Marcus's presence sent my brain spinning in a

thousand new directions, none of which provided a reassuring explanation for why one of us was lying—*naked*? Yes, oh, my god, I was completely naked from the waist down—in a bathtub. The gold-flecked sweater I'd picked out earlier that night clung to my breasts and shoulders. Soaked through. It was the only item of clothing on my body.

"Sorry." Marcus cringed, looking down at me. He pulled his hand away from mine and rested it unsteadily on his knee, which was at the level of my shoulder. "Is the water . . . is it warm enough?"

The question was so ridiculous, I thought I might be dreaming. Then the water lapped against the abrasions on my thighs and from the way it stung, I knew I was not sleeping. I must have been unconscious before, when someone had put me in this bathtub, but now I was undeniably awake. And with each passing moment, I was becoming more and more alert. I recognized the familiar octagonal, stark white floor tiles and the gaudy gold fixtures of the Dolans' master bathroom where, less than a month ago, I'd waited on the same toilet lid where Marcus was now seated, playing on my phone while Liza changed out of her yoga clothes.

"Liza?!" I yelled, frantic. "Where are you?" There was no response from Liza. "Marcus, what the hell is going on?"

He stood up and extended a thick white bath towel in my direction.

"Here," he said, turning his face toward the wall in an absurdly inadequate gesture of propriety. I reached back as far as I could and grabbed the towel from his hand.

My legs had melted into the water. They would never support me if I attempted to stand up and dry myself off. Instead, I draped the bath towel over my lap in a pathetic attempt to shield my lower body from Marcus's view. It billowed briefly on the surface of the water and then sank down, clinging to my sore skin.

"Why am I here?" I demanded.

"I brought you up here because I thought . . . I don't know," Marcus stammered, still facing away from me. "Do you know what happened?"

"I don't remember anything," I said. The effort it took to speak was physically draining. My entire body wanted me to fall back asleep, but I needed to get out of this bathtub, get dressed, and go home. "Help me out of here, Marcus."

With his eyes trained on the floor, Marcus obligingly grabbed a fresh, dry bath towel and draped it across his broad chest. He faced me with open arms, waiting.

"I need your help, here," I said, grateful for the stubborn drowsiness that provided a mental padding for my pride. "I can barely move."

He leaned down and wrapped his arms around my back, keeping the towel in place between us. My skin burned beneath his touch.

"Ready?"

I nodded, wincing as he heaved me up and over the tub's edge. My bare feet skidded on the tiles, and I teetered, but Marcus grabbed my elbow to stop me from falling. He clumsily wrapped the towel around my chest, tucking it in below my armpits, and helped me come to a seated position on the closed toilet lid. Once we both felt confident that I wouldn't tip over, Marcus stepped back and leaned against the counter of the vanity.

"Now tell me what the hell is going on," I said. "Where are the rest of my clothes?"

"You seriously don't remember?"

"Oh, my god, Marcus!" I said. "Believe it or not, I'm not playing games here. I don't remember anything. Not a single fucking thing. So please. Why am I in your bathtub half naked, feeling like I've been hit by a bus?" I paused. "Where is your wife?"

Marcus took a deep breath. "Liza's passed out downstairs." He paused. "I'm pretty sure that's where she is, anyway."

"What time is it?"

"It's three o'clock in the morning," he said. "The party ended, like, an hour ago."

The party. I remembered now that Owen had felt ill at the last minute and decided to stay home. Liza's practice lasagna. But I'd arrived at the Dolans' just after eight thirty, I remembered, because I'd been a half hour late. If it was already three o'clock in the morning, if Marcus was telling the truth, then there were at least six hours I couldn't account for. How had I lost so much time?

"Everyone's gone home?"

Marcus nodded slowly. "Or crashed in an extra room. When I was taking the trash out to the bins I found you passed out on the back lawn."

"Outside?" It was freezing out there. "I didn't go outside."

"Maybe you were on your way home?" Marcus cleared

his throat. "What you had on was a mess . . . you weren't wearing the rest of your clothes . . . you were passed out, so I figured we'd get you washed up, cleaned up—"

"What kind of a mess?"

"Huh?" He didn't meet my eyes.

"My clothes," I said. "What do you mean, they were a mess?"

He made a reluctant gesture toward the sink, to the black clump of wet fabric inside it. My miniskirt. I remembered choosing it from my closet earlier that night, pulling the stockings over my legs at Owen's suggestion. But the memory ended there.

Marcus was talking again. "Your tights are torn up and your skirt . . ." His voice sounded like a tape recording that was gradually slowing down and down, getting lower and lower. ". . . it looks like mud, or blood, or something. I tried to clean it off . . ." he said, his voice lower still. "It's covered."

Rancid fluid seared my throat, splashing onto the bathroom floor and across my bare feet. I retched again, loudly, but there was nothing left to come up—I hadn't eaten dinner. And I must not have eaten anything at the party either.

Marcus kneeled in front of me, holding my hair away from my face. My vomit soaked through the knees of his jeans as he sat with me, waiting for my nausea to pass.

"Hey." Marcus's voice was full of pity, like his face. I was too exhausted to mind. "What can I do? What do you need?"

I needed to remember what had happened that night.

First, though, I needed to get into my bed and to sleep through the foreseeable future. For either of those things to happen, unfortunately, I needed Marcus's help.

"Could you go get me a plastic bag for my clothes?" I asked. "And are you sober enough to give me a ride home?"

He nodded, as if just remembering that he knew how to drive. "I'll bring you some of Liza's pajamas too." He disappeared into the bedroom. I heard him pull open a drawer and rummage among his wife's clothing for pajamas that a regular-sized adult could wear comfortably.

With Marcus gone, the entire bathroom took on a fabricated, unreal quality, like the set of a horror movie. Or one of those living dioramas on a Halloween hayride, where actors re-create the same gory performance over and over again, every night.

I inhaled slowly through my nose, trying to get a grip. The air was wet with the horribly sweet smell of regurgitated Cabernet. The taste scorched my throat. I swallowed heavily and dragged my left foot across the bath mat, watching the plush fibers become filthy with my vomit.

Given how my body felt, I wasn't shocked by the hideous reflection of my face in the mirror. Scarlet abrasions crisscrossed my thighs, pelvis, and forearms indiscriminately, as if I'd survived a knife fight with an untrained opponent. The shallower cuts along my hands had puckered in the bath. My right cheekbone was bruised purple; in the morning, the eye would be blackened shut. The earlobe next to it was caked in blood. When I touched it, the cartilage split in two between my fingers. At some point that night, in addition to my memory and dignity, I'd lost one of the sharp-winged little birds.

"I'm missing an earring," I said to Marcus as he drove me back to my house.

He stared at the slick black road ahead. "You are?"

"Liza gave me these earrings," I said. "They're special. Could you keep an eye out for it?"

"Sure, Julie."

It was an absurd request, given everything that had happened that night. There were so many other, more important things I had to ask Marcus. So many answers I should be demanding from him. But it took all the effort left within me to stay awake, and soon Marcus's pickup truck was turning into the circular driveway in front of our farmhouse.

The white lights of the Christmas tree offered a warped, cheerful welcome through the handblown glass of the parlor's front window. Earlier that month, we'd untangled the mismatched strings of lights and draped them around the Douglas fir, pushing them between the needles along with a handful of heirloom ornaments. I'd made mulled cider. Owen had spiked it. He'd sung along to Zooey Deschanel covering "Sleigh Ride," shimmying his shoulders under the mistletoe like a fool. From outside, the moment felt unreachable, impossible now.

"You okay?" Marcus asked.

"I think so," I said, although it wasn't true. Since Marcus had helped me out of the bathtub, I'd been forcing myself not to focus on the searing pain between my legs. It was bone deep, a new kind of pain. After the duration of the short drive, my vulva felt as if it had been cauterized.

Marcus leaned across the passenger seat to hand me the bag containing my wet clothes. "Crazy party, huh?" He grinned uneasily. Then he pulled the door of the pickup truck shut and drove away.

Daisy greeted me at the front door and barked once, halfheartedly.

"Good girl." I shushed her, and she nuzzled my ankles.

The house was quiet; undisturbed. As I climbed the stairs to our bedroom, my body screamed at me with every step. The persistent pain spread from my vulva to my upper thighs and lower belly. It felt as if I'd been sliding down a bannister with legs splayed, only to slam into the unforgiving newel post. I knew what it meant. I was far too fatigued, though, to investigate.

Upstairs, Owen was sleeping soundly. The bathroom door creaked as I nudged it open. He didn't stir but I left the lights off anyway. I placed the plastic bag containing my soaking wet sweater, stockings, skirt, and underwear on the vanity. Twigs and other debris stuck to the fabric, poked through the plastic. I'd have to remember to put in a load of laundry in the morning.

The flannel pajamas that Marcus had found in Liza's drawer were at least three sizes too small for me, and the soft fabric felt like sandpaper against my sore skin. I removed them, cringing, and dropped them into the laundry hamper next to the shower. I thought about pulling back the curtain and standing beneath the hot water, letting it stream over my shoulders, down my back, rinsing me clean. It would scald the open wounds. The pipes would whine, and Owen might wake up. Even if he slept through the noise of the shower, I'd have to dry myself off afterward, and our bath towels weren't nearly as fluffy as the ones at the Dolans' house. I thought about the nubby fabric, how it would scrape, and decided against the shower. I was too exhausted to remain standing anyway.

Draping my fleece bathrobe around my shoulders for warmth, I lowered myself onto the tile floor with my back against the door. I gingerly tucked my knees beneath my bathrobe and pulled up the search bar on my phone's screen. *Sexual assault,* I typed. That was too broad, obviously. *Sexually assaulted in Lee, Massachusetts,* I typed instead, and pressed the first link, which brought me to the website for a place called the Elizabeth Freeman Center. There was a phone number for a 24/7 hotline and the words *You are not alone. Call us.* Then in Spanish: *No están solos. Llámenos.* I dialed the number.

"Hello?" The voice was friendly, alert, despite the early hour.

"Hi," I said. "I was assaulted, I think. Earlier tonight."

"Are you safe?"

I knew what she meant, but I imagined another kind of safe. A black lockbox the size of a refrigerator, sealed shut with me inside it. No air, no way out of the dark.

"Are you safe?" the operator repeated with urgency. "What's your name?"

"Yes, sorry, I'm safe now," I said. "My name's Julie. I don't even know what happened."

"You have nothing to be sorry about, Julie," she said. "Many people feel confused after a sexual assault, but you called the right place. I'm here to support you. If we get disconnected, is it okay to call you back at this number?"

"Yes," I said, but I'd stopped listening to her. I was imagining the confused people she'd mentioned, all those many sexually assaulted people. The ones who weren't safe. I imagined trafficked teenagers, destitute women living on the street with nowhere to go, victims who hadn't blacked out, who remembered in excruciating detail exactly what had happened to them. They were the ones who needed this hotline, not me. They'd be stranded, unable to reach the operator as long as I was tying up the line. "I'm sorry," I said.

"You have nothing to be—"

"I'm sorry," I said again, and hung up.

The phone vibrated immediately in my hand. It was the operator from the Elizabeth Freeman Center, calling me back as promised, but I screened the call.

Daisy was waiting outside the bathroom door. She watched me climb into bed, then shuffled over to her dog bed in the corner and settled back into it, swishing her tail. As far as she was concerned, both of her owners were home—safe—and all was right with the world.

Next to me, Owen's exposed back rose and fell with unconscious breath. I leaned toward him and breathed in despite myself, expecting to smell the salty-sour mix of sweat and stale vomit. Instead, I inhaled a whiff of pine soap. He must have recovered enough to take a shower before falling asleep. He hadn't bothered to put on pajamas, though.

"Owen." I whispered his name like a prayer. My hand hovered above his warm skin, the celestial freckles of his shoulder.

He didn't respond.

I parted my lips to say his name again, tightened my throat to prepare the long vowel sound, but then I thought better of it. Closed my mouth. I didn't try again.

Owen needed rest to fully recover from his food poisoning. Besides, I didn't know what I'd say to him if I woke him up. I still couldn't even remember what had happened tonight. After I got some sleep in my own bed, my brain would function normally again, and the events from the party would come rushing back to me. I'd tell Owen all about it in the morning. As soon as I made that decision, sleep encircled me like a tomb.

CHAPTER 4

I woke up drenched in shame. The bedsheets clung to my limbs and chafed the raw skin. As my brain flickered awake, it retrieved sharp fragments of memory. The thick white bath towel billowing over my body in the tub. The knees of Marcus's jeans pressed into my vomit on the octagonal tiles. The pity in his eyes.

But nothing from the hours before that.

Bile rose in my throat, and I swallowed it back. I couldn't understand how I'd blacked out for most of the previous night. Memory loss on that scale had never happened to me before, not even as an undergrad, when I'd been drinking most weekends. At the Dolans' party, I'd indulged in a couple of glasses of wine, at most. Nowhere near the amount of alcohol that would cause all-out amnesia.

The mattress shifted. Lazily, Owen scooted up behind me and kissed the back of my neck, below my left ear.

"Good morning, Juju Bear," he murmured, using his favorite nickname for me. His touch was tender, but it stung.

More bile. I swallowed hard. When my voice came out, it was coated in a dirty film. "Morning, babe," I said. "Someone's feeling better, huh?"

Owen sighed contentedly. "Much better. Staying in last night was a good decision." Then he fell silent. I sensed him pull back from my body and examine it, first with curiosity, then with horror. The scrapes along my arms and shoulders, the bruises staining my back. The blood-crusted abrasions on my thighs.

Daisy watched us with concerned eyes, curled snugly in her bed at the foot of the mirror. She, too, could tell I'd been wounded.

Finally, Owen said, "You're a mess, babe."

"Sorry," I said compulsively.

"It's okay," he said, and I wished he'd told me I had nothing to be sorry for.

I wanted to tell Owen the truth, what I knew of it, to let him comfort me. I wanted to share with him all the confused feelings that battled in my heart, the ones I couldn't name. Even the worst part. The terrible thing I knew had happened last night with a thickening certainty. The reason my body felt broken, like an old plastic doll.

Owen had always been able to comfort me, even when he was a stranger. That's what he'd done on the night we first met, seven years earlier, at a rainy highway rest stop.

I wanted to explain myself to Owen, but I couldn't help thinking about the night he came into my life.

That night, I'd been facing another trauma. Moments before I met Owen for the first time, I'd been waiting to die. On the rainy drive back to the Rhode Island School of Design from an internship in Boston, my sedan had spun out across Route 95.

Amid the helpless screech of brakes and whizzing lights, I first registered shock, then fear. Finally, in the split second before the guardrail brought my trajectory to an abrupt halt, I was overcome by awareness that this moment, no, now this one, would be the last moment I'd ever notice. After that, everything would be the same as it was for me before I was born, and there was no stopping it, there never had been any stopping it, and now it was here, and now it *must be* here, and *now* . . .

The tow truck driver had given me a lift to the closest rest stop along Route 95, somewhere near the Blue Hills. I took shelter from the whipping rain beneath the concrete overhang and waited for my roommate, another student at the Rhode Island School of Design, to pick me up. It would have been an hour-long drive in mild weather, and god knew how long it would take her to reach me in this storm. I'd never felt so alone. Then a Subaru station wagon pulled into the rest stop, and Owen climbed out, a broad-shouldered figure in an athletic raincoat. He jogged through the sheets of rain billowing across the parking lot and shrugged off his hood when he reached the protection of the overhang.

"Nasty night out there, isn't it?" When he smiled, friendly creases appeared around the corners of his amber eyes. From the smoothness of his forehead beneath a full head of dirty-blond hair, he must have been about my age, twenty-two.

I tried to read his face, at least four or five inches above mine because of his height. I couldn't decide whether he was making polite conversation before going inside to use the restroom or whether he was biding his time, waiting for the right moment to lunge sideways and drag me kicking and screaming back to his station wagon.

"Hey, how'd you even get here?" He scanned the parking lot. "Where's your car?"

"I've totaled it," I said, and immediately scolded myself for revealing that I was stranded here with no escape vehicle, no way to drive myself away from him and this creepy rest stop, should he give me cause.

"What?" he said, aghast. "You mean, just now, you got into a car accident?"

Regretting my decision to overshare, I hugged myself tightly and nodded.

"But—are you okay?"

By no measure of the word was I "okay" after what had happened that night. "I'm sure I'll be fine," I said.

"Do you need a ride somewhere?"

"My roommate Bethany is on her way," I said. "We don't live that far away."

"Maybe I could get you a snack?" He gestured to the vending machine beside us, then noticed the tattered OUT OF

ORDER sign taped onto it. "Or not. Wait!" He crouched down and reached into the machine's dispensing compartment.

"What are you doing?"

He slowly retrieved his forearm and stood up triumphantly. "Ta-da!" He presented me with a plastic bag filled with red candies. "Can I interest you in a"—he read from the label on the front of the package—"Juju Bear?"

"Those are so disgusting," I said. "No wonder someone just abandoned them in there."

"Are you kidding? I love Juju Bears." He stashed the plastic bag in the pocket of his raincoat. "I'm saving these for the drive. You can't find them anywhere."

"That's because nobody likes gummy candies that are also spicy! They probably stopped making them." I laughed a little, too, in spite of myself.

"I'm happy to wait with you for as long as you need me to," he said.

"Thanks, but I'll be all right. I'm sure you've got somewhere to be."

"Just on my way to my mom's, in Norwood." He shrugged. "I take her to Mass most weekends."

"Mass?"

"You know, church, for Catholics. My name's Owen, by the way." He held out a sturdy pale hand.

"Julie," I said.

"Good to meet you, Julie." He was still holding on to my hand. "You could go by Juju Bear, if you wanted." He chuckled self-consciously. "I'm sorry. That was a weird thing to say. I'm sorry about your car too. Have a good night." He dropped my hand and disappeared into the men's restroom.

Now that I'd told him to get lost, I wasn't sure that I'd feel safer after he drove away. I checked my phone. No update from Bethany yet. I considered texting her to check on her arrival time but decided not to distract her. She'd be taking it slow in this weather.

The sound of a flush was barely audible over the rain that pounded the pavement a few feet ahead of me. Then came the burst of water from a faucet. Like that of the women's restroom across from it, the men's restroom door had been propped open with a stone. I stepped sideways, cautiously, and peeked behind it.

"Here I am!" Owen appeared in the doorway, jovial.

"I wasn't looking for you," I stammered. "I mean, I was just . . ."

"Checking to make sure I didn't die in there?"

When he said those words, my chest constricted viselike around my heart, unexpectedly, and I couldn't breathe.

Owen's eyes softened when he saw my expression. "What is it?" he asked. "What did I say?"

My mind had been spinning since the moment my sedan had slammed into the guardrail earlier that night. The police had arrived with lights flashing, I'd explained how I'd lost control of my car on the slick highway, and the tow truck driver had taken me to this rest stop and dropped me off to wait for my roommate. I hadn't allowed myself to process the new truth of my situation.

With a careless joke from this stranger, my whirling

thoughts snapped into focus on the thing that had happened. The terrible thing that had caused me to lose control of my car. The thing I didn't want to be true but that always would be true, from now on.

"I can't believe I'm crying." I couldn't remember the last time I'd cried when I was by myself, nevermind in front of a stranger.

"No, it's . . . you're probably in shock. Do you need a tissue or something?" He shoved his hands into the pockets of his jacket. "I could grab you a paper towel or some toilet paper from the bathroom."

"Don't worry about it."

"I think I have some napkins in my car."

"I'm all done," I said, shaking my head. "I'm okay."

"Are you?" His voice held genuine concern.

Maybe I could be honest with Owen. He was friendly, disarmingly kind, and so far, he hadn't raised any red flags for me. Maybe I could tell him the whole truth, then watch him climb back into his station wagon and drive off into the rainstorm. I'd never have to see him again. I'd never have to witness his pity for me and my circumstances.

"My parents died in a plane crash tonight," I said. There it was. The reason I'd totaled my car, the disaster that had brought me to that highway rest stop. The fact that made everything different. It was the first time I'd said the words aloud, and they sounded false, like a poorly planned lie.

"Oh! Shit." He took his hands out of his pockets and raised his arms, as if he might hug me. If he tried to, I wasn't sure I'd stop him. He raked his fingers backward through his hair instead, tugging on the ends. "There was a plane crash, tonight? What flight was it? They didn't mention it on the news—"

"Not a commercial jet." I cut him off. "My dad liked to fly. He crashed their plane with the two of them on board."

My throat was closing and I swallowed heavily, not daring to look up into Owen's face. My mother had been the only passenger on my father's Eclipse 500 Very Light Jet when, approaching Nantucket Memorial Airport in the minutes before eight o'clock that night, its landing gear had failed. My father had attempted a belly landing on the runway; that had failed too. I'd never been inside the airplane, couldn't even picture it in my mind. I couldn't imagine how it must have looked as it exploded on the tarmac with Charles and Patricia Merritt inside. Other than public knowledge about my mother's acclaimed research career, and the fact that my father enjoyed flying, I knew almost nothing about the lives my parents had been leading. I couldn't guess what they might have been talking about in the moments before it became clear they were going to die.

They'd sent me away to boarding school and summer camps for most of my childhood, hiring nannies to keep me out of their business in the rare periods when we'd lived under the same roof. Once I'd left for RISD, my face-to-face interactions with my parents had further diminished. When I'd visited their home in Needham over holiday breaks, my most substantial interactions had been with the family cook, Miranda. She was the one who'd called me that night to tell me the news that they were dead.

"I'm so sorry," Owen said. "That's awful." He rested a hand on my upper arm and to my surprise, I didn't recoil from him.

"Thanks," I said. "I mean, it *is* awful. When I got the call, I started crying and I couldn't see straight, and with the shitty driving conditions . . ." Once I'd hung up the phone, it hadn't been grief so much as shock and disorientation that had caused me to lose control of my car in the storm. "I thought I was going to die too," I said.

I finally raised my eyes to meet his and when I did, I knew I'd been right to trust him. His face was open; he was genuinely content to listen to a stranger's heartbreak. I wasn't used to that kind of compassion. "Anyway." I cleared my throat. "Your mom's expecting you, right? You should go."

Owen glanced at the time on his phone. "Yeah, she's probably worried. I get worried about her, too, living on her own. It just seemed like you wanted . . ." He shrugged one shoulder. "I don't know. But like I said, I'll stay here as long as you need me to."

A pair of headlights turned into the rest area parking lot, and I recognized Bethany's white SUV. My heart dropped. Owen was a strange man I'd met randomly at a rest stop, but I already knew that I didn't want to trade his company for Bethany's.

"Hey," he said, "I know this is kind of weird . . ."

"Let me give you my number," I blurted.

To my relief, his face relaxed into a smile. "Yeah, okay."

"What were you going to say?" I asked.

"I was going to get your number."

Bethany's SUV pulled up to the curb beside us and idled there. The driver's window lowered.

"Hey, Julie! I made it!" Bethany called to me over the slowing rain.

I rattled off my phone number to Owen and made my way to the passenger side of the SUV, being careful to avoid stepping in puddles. My stomach churned as I imagined having to tell Bethany the news about my parents' deaths, having to field her inevitable questions. But I felt more capable, sturdier, after confiding in Owen. I hoped he'd text me and then immediately scolded myself for hoping.

"Thank you so much for coming to get me, Bethany," I said, closing the passenger door. "Let me give you money for gas." Through the windshield, I watched Owen lowering himself into the driver's seat of his station wagon.

Bethany snorted as she put the car in Drive. "Damn straight you're paying for my gas *and* you owe me, like, a thousand trips to the airport."

My backpack buzzed at my feet. I reached down to grab my phone from the zippered front pocket. "Obviously," I said. "You really came through for me tonight."

"I am already having the *worst day*"—Bethany twisted her neck around to check for oncoming traffic before pulling out onto Route 95—"like you wouldn't even believe, and now I've spent my whole night just, like, trying not to *die* in this fucking *torrential* rain."

I looked at the number on the screen and recognized the 617 area code. The text message said simply, *Hey this is Owen.* I couldn't believe it. It wasn't that I'd expected him *not* to text, but seeing the words on my screen still caught me off guard.

"You're right," I said to Bethany.

She continued as if I hadn't agreed with her. "Some of us have to pay for our own gas, so again, yes, hit me up for like, twenty. Not *everyone's* parents are heirs to fucking *Mayflower* money." She removed both hands from the steering wheel and slid one palm against the other, as if carelessly distributing dollar bills. "How are those assholes, anyway?"

"Can you keep your hands on the wheel?" I needed to tell her my parents were dead before she continued repeating the profligate insults she'd heard me use against them in the past. Everything was different now.

Bethany kept talking. "Have they even acknowledged that you're about to graduate? Fucking assholes," she said without waiting for me to respond.

I attempted to make my mouth form the words. *Plane crash.* It didn't work.

Instead, I redirected the conversation. "You had a bad day?"

"Oh, my god. It's my senior project. I got assigned the. Worst. Team. Ever. Let me tell you . . ." And she began berating an unfortunate handful of our fellow students for their perceived inadequacies, from hair twirling to laziness to not understanding that Bethany had the best ideas.

I half listened while trying to decide how to respond to Owen's text. I wanted to answer him promptly, since he'd wasted no time texting me. But my mind was too scattered from the events of that night to come up with anything clever to write.

I saved his number in my contacts list and texted him back: *You're in my phone as Owen Rest Stop Guy.*

A moment later his response popped up on my screen: *You're in my phone as Juju Bear.*

What stood out about that night, besides meeting the man who'd become my husband, was how easy it had been to avoid sharing the truth about my parents' deaths with Bethany. I'd suffered the worst trauma of my life, and then I'd sat in the passenger seat beside my roommate for the entire hour-long drive back to RISD without saying a word about it. Lying by omission.

"Juju Bear," Owen said now, propping himself on his elbow beside me in our bed. He searched my face. "What the hell happened?"

Here is what I wanted to do: 1) tell Owen everything I could remember and let him comfort me 2) march over to the Dolans' house and demand that Marcus explain to us what he knew 3) report the crime and 4) seek justice, making sure whoever attacked me last night could never hurt anyone else.

Here is what I did instead: I lied to Owen.

"I walked home drunk," I said. "Through the woods."

"You took that overgrown path alone, in the dark? Drunk?"

"I guess so," I said. That part wasn't completely untrue. Marcus hadn't told me much, but he did say he'd found me on his back lawn, after I'd tried to walk home drunk.

"Why're you such a mess?" Owen asked, still groggy. "You fall down or something?"

"I tripped," I said, hating myself. "There was a . . . fallen log. I tripped over it."

"What did you land on, your face?"

"I guess so." I had the dreadful sense that my life, like my mother's when she'd strapped herself into the passenger seat of my father's jet for the last time, was hurtling toward disaster, out of my control.

"I *told* you it's dangerous to walk through those woods at night," Owen said. He reached out and fingered one of my curls, still damp from the Dolans' bathtub. "You showered already?"

"When I got home," I said quickly. "I showered before I came to bed." I'd *considered* taking a shower, at least.

"Really?" He glanced at the door to the bathroom, which was ajar. "I didn't hear you."

"I was quick," I said, feeling filthy. "You must have slept through it." This would be the part where he would catch me in a lie.

"Let's both take it easy today," he said. "Want me to make waffles?"

At first I thought he must be pretending to believe me. Maybe he was planning to play it cool, then he'd look for holes in my story with which to confront me later. But playing a psychological game like that would never occur to Owen. He trusted me. He believed my bullshit story about tripping over a log in the woods, and now he was moving on to breakfast plans. I was going to get away with this lie.

Couldn't he tell there was something terribly wrong with me? He knew me better than anyone. I felt as if I should look different to him, somehow. In a crevice of my heart that I wasn't proud of, I resented him for not following up my story with more questions, for not sensing that there was more to the events of last night than what I was sharing with him. He didn't even ask about the wet clothes in a plastic bag on top of the vanity, just tossed them into the washing machine with his next colored load.

More surprising, though, than Owen's willingness to believe my nonsense was the ease with which the lie had flown, unprepared, from my mouth. I never lied to Owen. I didn't know why I'd done so now, but there was one thing I knew for certain: I didn't want what Marcus had told me to be true. I didn't want any of it to be true. Not waking up in the Dolans' bathtub; not finding my soggy, bloodied clothes in their sink; not vomiting wine onto their bathroom floor. Not whatever happened to me before Marcus found me outside on his back lawn.

I didn't want it to be true for me, and I didn't want it to be true for Owen either. As soon as it was out there between us, I would never be able to take it back. It would become an inescapable, devastating part of both of our lives. I told myself that by not saying it out loud I could keep it from becoming real for him. I told myself I could protect him.

NOW

CHAPTER 5

FOR THE THREE months since I gave birth to Thomas, I've been watching a teetering carousel spin round and round, unable to climb back on. The mornings and nights have passed by in a ghastly blur, dragging me toward Thomas's due date, September 13. The day he should have been born is the day he is finally allowed to come home from the hospital. Today.

Waning sunlight pierces the front window, casting the parlor in bronze as my husband feeds the baby. Thomas looks up at Owen contentedly, cheeks and throat pulsing. He's learning how to suckle. If I had my watercolors with me, I'd capture this parlor scene before the light changed.

I've always enjoyed using that word, *parlor,* to describe this room at the front of the house. It's where we've put

Thomas's crib, for now, until we get around to painting the nursery. Despite its distinctive multi-pane window looking out to the front yard, the parlor feels private, a special nook for creating art or for pondering existential questions. It was the first room I focused on renovating after Owen and I moved in. I sanded and refinished the original pine floor planks with painstaking care, eventually covering the less-than-beautiful spots with a Turkish kilim carpet in rich, earthy hues of crimson and chamomile.

At some point while I was at St. Elizabeth's recovering from the C-section, Owen purchased the red rocking chair in which he's currently feeding Thomas. I came home to find it here, daring to occupy the spot in front of the fire. When it rocks, its runners tug against the weave of the kilim carpet, pulling the fabric in either direction. Its wood has been stained a vulgar red, which clashes with the exposed brick of the fireplace. With that rocking chair in the middle of the carpet and the davenport shoved back into the corner against the far wall, the parlor's balance has been unmistakably disturbed. It feels all wrong in here now. Off-kilter.

I foraged every estate sale in the Berkshires to find the perfect antique furniture for the farmhouse's five cozy rooms—six including the front entryway—and the davenport has always been my favorite piece. Its upholstery complements the pattern in the parlor's crewelwork drapes, but even more than for its visual appeal, I've appreciated the davenport for its function. It used to be mine and Owen's favorite place to sit together, sometimes with a book or a crossword puzzle, sometimes just to talk. It was on the davenport where he first brought up the idea of starting a family, over a year ago.

He had called and left me a voice mail during his half-hour commute home from work. I'd missed the notification, so it had taken me by surprise when he'd presented me with a pink cardboard box filled with paper strips meant for testing my pee.

"Half of these, the ones in this package, here, are to measure your LH, which is . . ." He squinted at the side of the box. "Lu-tein-izing hormone. That's how you know when you're ovulating. Your LH spikes."

"Thanks, I know about luteinizing hormone," I said, feeling accosted.

"Now, you have to pee on this every day," he continued. "And when you see the thin purple line, we know that's the day to have lots and lots of sex." He flashed me a mischievous grin. "We basically shouldn't stop doing it for forty-eight hours straight, just to be sure."

"And what are those other strips for?" I already knew what those other strips were for.

"Pregnancy tests!" Owen exclaimed. "If we get it right, with the sex and the timing, then this is how we'll know it worked. Look." He thrust the box at me. "They show one line when you dip them in regular pee and two lines when you dip them in pregnant pee."

I couldn't put my finger on why, but his enthusiasm for monitoring my bodily functions crossed an unarticulated boundary. We'd discussed having kids in the future, casually, but I'd given him no indication that I was ready to start trying to conceive right this minute. Or whenever my LH spiked.

"Hold on a second, Owen," I said.

Owen, unfortunately, did not hold on a second. "I also got some of these," he said, reaching back into the pharmacy bag. He pulled out a sleeve of those three-ounce paper cups that people keep on the bathroom counter to wash down pills. "For you to pee in," he explained.

"I get it!" I shouted, surprising us both. "You want to get me pregnant."

"Well, yes," he said matter-of-factly. "I thought you'd be excited."

"You thought I'd be excited? About *your* decision that it was time for me to get pregnant?"

"What?" he said, hurt. "That's not what I meant. I thought you wanted to start a family."

"I do, eventually," I said. "But this is so . . . presumptuous of you. First of all, I'm not done renovating the house. In case you haven't noticed, we still live in a construction zone."

"There's really only the nursery left."

"Which I won't be able to work on if I'm pregnant."

"We can hire Eddie's guys to do the labor."

"And you've been so busy at work lately—"

"It's tax season." He interrupted me. "Julie, I could quit tomorrow. I could even be a stay-at-home dad and take care of the baby full-time. We don't need the income, you know that."

He wasn't exaggerating. Owen was an asset to the family

law firm in Lenox where he'd taken an accounting job soon after we'd moved here, but he'd never been the type to concentrate on advancing up the corporate ladder. The purpose of a career, in Owen's mind, was to serve and set an example for his children, his family—the only thing that really mattered to him. I believed him when he said he'd be delighted to take on the role of our future kid's primary caregiver. For it to all come together, though, he needed me to play along.

"If you're serious about quitting work and staying home, I like that idea," I said. "But I'm still the one who has to be pregnant. I'm the one who has to *have* the baby. And I don't know, I'm just not ready."

"What are you afraid of?"

"Pregnancy wasn't easy for my mother, mentally or physically," I said. "The doctors made her stay in bed for the last few months leading up to my birth."

"You never told me that," Owen said. "Was there something wrong with you—with the baby?"

"No, I'm pretty sure I was healthy," I said. "It was Patricia they were worried about."

"Why?"

"She never talked about it with me. I wouldn't even know about the bed rest order, except I overheard her complaining to my dad years later," I said.

"Is there a way for you to find out what was wrong with her?" Owen asked. "When she was pregnant with you?"

"Miranda would know."

I thought of the sprightly Italian-American cook whom my mother had hired immediately after marrying into the Merritt family. Miranda had worked at my parents' Needham estate nearly every day for two decades. Her semolina ravioli, hand folded and stuffed with fresh ricotta, had reminded Patricia of her childhood in East Boston. I thought of the exhaustion in her voice the night she'd called me to report my parents' death. *There's been an accident.*

"Can you still get in touch with her?" Owen asked.

"I'll send her an email," I said. "But Owen, it's more than the physical stuff my mom went through. I guess I'm afraid because, you know, my own parents were . . . *not* parents."

"You're not the same as your parents, Julie," Owen said.

During my lifetime, my mother had likely spent more time one-on-one with her individual graduate students than she had with me, her daughter. She'd been raised in East Boston by Italian-American grocers, grandparents who'd died before I was born. At some point during her scholarship-funded Ivy League education she'd met and married Charles Merritt, who was content to fly planes between his friends' summer homes and "play with" his family's outrageous generational wealth by backing whichever political candidate was currently hosting the most glamorous fundraisers.

"There was nothing stopping either of them from bonding with their only child," I said. "They didn't even try. What if it's the same way for our kid? What if I'm just as bad as they were?"

"I'm not your father, Julie," Owen said. "And you aren't your mother."

"I know that," I told him. "And you never even met them.

But I might have inherited something, that weird part of their personalities, the part that just couldn't . . . couldn't love a child."

Owen shook his head. "That's impossible, Juju Bear. I may have never met your parents but I know *you*. You'll be a good mom. Can't you imagine it? Our life as a family?" He wrapped both arms around me. "Sitting here on the window seat, coloring pictures with a cute little kid? *Our* cute little kid?"

"We are almost thirty," I conceded, leaning against his chest.

"Don't you think it's time to start planning for a family?"

"Maybe you're right," I said. "But don't surprise me with it like this."

"I'm sorry, Juju Bear." Owen took my hands, contrite. "I shouldn't have sprung the LH strips on you."

"You could have at least run it by me before you sashayed in here with a box of pregnancy tests."

"I'm sorry," he repeated. Then, after a beat, "Did I really *sashay* in here?" He jumped up and performed an exaggerated lean, as if he were a marionette. "Like this?"

I couldn't help laughing at him. "Get back down here," I said, pulling him onto the davenport with me. "Let's talk about having kids again later, after I've had some time to get used to the idea."

"Okay, but when?" Owen clasped his hands in a playful gesture of hope. "Next week? I don't want to pester you, but I don't want you to forget."

"I'm not going to *forget*," I said. "How about January,

in the new year? And then we can come back to it, once a month after that, to see if we're on the same page."

Owen agreed to the monthly check-ins. I sent off a quick email to Miranda, asking what she remembered about my mother's symptoms during her pregnancy. I doubted she'd respond. The email didn't bounce back immediately, though, so at least the address was still in use. Then Owen started in on one of his legendary foot massages, and we cuddled on the davenport until it was time to make dinner.

That's how we used to be. The davenport was a place to solve our problems, to cozy up and conspire in front of the hearth, like they sing about in Christmas carols.

Now, the davenport is the coldest seat in the room. I would know, because it's where I find myself huddled, alone, keeping Owen silent company as he presses a bottle to Thomas's eager mouth. He'll have to do it again in two to three hours. Because I cannot keep my son alive.

It's not like I didn't try to feed him breast milk. I went to him every day while he was in the NICU, cradled him close while he emitted desperate creaking noises. His mouth would grope like a fish suffocating on a hook, but it would not latch. I'd adjust the position of the swaddling blanket beneath his yielding red chin and try again. It hurt, in a way that was beyond visceral, to let the baby down like that. Eventually the failure became unbearable, and I watched him learn to suckle at a bottle instead. I gave up.

Owen doesn't appear to notice the baby enthusiastically blinking up at him. Instead, he stares straight ahead at the wall panels behind the davenport where I'm sitting. His eyes bore through me as if I'm not in his line of sight, also trying to be worthy of his attention.

On the side table beside the davenport lies a paperback book. Written in a curly, sans serif font across an image of a sullen-looking pregnant woman is the title *Healing from Trauma*. One of Owen's leather bookmarks dangles between the pages from a spot he's saved. That bookmark is no doubt my husband's way of sending me a message. Now that Thomas has come home from the hospital, Owen's ready for me to be healed and functioning. It's past time to get it together and address everything I've been failing to do since the baby was born.

Healing from Trauma beckons to me from the side table but I can't bring myself to pick it up again. It's not the title that stings, but the words below it: *by Dr. Patricia Merritt.* My mother. Her life's work. The standard-bearer when it comes to self-guided trauma healing. It was published a few years before my father crashed their plane and killed them both. I wonder how she'd feel if she knew I was reading her book. Rather, I wonder how she'd feel if she knew I'd been *instructed* to read her book by Dr. Bridges, the clinical psychologist I'd met for a single video appointment during my truncated pregnancy. I read through a handful of pertinent sections months ago, even highlighted some of them, but I haven't opened *Healing from Trauma* since Thomas was born.

Owen knows how annoyed I was when Dr. Bridges recommended my own once-absent and now-late mother's book, but I'd perused it anyway because it was the only lifeline I'd been thrown. The book's main insight—basically, trauma victims must reconnect with their bodies in order to feel like themselves again—was impossible for me to put into practice while I was pregnant. If I was disconnected from my body then, it's even worse now. My mother's book won't have the answers to why I'm feeling this way, three months after giving birth.

The word *feeling* isn't right, though, to describe my current state of existence. I don't feel much of anything except, perhaps, lonesome. I'd expected to be in physical pain after such an invasive surgery as a C-section, but since I'm not breastfeeding Thomas, I can take prescription painkillers, and they've been doing the trick. Even the persistent ache that plagued my entire lower body throughout the pregnancy has dissipated, all thanks to the lovely narcotics they sent home with me when I was finally able to leave the hospital.

No, I don't feel very much, these days. What I am doing instead is *failing,* spectacularly. Failing at motherhood. Failing to adjust to everything that's changed.

That's why Owen left my mother's book out on the side table for me to find. There's something wrong with me, something that wasn't wrong before, and he's recognized the shift. Maybe it's a chemical imbalance, like the stage fright that Liza treats with beta blockers. It's possible, in the way that anything becomes possible once the worst has already happened, that this void of feeling has nothing to do with the trauma of the night I've forgotten. Maybe it's as simple as I'd feared. I wasn't cut out to be a mother.

THEN

CHAPTER 6

IT TOOK OVER a month to finish the job at the Bidwell House. During that time, other than a mail-order at-home STI kit that cost $149, I focused only on work. I brought it home with me, spreading out the plans across the kitchen table so Owen would see. He was distracted with tax season, meanwhile, and didn't pry. He had no idea I'd been attacked; after the morning I'd lied to him about my injuries, he hadn't asked again. Liza was the only other person who might have noticed that something was horribly, irrevocably wrong with me, and she'd been conspicuously absent since the night of her holiday party. In the days before Christmas her mother fell and broke a hip in the New York apartment where she lived alone, and Liza rushed down there to care for her. We exchanged a few vague text messages, mostly about her mother's condition. We never had a chance to speak. I never told her how her husband had found me on their back lawn or how I'd woken up in their bathtub, naked and battered. Apparently, neither did Marcus.

Six weeks after the night I still couldn't remember, four days before my twenty-ninth birthday, I waited on the davenport for Owen to return home from the office.

The sound of Daisy charging down the front staircase alerted me to Owen's arrival before his key turned in the lock.

"Juju Bear?" His voice filled the entryway with warmth even as the night's chill burst through the front door behind him. "What's going on?" He crossed the parlor and sat down beside me without bothering to remove his peacoat. From the way he looked at me, the expression on my face must have been alarming.

"Owen," I began. I hadn't wanted any of this. I'd resisted speaking the truth into existence for him, but now there was no other option. There was no other reality, and I couldn't pretend any longer. My mouth felt too clumsy to shape the words, but the truth I needed to tell him forced its way out into the space between us. "The night of the Dolans' Christmas party, six weeks ago, I think I was raped," I said. "Someone raped me."

He inhaled sharply, wrapped me in his arms, and held me against the cold wool of his coat, without saying anything. I felt his chest rise beneath my cheek.

"I'm sorry," I said.

"Don't be *sorry*," he said. "It's not your fault."

I knew that the rape wasn't my fault, of course. That wasn't what I meant. I was sorry in the way you were sorry when someone died. Sorry any of this had happened, sorry to be the bearer of bad news, sorry our lives were now ruined.

But Owen had misinterpreted it as an apology *to him*. As if that was the reaction he expected from me. It made me irritated with Owen, and I didn't want to feel that way. I shouldn't have compulsively apologized to my husband in the first place. That was a bad habit.

"I mean, I'm sorry for not telling you right away," I said truthfully.

Owen didn't respond. He didn't tell me not to be sorry about lying; that part *was* my fault. Instead, he controlled his breath, apparently trying to calm us both down.

"Let's breathe in, together," he said, and his voice shook. But he inhaled deeply, steadily, and waited until I matched his breath.

Then, with his lungs full, he whispered, "Out together," and released the air gradually through pursed lips.

I followed his example, matched his breath pattern, and felt my heart rate slow down a bit.

Again. In together, we breathed, and out together.

I'd seen Owen use this breathing exercise on his own, after getting off the phone with his mother. He'd never included me before, though. I loved him for helping me calm down my nervous system, for using his breath—the very thing keeping him alive—to help keep me alive too. When my breathing returned to normal, Owen created enough space between us to look down at me. His face was streaked with tears.

"You said that you think you were raped." His jaw twitched. "What the hell, Julie? How could you not be sure about something like that? Who was it?"

"I don't know. I mean, I only know I was raped because Marcus told me, and because—"

"Marcus?" Owen interrupted. "It was *Marcus*?"

"No," I insisted. "Marcus is the one who found me outside, all beaten up. I don't think he knows much more than I do."

Owen sat back. "Outside?"

"That's the thing," I said. "When I try to remember what happened that night, I can't. Most of the party is completely wiped clean. Someone must have put something in my drink."

He watched me carefully as I spoke, and I thought his eyebrow twitched with surprise. Or skepticism. It must sound awfully convenient, how I'd forgotten the details. The back of my neck and shoulders prickled with creeping fear. He was doubting my story.

"It's the only explanation." I barreled onward. "Marcus found me on his back lawn and brought me inside. He put me in their bathtub, and that's where I came to."

"In their bathtub," Owen repeated. "And you don't remember anything before that?"

"I remember getting to their house. Seeing Liza, having a glass of wine, and not much else."

"That's fucking crazy." He stood up. "We're going over there. *Fuck* Marcus. If he won't tell us what he knows, we can hire a private detective, track down everyone who went to that party, whatever it takes."

"No!" I said quickly. "I can't face him, Owen."

"Then let's go to the police." He offered me both his hands so he could pull me up with him. "They'll launch an investigation."

"No, no, I can't." I shook my head frantically, squeezing my eyes shut. "Owen, I can't."

After a moment, I felt him collapse back onto the davenport next to me. "Okay, okay," he said, slightly subdued. "We can talk about it later."

I didn't want to talk about it later.

"But if you don't want to report the rape or confront Marcus, why are you telling *me*, now?" His voice broke. "Why not weeks ago, right after it happened? Did I do something wrong?" His eyes were pained, earnest. "Why now?"

It was time for me to break his heart. Mine would break, too, structurally dependent as it was upon Owen's. I wondered if it would feel better or worse to do the breaking physically, and imagined the two of us with our torsos split open, ribs cracked, hearts crushed into pulp like overripe stone fruit. This would be worse.

"I'm pregnant," I said.

Owen's eyes filled with disbelief, squinting at the corners, as if asking me to hurry up and deliver the punch line. Then his face was overcome with such disappointment that it was all I could do not to look away from him.

He leaned forward over his lap and cradled his forehead in his palms. "How do you know?" he asked the floor.

I'd known the morning after the Dolans' party. From the deep and lasting ache in my abdomen, I'd known my body had experienced more than a violent invasion. It had been transformed. Against my will, my body had become a host for the invader's offspring. Viscerally, biologically, I'd known.

But knowing something is not the same as letting yourself believe it.

"I missed my period," I said. "And then this morning at breakfast, you brought up our recent . . . lack of physical intimacy." We both cringed at my clinical euphemism. I'd promised him monthly check-ins back in December, and he'd waited until that morning to bring up the topic of family planning again. "I decided to find out for sure."

"You took a pregnancy test?"

"More than one."

I told him how I'd spent the day peeing into the three-ounce paper cups and using up the paper strips from the kit he'd surprised me with. The kit he'd intended for me to use to plan my pregnancy with *his* child. I'd tested, chugged water, tested, eaten a saltine cracker, tested again, and so on. I'd lined up more than a dozen cups along the vanity in our bathroom, each containing a tiny rectangular strip of paper displaying two matching bright-purple lines, and then I'd gone out to the pharmacy and purchased a variety of new, different kinds of pregnancy tests.

They'd all been positive too.

Owen sat back on the davenport and tugged at the ends of his hair. "What do we do now?" he finally asked.

"I don't know what to do." I moaned. "Should we have a baby? A rapist's baby? I could have an abortion." The parasitic fetus in my body would never feel like a real person, anyway, I reasoned. "I should have an abortion."

"When it comes to the pregnancy," he said, "it's up to you. It's always been up to you."

I almost reminded him how he'd tried to convince me I was ready to get pregnant a few months earlier. But if he'd come around to the belief that it was my decision, there was no need to rehash that argument. There was no space for bickering now, anyway.

"I need to make the best decision," I said. "And right now, no decision feels okay."

"Then let's find a doctor, sit down with a professional counselor, consider all our options, figure out what will make us—" Owen cleared his throat. "What will feel the least bad, I guess."

I nodded. "You're right."

"I am?" He raised his eyebrows. "That means we should report the rape so the police can start investigating."

"No, I don't think so," I said. "Especially if we end up with a baby."

"*Especially* if we end up with a baby, don't you want to know who the guy is? It will be the kid's biological father." I loved Owen for not needing to reassure me that he would become the child's father in all ways that mattered. He'd never known his own dad, a grifter who'd bailed on Owen's mother while she was pregnant. I'd never once heard my mother-in-law, Diana, speak of the man. Owen only referenced his dad as an example of the precise type of person he hoped to avoid becoming. He wanted the chance to shape himself into a different kind of father.

But I didn't like his suggestion. Whether the person who'd attacked me was a stranger who'd been hiding in the woods or one of Marcus's employees from the Christmas party, I wasn't ready to find out. I was terrified to give my fear a face.

"What if when the kid's born it looks nothing like me and everything like *him*?" I asked wildly. "What if it has the rapist's eyes? Or his personality? How am I supposed to feed, clothe, and love that child?"

Owen didn't say anything, and I was grateful. There was nothing he could say. After a moment he stood up and removed his coat, and the space beside me where he'd been sitting felt instantly cold.

"Where are you going?"

"To make some tea," he said. "We can sort this out."

We spent the rest of the night and most of the following morning discussing what we were going to do next. I regretted not confiding in him sooner and told him so. At some point, Owen made another pot of tea. More than once, when I felt overwhelmed, we repeated the breathing exercise of inhaling together, holding our breath, and exhaling together slowly.

We decided that the next day we would do three things. First, we'd select a prenatal care facility where I could talk to a counselor about how to proceed with the pregnancy, and we'd make an appointment. Then we'd drive together to the Dolans' house to ask them what they knew about what had happened to me at their holiday party. Finally, we'd bring whatever we found out to the police station to file a report. The police would know what to do next.

As the frosty glow of morning filled the parlor, we padded upstairs together to get some sleep. I didn't feel hopeful, exactly, but it was comforting to have formed a plan. Most importantly, I wasn't lying to Owen anymore. I'd never lie to him again, I told myself. No more secrets.

CHAPTER 7

OWEN SHOULD HAVE told his mother not to come. I was in no mood for company, least of all Diana's. She'd called that morning to inform Owen that she'd be stopping by and leaving us in charge of her four-year-old goddaughter, Sadie, who was currently in her care, while she visited a new mother in neighboring Sheffield "for just a few hours." As we waited, Owen paced and tugged at the ends of his hair. I sat rigidly to avoid wrinkling the crisp teal dress I'd ironed for my mother-in-law's unsolicited visit.

The previous evening had been spent researching a prenatal care facility online. We'd eventually chosen Dr. Hasan Syed from the list of gynecologists in our insurance network based on positive reviews from former patients, the convenient location of his office, and the fact that he had an opening the following Monday. Making that appointment was the first step in our three-step action plan.

We should have been at the Dolans' house already, grilling them about the holiday party and taking notes. Instead, we'd spent the morning preparing for Diana's inevitable judgment, cleaning our house until it was nearly acceptable by her standards. The rooms weren't childproofed, but Sadie was a well-behaved four-year-old, resilient, clever. At least we'd removed everything fragile from the lower shelves.

Owen had promised not to mention the pregnancy to his mother. After the appointment with Dr. Syed coming up on Monday, if I decided to have an abortion, we'd never have to tell Diana about any of it.

The doorbell rang. Owen squared his shoulders to greet his mother.

"The traffic on the Mass Pike was unbelievable," Diana said as she stepped inside. Sadie followed her godmother, eyes downcast. "And why *Lee*, of all places? There's Lenox right next door, or Stockbridge, for Pete's sake."

Our old mill town's economy had slumped in the mid-twentieth century and never fully bounced back, which meant it was still affordable for the families who'd put down roots when industry was booming; they hadn't yet been priced out by the wealthy city dwellers seeking second homes near Tanglewood.

"I drove by an old mill building that must have been longer than a dozen city blocks," she continued, "and its windows were *shattered*, all on one side, like it had been shot up in a drive-by or something."

"Hi, Diana," I said. Then, squatting down, I said, "Hi, Sadie. We're so glad you're here." As the words left my mouth, they became true, and Sadie returned my smile. Diana's eyes moved deliberately from my unruly curls down to the inevitable creases across the lap of my dress. "Julie," she said, grimacing. "Happy birthday, isn't it?" Then, to Owen, "Give your mother a hug."

"Good to see you, Mom," Owen said, obeying her. "Julie's birthday isn't until the fifth, remember. Would you like some iced coffee?"

"I'll just have a cup," Diana said, leading the way into the kitchen. "But I have to get to Sheffield." She took a seat at one end of the table, reflexively arranging the pockets of her tea-length, floral skirt on top of her lap to avoid sitting on her rosary beads. She used the string of pea-sized wooden beads so often that she only wore skirts with pockets so she'd have somewhere to stash them. A consistent performance of her type of perfection.

"Will you draw with me?" Sadie asked, noticing the sketchbook and colored pencils I'd arranged on the kitchen table.

"I was hoping you'd want to," I said. "But first, I need you to look around the parlor and find the three best objects to draw. All different shapes and sizes."

"Three objects," Sadie said, beaming at the familiar assignment. "For a life, still," she said. "We'll make a life, still."

"You got it," I confirmed. "A still life."

"Still life," Sadie repeated to herself as she headed for the parlor.

Of all the christenings of all Diana's godchildren, Sadie's

was the only one to which I'd been invited, nearly four years ago. When I remembered that day, the humidity stood out in my mind as much as the fact that we'd arrived late to St. Catherine's. It had been a historically hot summer, and that Sunday in particular had been classified by local weather reporters as "a real scorcher."

Sadie's christening was one of four taking place in the middle of a regular Sunday Mass, and the pews were nearly full when Owen and I arrived. We crept in the back and paused for a moment to close the huge wooden doors behind us without accidentally slamming them. Then I followed Owen up a side aisle to the front of the cavernous church, where Father Eagan presided at the altar. The late morning sun sliced through the stained-glass windows and made his face appear kaleidoscopic.

Diana sat in the front pew beside the biological parents and corresponding godparents of the other babies who were to be baptized. The mothers and godmothers wore conservative cap-sleeved dresses; the fathers and godfathers wore starched suits with sweat-soaked collars. Large fans positioned at the front of each aisle blew the August air around loudly but ineffectively and the red-faced couples used their paper programs to alternately fan themselves, each other, and the three sleeping infants among them. Like the other soon-to-be-officially-Catholic babies, Sadie was fast asleep in her ridiculously long embroidered christening gown. But neither of her parents was anywhere to be seen, as far as I could tell. Instead, Diana cradled baby Sadie in the crook of her elbow, with her gaze trained on Father Eagan.

For Owen's sake, I wanted to make it clear that I was a part of the Porter family, and that meant participating in the sacrament of Sadie's baptism. We stood with the rest of the congregation and repeated specific phrases about how we planned to raise Sadie in the Catholic tradition. Regardless of how I felt about the faith-related commitments, I decided that I was making a real promise to that little girl. Even then, part of me suspected the time would come when Owen and I would need to step up to take care of Sadie.

"You know Sadie's mom? Kristen?" Owen whispered as we waited outside the church for the crowd to disperse. "I asked one of the deacons. It's heroin this time. Mom must be pissed."

As if summoned by her son and determined to prove his assumption right, Diana marched out of the church visibly distraught. She pressed the sleeping baby into my arms and snapped, "Hold Sadie while Owen and I clean up in the sacristy."

They both volunteered as lay Eucharistic ministers at St. Catherine's, Diana almost every day and Owen whenever she roped him into attending Mass with her. Their duties in the sacristy involved washing the chalices, folding the napkins, and reordering the various other accoutrements that Father Eagan and the altar servers had used during Mass. As I attempted to gather the billowing bright-white christening gown around Sadie's tiny body, Owen followed his mother back into the church to help clean up.

The door shut behind them, and I was surprised to find myself face-to-face with Father Eagan, still in his ceremonial robes. I assumed he was looking for Diana, having finished sending off his less devout congregants.

"Diana's gone back inside to clean up," I told him. He stopped walking, and I realized that I'd failed to greet him formally before speaking. "Father," I added. It was the term of respect I'd heard Owen and Diana use every time they'd referenced him or any other priest, directly or indirectly—"Father"—but I didn't like the texture of it in my mouth. It felt chewy in the wrong places, like overcooked pasta.

"Thank you for being here, Julie," the priest said warmly.

"Yeah, I mean, of course." I waited, surprised at his initial friendliness. I'd never interacted with a priest before, one-on-one. I wasn't sure what to expect from this man who believed himself to be holy.

"Diana suggested that we offer a prayer for you, and for the souls of your parents," he said, in the same benevolent tone of voice. "I wanted to talk to you first. To see if being included in the Prayers of the Faithful was the kind of thing you'd appreciate."

"Sure," I'd said. "Thanks."

It surprised me, when I thought of it now, that Diana had offered to rally all those faithful, praying people to put in a word with God on my behalf.

If what the parishioners at St. Catherine's believed about the afterlife turned out to be accurate, if what they preached about rules and consequences was true, then no amount of praying would save my parents' souls. Nor, for that matter, would it save mine. I put very little stock in the effect of Catholic prayer, but it couldn't *hurt* to be on the receiving end of all that positive energy. I wondered if they'd ever gone through with it.

"Who are you meeting in Sheffield, Mom?" Owen asked, pouring iced coffee into three glasses over by the sink. I leaned my weight against the kitchen island.

"Imogen," Diana said. "She's a child of God and I'm about to become her godmother." *Godparent* was usually an honorary title, occasionally requiring its bearer to mail a congratulatory check or perform some light spiritual mentorship. Diana, though, took the role exceedingly seriously. She was godmother to multiple children across New England, for whom she took varying degrees of responsibility.

"That's nice, Mom." Owen put a glass of iced coffee down in front of his mother and another one on the island beside me.

"It *is* a big honor, indeed." Diana's eyes lit up with pride. She lifted her glass to her lips and held it there, poised above her chin, as she spoke. "Imogen's mother struggles with her mental health," she said. "She doesn't always have a place to live, but the grandparents are in Canton, right near me. Some of us at St. Catherine's are helping her and Imogen move out there." She returned the glass to the table without having sipped from it.

"Oh, my god," I said. "What's her name?"

"Julie," Diana snapped, startling me. "I'm sure I've told you about taking the Lord's name in vain."

Owen's eyes were glued to the condensation on the side of his iced coffee glass.

"Anyway, I'm happy to do it," Diana continued quickly.

"Imogen's mother—her name is Shana, Julie—is one of the women we helped at the CPC." Besides volunteering as a Eucharistic minister at Mass every morning, Diana spent a few afternoons a week working at the crisis pregnancy center affiliated with St. Catherine's.

"And Shana chose you to be her daughter's godmother?" Owen lowered himself into the empty chair beside Diana.

"It's the least she could do." She finally sipped her iced coffee. "I'm the one who saved her baby, you know. She was off her medication when she got pregnant. She came into the CPC looking for an abortion."

"Oh, my god," I said again, nearly choking on my iced coffee.

Diana's reaction was immediate and characteristically disproportionate. "Julie, you really have to stop taking the Lord's name in vain if you're going to be a part of this family."

My face burned.

"Mom, Julie *is* our family." Owen spoke up, finally. "We've been married for over four years."

Diana narrowed her eyes. "You can call it whatever you want to call it, but *our* family believes in sacraments."

I'd never regret the way we'd gotten married. The two of us and our love, no flashy parties or over-the-top romantic performances for people we hardly knew. In addition to resenting our elopement, Diana had been furious that we'd eschewed a Catholic ceremony. What bothered her the most, I suspected, was that I'd refused to get confirmed by Father Eagan. She couldn't stand the idea of having "pagan" grandchildren. It was why, over four years later, she was acting this petty.

"We're married, Mom," Owen said. "It counts. I'm going to have some more coffee. Anyone else?" He pushed his chair back and rose, clearly eager to redirect the conversation.

Diana glanced up to answer his question and as her eyes landed on him, Owen touched me. He placed his hand lightly on my lower belly in that reflexively possessive way men sometimes do. It was the first time he'd made that gesture since I'd told him I was pregnant, and it surprised me.

I flinched.

Diana's eyes widened. "What was that?"

Owen yanked his hand away too quickly, answering her question.

But she needed to be sure. "Are you pregnant, Julie?" She nearly shrieked.

My stomach churned. Owen looked to me in panic.

"Diana . . ." I began shakily. I took a deep breath and when I spoke again, thankfully, my voice was sturdy. "Diana, I was raped," I said. "A little over two months ago. And I got pregnant. Pregnant with the rapist's baby."

When those words came out of my mouth in that order, they sounded absurd, fabricated, as if the situation they described could never occur in real life. As if we were all characters in a television series whose writers had gone on strike.

Diana pressed both hands to her heart. She said tenderly, "Julie, I am so sorry that happened to you." Then she outstretched her arms, offering me a hug. "Honey, I am so, so sorry."

I leaned against her, dubious at first, then grateful as she held me. It felt like the kind of hug a mother might give her own, beloved child; it was a new and welcome feeling for me. No one had ever wanted to be my mother. Maybe Diana would be able to fill that role for me—the role she'd always filled for Owen. The thought embarrassed me but I let myself entertain the possibility that *mother-in-law* might take on new meaning between us now. This tragedy, the aftermath of the rape, could become the turning point when Diana would start treating me like a member of the Porter family.

She pulled away from me and crossed the kitchen. "The pregnancy will be challenging for you, of course," she said as she reached the wall-mounted telephone and placed her hand on the receiver. "But we can get you in at the CPC as early as tomorrow morning. Let me just give them a call."

She was about to book me an appointment at her god-damn crisis pregnancy center. They wouldn't be able to manipulate me, but the prospect of letting them try made me want to retch. As soon as she made that call, all her fellow volunteers and probably most of the parishioners at St. Catherine's would know about the pregnancy. Owen would start receiving congratulatory greeting cards. Even if I could stomach sitting through an appointment at the CPC, I couldn't let the news get out this way.

I opened my mouth and heard myself say, "I'm not sure whether I'm going to go through with the pregnancy, actually."

"Even more reason why you need an appointment," Diana said, undeterred.

"Mom, wait."

"Excuse me?" Diana placed the phone back on its mount and turned to her son, her expression unreadable.

"Julie and I know that we want to start a family of our own," he said, "someday soon, even, but this probably isn't the right way for that to happen."

Diana didn't answer.

"I want to have *Owen's* child," I said, hoping that would resonate with her.

She was looking at Owen, not at me. "The answer is no," she told Owen.

"No?" he repeated back, dumbfounded.

"I don't . . ." I began to explain that it wasn't a yes-or-no question, that we hadn't been asking for her permission in the first place, but she interrupted me, speaking evenly.

"God is present in the creation of every life, including the one you are blessed to be carrying," she said, finally turning to glare at me. "No, you will not kill this baby."

It sounded terrible when she put it that way. I wasn't surprised at the intensity of her reaction, though. I'd always known how she felt about abortion. Whatever respect she'd ever had for my life was now secondary to her feelings for the blob of cells multiplying inside my uterus.

"Mom, she was raped," Owen said.

"Thank you, Owen. Julie's already told me that," Diana said. "It seems as if you take her word for it."

She couldn't possibly mean that she suspected I hadn't been raped. Because that would mean she believed I'd gotten pregnant by having consensual sex with someone other than Owen. It would mean she believed I was capable of being unfaithful to her son. Furthermore, it would mean she thought I was lying to them both about what had happened. She'd never thought highly of me, but even Diana wouldn't go that far.

"It's a lot to process," I said slowly.

Diana finally spoke to me, her voice saccharine. "You seem to be managing quite well, Julie," she said. "For a rape victim."

I was speechless. How dare she treat me this way in my own kitchen? Examining her face for any sign of empathy or solidarity, all I saw was a woman who had made it six decades without meeting a pregnant victim she couldn't find a way to blame. No matter how I responded—whether I maintained my composure or gave in to the angry tears gathering in my throat—she'd construe the reaction as proving my guilt.

"Mom, that is out of line," Owen said. "Julie *has* been managing well, given what happened, and I believe her."

Diana opened her mouth to deliver a retort but he wouldn't let her interrupt.

"Whatever Julie—whatever *we*—decide about the baby, you need to trust us that it will be the best decision for our family," he said. "We are not going to live our lives on a rapist's terms."

I'd never heard him speak to his mother that way and from the look on Diana's face, neither had she.

"What's . . . *arapisterms*?" Sadie asked blithely, returning from the parlor. In her hands she carried one of Owen's

L.L.Bean slippers, an antique brass letter opener, and a bookend in the shape of paintbrush.

"I'm sorry, I—I misspoke," Owen stammered. "It's just a nonsense word."

"Looks like you found the best three objects," I said, relieved Sadie hadn't overheard the word *baby*.

"Is that a letter opener?" Diana said through gritted teeth. "Put it down. You're not staying here."

Owen's face fell. "What do you mean, Mom?"

Diana stood up from the table, adjusted the rosary beads in her skirt pocket, and swiftly gathered her purse. "Sadie will be coming with me to meet the new baby in Sheffield," she announced.

"But the life, still . . ." Sadie whined.

"You can draw a still life in Sheffield," Diana said. "You'll love meeting baby Imogen. Your new godsister!"

Sadie reluctantly returned her treasures to the parlor.

"Mom, wait." Owen trailed his mother to the front entryway as if he were a child again himself. "I don't understand."

"No, I'm afraid *I* don't understand," Diana said. She hurried Sadie out the front door ahead of her. "A letter opener, just lying out, for Pete's sake," she said. "This house is not safe for a child. Not safe at all."

NOW

CHAPTER 8

THE BABY SQUIRMS in Owen's arms, jolting us from our respective dazes. *Thomas.* I need to get used to using his name. Owen is the one who chose it. As soon as we saw on the ultrasound that he was going to be a boy, Owen began to brainstorm potential names with vigor. Each time he suggested something, though, I'd imagine how the boy bearing such a name might grow up to look, how he might behave, and I'd find myself resenting that small person named Jacob or Francis or Michael. As long as we avoided my father's name, Charles, I was content to leave the final selection to Owen. It seemed like a convenient way to demonstrate his unique nonbiological connection to the baby.

"There you are." I tease my husband gently with the phrase he uses to welcome me back to the room when I've been distracted, off in space like that. We haven't been speaking playfully with each other lately, and I'm hoping he'll notice the invitation in my voice.

Owen's amber eyes align with mine, long enough to register that I'm there. He seems startled by the discovery, as if I'm the last person he expected to find sitting across from him in our own parlor.

"Juju Bear . . ." he says, barely loud enough for me to hear. His eyes are suddenly desperate. I'm about to stand and go to him, rest against the bulk of his upper arm, and kiss the top of Thomas's head, cradled there.

Before I can move, though, dim light fills the front window as the lanterns that line our brick walkway flicker on, triggered by their motion sensors. We hear the unintelligible conversation of two voices approaching, one deep and resonant, the other delicate, like ice clinking against the sides of a glass. Marcus and Liza. They've walked around to the front of our house instead of cutting through the woods and across our back lawn, like they usually do, weather permitting. It makes their arrival feel oddly formal.

Owen sighs with apprehension. "Alexa, Play," he tells the smart speaker on the mantel, and a laid-back mix of singer-songwriters covering the Beatles starts up from where it left off earlier. The music immediately makes the house feel less like a bottomless pit of misery and more like an appropriate place to welcome guests.

A rich, burly alto voice sings Paul McCartney's lyrics in a lower key, Mother Mary's words of wisdom. Let it be, she instructs. I used to think those lyrics were pretty good advice. And it's not the meaning of the lyrics that bothers me now; rather, it's something about the repetition. Those three words, over and over. *Let. It. Be.* It's unsettling.

Owen stands, holding the baby out unnecessarily far away from his body, as if that space will protect it somehow. I watch him carefully place the bundle, heavy and still now, into the crib. He leaves the parlor to greet Liza and Marcus as the sun finishes its descent.

Our moment of connection has disappeared with the day.

THEN

CHAPTER 9

FROM THE LOOK on Marcus's face when he opened the front door, it was obvious he knew why we were there. He fumbled to finish buttoning his wrinkled flannel shirt.

"What's up, you guys?" His tone was casual, insincere.

"Have a sec?" Owen asked.

"Come on in." Marcus stepped aside, scratching the stubble on his chin. We followed him into the Dolans' grand foyer. "Can I get you anything to eat?"

"No thanks." Owen was curt. "We're on our way over to the police station." He paused, and we both watched Marcus straighten up to his full height.

"Police station," Marcus repeated, his tone flat. "What for?"

"To report what happened at your party," I said.

Marcus snapped his head toward me. "You remember what happened?"

"No," I said. "That's why we're here."

He wiped his hands on the front of his paint-stained jeans. "It's a shame you couldn't make it out," he said to Owen. "Julie said you caught a bug or something? You missed a crazy party."

"She told me what happened."

"I thought you said you didn't remember," Marcus said.

"I told him how you found me, how I was . . . raped." I hated saying that word, especially in relation to myself. It immediately defined my role in the conversation when I identified myself as a victim. Unlike Owen and Marcus, something I hadn't wanted to happen had happened to my body, and I'd been powerless to stop it. Suddenly, I was no longer on equal footing with the two of them, the Not-Victims.

Marcus still looked confused. As he opened his mouth, I knew what he was going to ask. If I didn't remember any new details, why had I waited until *now* to tell Owen about the rape? "But how come—" Before he could finish, I cut him off.

"I'm pregnant, Marcus," I said.

"Whoa." He looked back and forth between me and Owen, apparently bewildered by the news. "Are you . . . keeping it?"

Immediately, I regretted telling him.

Owen was watching me, surprised, waiting to see how I'd answer. We hadn't made an explicit plan for this; we hadn't discussed what we'd share with Marcus and what we'd keep from him. We'd arrived at the Dolans' house prepared to grill *them* for information, not dish our own.

"We don't know yet," I said. "We're trying to figure out what happened."

"Is Liza still in New York?" Owen asked, peering into the kitchen behind Marcus, as if she might have been sitting there at the table this whole time, silent and antisocial. "Maybe she remembers something."

"Yeah, she's with her mom," Marcus said. "She hasn't been back in over a month." His voice was sheepish, and for the first time I noticed several empty beer cans strewn across the kitchen table and an open trash bag in the corner of the foyer. "I had a couple of guys over last night," he said by way of explanation, then followed up quickly, "None of them were at the party, though."

"Who *was* at the party?" Owen asked.

"There were . . ." Marcus raised his eyes to the ceiling, mentally counting. "Eleven? Eleven or twelve of my land-scaping guys, and a handful of them brought dates. And Donny."

"I'm going to write this down," Owen interrupted, pulling out his phone and opening the note-taking application. "What are their names?"

In total, there were twelve of Marcus's colleagues and landscaping employees on the list, including his brother,

Eddie, ten of their spouses/dates, and Donny. Counting Marcus and Liza, that made twenty-five people the police could interview to find out what had happened to me that night.

I'd been expecting to become nauseated all over again as Marcus rehashed the events of his party. Or maybe, I thought, I would cry. Finally. But as Marcus answered Owen's follow-up questions and promised to call his employees who'd been at the holiday party to "look into the incident," I didn't feel the expected wave of nausea and I certainly didn't start crying.

Instead, I experienced no connection to Marcus's words at all. It was my body he described having discovered in a freezing, bloody pile on his back lawn. It was me whom he'd brought inside to "clean up," as he put it. But from the effect his story had on me, it could have been the plot of a TV show he'd been binge-watching the week before, or details from a disturbing article he'd read online. It could have been a complete lie. Overall, Marcus didn't provide any details surrounding the rape beyond what he'd explained to me while I was half naked and terrified in his bathtub the night of the party.

It would have been better if Liza had been home. Part of me suspected she was purposefully avoiding me, no matter the situation with her mother's health. Six weeks was longer than we'd ever gone without at least talking on the phone, and it wasn't like Liza to be out of touch. Still, she didn't deserve to be blindsided by a police investigation, and I wanted to talk to her before a detective did. I didn't have the luxury of waiting for her to get back from New York, though, before reporting the rape. I'd already wasted enough time.

•••

We drove directly from the Dolans' house to the police department on the second floor of Lee Memorial Hall.

"I'm right here with you," Owen whispered, giving me as much of a side-hug as possible in the doorway of the police station's conference room. The weight of his arm across my shoulders reassured me. This was the next right thing to do, the third step of our three-step action plan. It was time to report as much as I knew about the rape. The idea that I was about to try to report a crime I couldn't even remember seemed impossible. But after talking to Marcus, at least we had a list of names, which was more information to work with than we'd had two nights before, when we'd come up with this plan.

I stepped across the threshold into the small, window-less room. The only furniture comprised one long, metal table and a handful of never-been-cleaned folding chairs. Rust-colored upholstery frayed at the seams where count-less fingers had nervously peeled and picked at it.

"Have a seat."

An officer entered the room behind us, carrying a yellow lined notepad and a ballpoint pen. He shut the door. Officer Bose, according to his name badge, was a short, sturdy man who looked about our age but with much less hair than Owen. He had combed the remaining tuft sideways, attempting to disguise his baldness. I imagined him examining his scalp that morning while getting ready for work, smoothing drugstore pomade between his palms and then across the sparse, struggling hairs.

Officer Bose strode to the folding chair on the far side of the table and waited behind it without sitting. He watched me as a warden might watch an unpredictable inmate.

Owen moved to take a seat, motioning for me to follow.

I willed my body to sit down beside him in the remaining folding chair. Its metal legs whined and snapped into place below me. I wished I was the one holding the cell phone with the list of twenty-five names; my anxious hands craved the comfort of an offering, something to show for myself. I inhaled the stagnant air and tried to focus on the feeling of my lungs expanding outward against the fabric of my sweater.

Officer Bose tossed his notepad onto the table with a loud thwack. He lowered himself into the chair across from us and folded his thick, red hands on top of the yellow lined paper.

"I'm Officer Ryan Bose," he said. "It's my job to help you. You said on the phone that you were sexually assaulted back in December? The twenty-second?"

"Yes," I said.

"Okay, I know it was a while ago, but I need you to tell me everything that happened."

"I don't remember much," I said.

"Everything you remember."

"I went to a party at our neighbors' house," I said. "Marcus and Liza, the Dolans. The next thing I remember is waking up in their bathtub, half naked. Marcus was there. He said he'd found me unconscious out on their back lawn and brought me inside when he realized I'd been attacked. It felt like I'd been raped, but I didn't know for sure until a few days ago when I found out that I'm pregnant."

Officer Bose brought the notepad toward him, so I couldn't see what he was writing, and jotted a few words. Then he looked up at Owen. "Where were you?"

"At home," Owen said. "I had food poisoning."

"Huh. Bad luck." Bose wrote something down. "What time was it when you arrived at the party?" he asked me.

"Around eight thirty," I said, "but it started earlier. I was late."

"And how did you get there? Did you drive?"

"I walked," I said. "We live right through the woods."

"And when did you go outside?"

"What?"

"You said your neighbor found you outside," he said. "What time did you leave the party?"

"I didn't," I said. "I mean, I don't remember when. That's just what Marcus told me."

"Okay. And before all that happened, what were you doing?"

"I remember talking to our other neighbor, Eddie Dolan. He's Marcus's little brother."

"And before that?"

"I was hanging out with Liza—she's Marcus's wife, they

were hosting the party—and this other guy, too, Donny Rocket."

Officer Bose raised an eyebrow. "That his real name?"

I shrugged. "I only talked to him for a second, in the pantry—"

"You were *in* the pantry?" he interrupted.

"It's a whole room, in their house," I said. "A butler's pantry, not a closet. That's where the wine was."

"Got it." Officer Bose wrote something down on the notepad. "And how much wine did you have to drink, Julie?"

"I only remember having a couple of glasses."

"Who served it to you?"

"The first glass, Liza poured. Then Marcus gave me a refill."

"Marcus gave you a refill," Bose repeated. "And the next thing you know, you're naked in a tub with this guy?"

"He wasn't in the tub *with* me," I said. "And I wasn't naked."

Bose scanned the words he'd written down since we came in. "But then—why did you tell me you were naked?"

"I was half naked," I said. "From the waist down."

"You were *half* naked," Bose repeated, looking up with his brow furrowed. "Are you sure, Julie? It's important that we get all the details correct, especially since I'm guessing you didn't acquire a sexual assault forensic exam."

"I'm sure, I was half naked," I said. "But—sexual assault forensic exam? I'm sorry, I don't know what that is."

Officer Bose didn't exactly roll his eyes. Rather, he bulged them out at me in an expression similar to one I'd seen on the faces of people waiting in line at the Department of Motor Vehicles or nannies wrangling toddlers in grocery stores.

"You might have heard it called a rape kit," he said. "They gather evidence from your clothes, on your body, inside your body." He made a rapid, wiggly motion with his hand that was meant either to demonstrate the general shape of a vagina or to dismiss vaginas categorically.

"No, I . . . no. I didn't do a rape kit," I said. "Should I go to the hospital and do that now?" The question came out sounding wrong, as if we were all listening to a warped recording of someone's misguided impression of what a rape victim ought to sound like.

"Now?" Bose squinted at me. "It's been two months."

"Six weeks," I corrected him.

"She just told you," Owen said. "She was unconscious and our neighbor put her in a bath before she could have gone to a hospital to even request a rape kit."

"Is that right, Julie?" Bose asked. "When you woke up, you were in the bathtub? Or did you wake up, and then get into the bath? I just want to be sure I have the details straight here."

"I was already in the bathtub."

"Got it," said Bose. "And now you're pregnant. Have you told Marcus?"

"We just came from his house," Owen said. "He gave us the names of all the people who were there, at the party. There are twenty-five of them. They would probably talk to you if you call them up and ask them what they remember."

Bose nodded and sat back in his chair, rested one ankle

on the opposite knee. "You could also do a DNA test, once she has the kid."

"Once she has the kid?" Owen's voice expressed my own incredulity. "That's like, nine months away."

"They have ways to test the DNA of unborn babies." Bose folded his sausage-link fingers across his belly. "Happens all the time with paternity disputes. It's pretty invasive, though, so you'll probably want to wait the nine months. Sorry—it's been *six weeks*, right?" He glanced at his notes. "So you've got just over seven months, when you do the math."

"I'm not sure I'm going to continue the pregnancy," I said. "Here's the list." I took Owen's phone from him and placed it on top of the table between us and Bose. That list of twenty-five names was the only thing with which I'd armed myself.

Bose leaned forward to glance down at the list on the screen but didn't touch the phone. He narrowed his eyes at me. "You're going to have an abortion?"

"I don't know yet. I mean, maybe."

Bose let out a long sigh and sat back in his chair again. "Why didn't you report the rape the day after it happened, Julie?" he asked. "Why not have your husband bring you down to the station right away?"

I couldn't stand the way Owen was looking at me.

Officer Bose had asked the question I'd stopped Marcus from asking, the question Owen was dying to have answered. He'd assured me that he believed me about what I could remember and what I couldn't, and I knew he wouldn't lie about that. But once Bose put the question out there, my husband's eyes implored, *Why didn't you tell me sooner?*

"I don't know," I said.

"The part I really don't understand is the bath," said Bose. "You and Marcus put your clothes in the sink and washed everything off your body. Why?"

My stomach dropped. Since I hadn't done a rape kit, those pieces of clothing were technically the only proof that a crime had occurred. If Officer Bose or anyone else was going to figure out what had happened to me that night, my body itself would have carried the most important pieces of information.

But Marcus had destroyed the evidence.

Bose rested his elbows on the table and pressed together the tips of his stubby fingers. "Semen, blood. Julie, that stuff could have been tested for DNA. Then we might have had something to work with," he said. "But you and Marcus washed it all away."

You and Marcus. It was the second time he'd grouped those words together like that. I didn't like it.

Owen's shoulders had slumped forward considerably since we'd entered this enclosed space. From the grimace on his face, I could tell that he understood what was happening as well as I did. Officer Bose had invented his own version of the night I'd forgotten, a version that didn't involve a rape at all.

"That's not fair," Owen said.

Officer Bose looked like he might laugh in Owen's face. Instead, he stood up abruptly. "We've got the report, so we'll look into it," he said.

I couldn't find my voice to answer him. It didn't matter; there was nothing I could have said. Officer Bose was escorting us from the station with a less-than-reliable promise to investigate, and we could take it or leave it. The time for speaking had passed.

NOW

CHAPTER 10

THOMAS MAKES A choking noise and regurgitated formula pools in the corners of his mouth, trickling down his chin. He's messy, but peaceful. Safe. His eyelids flutter back into the enchanted sleep that only infants can conjure.

While I've been standing here remembering the events leading up to Thomas's birth, the parlor around us has grown dark. Ever since I became a mother the hours don't pass in a way that makes sense. I'll find myself waking up on the davenport or in bed beside Owen, without remembering having fallen asleep. A single day might stretch on for what feels like weeks, as flimsy and convoluted as the tape from an unwound cassette. Other times, the daylight skips into darkness and back again, over and over, like a broken record.

It's a good thing I don't have any design work right now. I'd never be able to keep track of a deadline. This time at home was planned, starting from Thomas's due date. The idea was to give myself a self-managed maternity leave, to let the baby's schedule dictate the rhythms of our household. At night, he sleeps between me and Owen in a platter-sized portable bed, protected from the weight of our sleeping bodies by a bumper cushion. It was a gift from Diana, who informed us that co-sleeping helped some of her godchildren's parents with family bonding. That's what Owen and I are supposed to be spending the first part of Thomas's life focusing on: bonding as a family. I hadn't expected this disorienting sense of powerlessness. This incapacitation.

Still, just now, the sound of Thomas choking strummed something within me. A new chord of panic. It must be what they call maternal instinct. There's no risk of him being mauled by a wild animal, or whatever biological fear wrenched my mind back to the side of his crib upon hearing him in distress. But my gut reaction is, apparently, to protect him. That's more than I've come to expect from myself lately.

The sound of stilted conversation leaks through the fireplace that connects the parlor to the kitchen. I can make out the voices of Owen, Liza, and Marcus in the stumbling rhythm of uncomfortable small talk. They're probably wondering where I am and why the hell I'm avoiding them.

The formula Thomas spit up a moment ago is beginning to soak into his onesie. I scan the parlor for something with which to wipe the delicate creases in his neck. On the ugly new rocking chair, Owen has discarded a muslin burp cloth adorned with frolicking baby elephants. Their mothers raise triumphant trunks beside them, paragons of wisdom and strength. When I look closer, though, the elephant babies and their mothers are soaked in vomit, drool, or another of my own baby's bodily fluids. Unable to use the burp cloth, I reach into the crib to collect the white goop from the side of Thomas's face. I'll have to stop by the powder room to wash my hands before joining Owen and our visitors in the kitchen.

As soon as I touch him, Thomas shrieks in recognition. It's not an unhappy sound, but it reverberates against the parlor walls like a siren in a well. His entire little body stretches and extends away from itself as if someone cruel has dipped him in ice water. As the baby sucks in air to make the noise again, Owen's silhouette appears in the doorway. For a moment, neither of us moves.

"I don't know what happened," I offer weakly.

Owen strides over to the crib and stands beside me. "Hey, shhh." He places one gentle hand on Thomas's chest and immediately the baby's body relaxes.

"Just a nightmare," Owen whispers as much to Thomas as to me. "Shhh. It was just a nightmare, right, little guy?" He picks up the baby and rocks him. They're facing away from me, toward the front window.

I pause behind them and press my hand against the lower part of Owen's back. He freezes but doesn't pull away from me. I move closer.

"This was always going to be tough," I say to my husband and to myself, making my voice tender. "It won't last forever, though."

I wait for the rise and fall of Owen's back as he breathes but it doesn't move. He's rigid. Holding his breath.

"We'll get back to where we were," I say. I try with everything in my being to believe it's true. "Once we get the nursery painted, we can move the crib upstairs. The rocking chair, too, if you want to keep it. Then we'll put the davenport back in front of the fireplace where it belongs."

Finally, the muscles in Owen's back relax. He turns around to face me and I lean against his broad chest, nuzzling Thomas, who is nearly asleep again.

"Breathe in together," I say, "and out together."

As Owen inhales and exhales deliberately along with me, I notice tears in the corners of his eyes. We stand there in the parlor, together, holding the baby between us. The last thing I want to do is to move away from Owen and Thomas. This is closer to Owen than I've felt in a long time.

A raised voice from the kitchen reminds me that Liza and Marcus are here, apparently having an argument. They only arrived a few minutes ago and they've already launched into bickering. Then again, I must have been standing in the parlor for a lot longer than a few minutes. It's possible they've been visiting for hours.

"I lost track of time again," I say to Owen. "I'll go catch the Dolans before they head out. I've been rude enough already."

"Okay," Owen says as he places Thomas back in the crib. "Shhh, you're okay, now."

Perhaps feeling my eyes upon his swaddled little body, Thomas shivers dramatically. Then he gives a heavy sigh and relaxes again as Owen pats his belly. I feel a surge of envy and loathe myself for it. It's not Owen's fault my touch caused Thomas to start wailing. It's not his fault I can't soothe my baby when he's upset. Of course, Owen is not a perfect parent either. The unpredictable emotional state of our newborn often baffles him too. But he is doing a much, much better job than I am.

In the kitchen, Marcus stands stiffly by the door to the back porch, impatiently thumbing at his phone. Liza finishes jotting something down on a notepad, tears off her completed note, and places it on top of a serving dish covered with tin foil—another "experiment"—in the center of our kitchen table. Even mundane gestures are striking when she performs them.

"I labeled and dated the casserole. Remember to eat it!" Liza shouts.

Now is the time to enter the kitchen, apologize profusely for making the Dolans wait, and thank them for the casserole. But doing so feels impossible, as if they're characters in a play from which I'm excluded by an invisible fourth wall. I don't respond to Liza. Instead, I take a step backward into the dark entryway, feeling like an intruder in my own home.

Marcus scoffs at the casserole dish. "They've always hated your experiments," he says. "Owen told me."

"As if he'd tell *you* that," Liza snaps.

On the table beside the casserole dish is a wire mobile for the baby's crib, wrapped in the kind of clear cellophane that's usually reserved for corporate gift baskets. Whoever placed it on the table a moment ago must have used considerable force, from the way the plush, felted animals bob maniacally on their wires.

A cardboard children's book is propped open on its edge beside the mobile. Another gift for the baby. The cover illustration depicts the recognizable, stern profile of a woman with dark-brown skin and a frilly white bonnet. Elizabeth Freeman, the eponym of the Berkshire County rape crisis center. Her famous nickname is emblazoned in Comic Sans font across the top of the book: *MumBet.* Below that, the subtitle reads: *Baby's Introduction to African American Heroes.* The crib mobile might have been Marcus's idea, but this board book was undoubtedly Liza's purchase. It's her characteristic way of encouraging Owen and me to educate Thomas properly from the beginning. It's also, I suspect, her way of sending me a message.

Liza was the one to fill me in about the history of Elizabeth Freeman, MumBet for short, and the Sedgwick family, beside whom she was buried just down the road. We'd been exploring Judge Theodore Sedgwick's old house, where MumBet had worked as a servant after he'd helped her sue for her freedom and win; she was the first enslaved person to do so in Massachusetts, according to Liza and to the humbling follow-up internet search I'd performed. It was the spring after Owen and I had moved to the Berkshires, and Liza was helping me scope out the Sedgwick property after I'd been hired to transform it from a private home into a universally accessible museum.

The Berkshire Hills were cluttered with once-private residences that now charged admission, mostly Gilded Age properties of the exorbitantly wealthy families whose art collecting habits my own parents had emulated. Summer "cottages," they called them. In contrast, the Federal-style Sedgwick house on Main Street had been continuously occupied by Judge Theodore Sedgwick's able-bodied descendants since its construction in the late eighteenth century up until its recent donation by the current generation of Sedgwicks. To retrofit a building that old without destroying its historical character would take considerable care.

I was only two years out of RISD and new to the area, but Liza had put in a good word for me with the director of the Berkshire County Historical Society. The Sedgwick House would be a career-making opportunity for me. Liza knew this.

"There's no ramp, or elevator, or anything," she'd said, reaching the top of the staircase in the grand foyer. We'd completed a brief tour of the house's landscaping, which would need stone embankments to allow for wheelchair-accessible paths, before the groundskeeper had let us in the front door with instructions to find him if we had any questions.

"I'll add a timber ramp outside, to match the siding," I said, following Liza over a threshold that would need to be lowered and into a large square bedroom at the front corner of the house. "And I'll need to widen almost all of these doorways."

The bedroom was about twenty feet in diameter and had been wallpapered a jaunty green, with an unused fireplace made from local marble. A peculiar aroma clung to the dust particles that were suspended, dazed, in the streak of sunlight streaming between the window sashes. I breathed in deeply, as if I might be able to detect a lingering perfume, a whiff of heartbreak, or some other hint of the lives that had come and gone over that threshold. There was something, but it evaporated before I could name it.

Liza strode into the middle of the wide-planked pine floor with the confidence of someone who lived there. Then she stopped short, suddenly, so that I nearly collided with her. She stared, unmoving, out the tall windows toward the maple trees beyond the front lawn, with a look on her face as though she'd suddenly remembered something important.

"What's up?" I asked, nonplussed.

She answered in an explanatory tone, as if we'd been interrupted in the middle of a conversation about the house's inhabitants. "She died here," Liza said. "It was awful."

"Who died here?" I asked. "Catharine? Edie?" In addition to the abolitionist author, Catharine Maria Sedgwick, whose book *A New-England Tale* had been on my English literature syllabus at Andover, the ill-fated Hollywood starlet Edie was the only other Sedgwick whose name I'd recognized when I'd applied for this job. But Edie Sedgwick was many generations removed from Stockbridge, and besides, I was pretty sure I'd seen in a documentary once that she'd overdosed in Southern California.

"No . . . Pamela Dwight Sedgwick. Catharine's mother," said Liza. "She *lived* here with her ten children. Well, seven of them." Her hand flew to the base of her throat, as if she was experiencing a visceral, painful memory. "One baby died after a day," she said. "Two others survived for almost a year."

"That was pretty common back then, right?" I asked. Liza had an interest in the region's seldom-told stories, and I usually appreciated her willingness to share what she'd discovered. But she wasn't communicating in the way one might convey a historical anecdote. Instead, she appeared to listen to the room around us, as if learning this information about Pamela Dwight Sedgwick for the first time herself, from some silent source.

"Theodore—they just called him The Judge—would stay away at work in Boston or Philadelphia for most of the year," she continued. "He left her here, with MumBet, to care for the children." Liza's face was rapt with grim concentration. "She hated it. She poisoned herself, Julie."

"What? Jesus, Liza. That's dark."

"It was September twentieth, 1807," she continued, ignoring me. "Here in this bedroom, with Catharine and MumBet. Right here." She made a gesture toward the center of the room, as if indicating a bed and two chairs arranged beside it.

"September twentieth? That's when Owen and I got married," I said, impatient. I was eager to continue exploring the house.

"She chose the wrong poison, though," Liza said, breathless. "She suffered. Her whole body spasmed, over and over, and she finally choked to death. It took hours."

"Speaking of death," I said, steering the conversation back toward useful territory, "I wonder if I can get my hands on Theodore's death registry. One of those lists they used to make, of everything people owned? That would really help when it comes to accurately furnishing this place."

Liza dropped the performance with a shake of her head. When it was time to leave the Sedgwick House and she raised her arm to wave to the groundskeeper, I noticed a detailed informational pamphlet peeking from her purse. She'd studied up on the Sedgwicks before we arrived, I realized with amusement, so she could prank me by pretending to commune with that poor suicidal woman, Pamela. I didn't mention the pamphlet to Liza, but I made a mental note to move forward in our relationship taking whatever she said with a generous handful of salt. It wouldn't be the last time she'd commit to a story, either comedic or creepy, to get a reaction out of me.

We walked across the street for lunch at the Red Lion Inn. Liza insisted on buying me a congratulatory gift of earrings she'd seen through the window at the gift shop there.

"We're celebrating!" she exclaimed as she returned to our table. She presented me with the pair of golden sparrows dangling from a white cardboard square. "To your career," she said, raising her glass of lemonade.

"To new friends," I'd toasted her, grateful for her willingness to vouch for me on the Sedgwick House project. She'd leveraged her professional reputation with the historical society on my behalf, an enormous gesture of good faith in her new neighbor.

The earrings were a generous gift, and I appreciated what Liza meant, but they were too gaudy for my style. Not to mention hazardous due to their sharply pointed wings. I'd stashed them in the top drawer of my bathroom vanity along with the rest of my rarely worn jewelry.

Come to think of it, I can't remember the last time I'd put them on before the night of the Dolans' holiday party. I still haven't found that missing earring, but now is not the time to bring it up with Liza.

She must have guessed—she must have known—how seeing the cover of the *MumBet* children's book would bring me back to that morning at the Sedgwick House. She'd have predicted the mixed feelings it would summon within me. This gift for Thomas is intended either as a message of reconciliation or as a reminder that I owe her.

"We can't just *leave*," Liza whispers to Marcus. "We haven't even met the baby."

"It's sleeping," he hisses. The condescension in his voice causes me to take another step back into the shadows. "We brought over your meal and your stupid gifts. Now we're getting the fuck out of here."

A clump of shame catches in my throat. I'm torn between wanting to speak up on Liza's behalf and wanting to disappear back into the parlor with Owen and Thomas, unnoticed. I hate the way Marcus is talking to her but I don't want to embarrass them by letting them know I've overheard them.

Liza doesn't seem concerned about her husband's tone. She tilts her head to the side and pivots away from him, arms akimbo. She takes a hesitant step toward the entryway, toward me, as if she can't decide whether to venture into the parlor or not.

"Owen?" she calls. Then, softly, "Julie?"

I wish Owen would respond for the both of us. I wish he'd bring the baby in here and say something silly, to dissolve the tension. But he must have taken Thomas upstairs quietly, or otherwise he fell asleep in the rocking chair as soon as he sat down. He's not coming to rescue me from this awkward scene.

"Nice try," Marcus says. "Let's go." He grabs Liza's upper arm too tightly and steers her toward the kitchen door. Something about the smirk on his face frightens me.

"Liza," I try to call, but my voice comes out as nothing more than a rasp. Without hearing me, she follows Marcus onto the back porch.

I hesitate in the doorway. Maybe if I'm overreacting to Marcus's hostile expression. Arguably, his face always looks that way. I have no reason to believe Marcus is a danger to Liza. She's never mentioned violence in their relationship. And this is the first time I'll be saying as much as hello to either of the Dolans since before Thomas was born. I don't want to worsen whatever friction exists between our families, or between the two of them as a couple.

It might be dark enough outside, though, that I'll be able to follow them into the backyard without being observed. That way, I can make sure Liza is safe without having to initiate a confrontation. I don't have a plan for what I'll do if I reach them. If Marcus is angry, if he does try to hurt Liza in front of me, it might be impossible to stop him. The idea that I could intervene against Marcus physically is laughable, but I could shout and wave my arms around, anything to give Liza time to run away.

I step out into the humid night. Crickets screech panicked warnings as I tiptoe down the porch steps behind the Dolans, moving silently and sticking to the shadows, like a child playing flashlight tag. The two beams from their flashlights bounce around in the darkness, pointed away from me, across various segments of our untended back lawn. *Whoooo-cooks-for-yooouuu* cries a lone screech owl as we approach the woods. At the hobbleberry shrubs, I hesitate. I haven't stepped foot on this path since before Thomas was born. I'm not sure I can bring myself to go any farther.

Then, just beyond the line of trees where the black night becomes blacker still, the two flashlight beams stop moving. I brace myself and enter the woods behind the Dolans. I can barely discern the outlines of their bodies among the gnarled, grasping tree branches.

". . . next time, I'm going over there by myself," Liza is saying.

"These fucking mosquitos are eating me alive," Marcus huffs. "Let's keep moving."

Their next words are indecipherable by the time they reach my ears, but the tension has dissolved from the timbre of their conversation.

Whatever instinct compelled me to follow them was clearly wrong. Marcus might be angry but he's not a threat to Liza. From what I've overheard, she's the one frustrated with Marcus about the way their visit unfolded. Soon, the two figures disappear into their own backyard.

I am alone in the woods. With that realization comes sudden and overwhelming disorientation, even though I've traversed this path dozens of times before. Stained silver by the September moon, nothing looks familiar.

I sense the dark presence of the Dolans' storage shed in the clearing before me. The wrought iron handles on its double doors are secured with a dead bolt. In the daytime, the shed has never struck me as anything but nondescript and functional. Now it looms ominously, and I feel exposed. Its weathered shingles seem to inhale and exhale among the trees.

I'm overcome by the sensation—the certainty—that someone is inside the shed, waiting. Drawing me closer, deliberately, inevitably. I take a step backward. Then I turn and sprint as quickly as I can back across the lawn, up the porch steps, and into our house, away from the Dolans and the woods and the shed.

THEN

CHAPTER 11

MY INITIAL PRENATAL appointment was the first Monday in February, the day before my twenty-ninth birthday. Owen parked the Subaru in front of a waist-high pile of snow edged in soot. A heavily salted cement walkway led to the unassuming single-story structure off Route 8 that was Dr. Syed's office.

Inside, the waiting room was painted the color of steamed milk. The sound of bright, rapid chatter burst like gunfire from behind the reception desk. A plump, pink-faced woman with blown-out gray bangs gave instructions to a very pregnant woman before turning her cheerfulness on me and Owen. She gushed for a few minutes about how exciting it was to be starting this journey together, handed me a tablet with a pre-appointment questionnaire, and directed us over to a row of chairs against the opposite wall.

I stared down at the tablet screen on my lap, forcing my eyes to focus on the text.

When was the first day of your last menstrual period? the questionnaire wanted to know. Since Owen had recently been pestering me about tracking my fertility, and since I'd needed to provide the same information when I called to make this appointment, I happened to know the answer: December 8.

Have you had any problems during this pregnancy? was the next question. *If yes, what?* A pixelated gray rectangle awaited my response. I dragged my finger around the touch screen until I'd typed the words *Someone raped me.* Answering an introductory question with such a brutal statement felt impolite. Audacious. But it was information the doctor would need to know, and, scrolling down to the bottom of the questionnaire, I didn't find a more appropriate place to provide it. The questions that addressed violence were all in reference to Owen, not some unidentified man in the woods: *Has your current partner ever physically hurt you?* I answered no. *Ever threatened you or made you feel afraid?* No. In the plastic chair beside me, Owen mindlessly tugged at his hair. It curled over the collar of his parka; he needed a haircut. He was perusing an article on matching family Halloween costumes from an outdated waiting-room copy of a parenting magazine. Owen made me feel many things, but not afraid. Never afraid.

The final portion of the questionnaire comprised a Likert scale for me to rank how often over the previous two weeks I'd been experiencing *Little interest or pleasure in doing things.* More than half of the days, I answered. *Feeling down, depressed, or hopeless:* Nearly every day.

"Really, Juju Bear?" Owen asked. I hadn't realized he was reading over my shoulder.

"Eyes on your own work," I said, pointing to his magazine.

"But . . . nearly every day?"

"Julie Porter?" The nurse who called my name was as pink and peppy as the receptionist, and nearly as plump.

Owen put down the parenting magazine and started to stand up with me, but she motioned for him to stay seated.

"We're just going to talk to Mom first," she said. "Thanks, Dad."

The nurse made pleasant small talk with herself as she weighed me and took my blood pressure at a station in the hallway. "You should start to see some weight gain soon," she said as she entered my vitals into her computer without looking up, "since you're eight weeks and two days along today."

"No," I corrected her. "I'm only about six weeks. The date of . . . conception was December twenty-second." *Conception* wasn't the right word, though. It was too hopeful, too promising. "That's when I got pregnant," I said. "That's what I put on the questionnaire."

She smiled playfully, as if I were a student of the English language who'd recently discovered that *i* came before *e* except after *c*, so I'd been misspelling *conceive.* "I haven't seen your questionnaire, honey, but when you made this appointment, you said the first day of your last period was"—she glanced back at the computer screen—"December eighth."

"Right."

"When we're estimating your due date, we start counting from the first day of your last period, not the day you actually conceived."

I did some panicked mental math. If I was already over eight weeks along in this pregnancy, that meant I was going to have even less time to make up my mind about whether to end it or not.

"Don't worry!" the nurse said when she saw my face. "You're not the first mother to find that out at this appointment. Everyone's surprised. But it just means you'll get to meet your little angel sooner than you expected!" She handed me a sealed plastic cup and a package of disinfecting wipes. "I'm going to need a urine sample from you," she said, directing me to an open door across the hallway. "Wash your hands before and after. The lavatory's through the exam room, and there's a compartment to deposit the sample when you're done. Dr. Syed will be right in." With a kindly pat on my shoulder, she bustled off, closing the exam room door behind her.

I was alone except for the diagrams of pregnant bodies posted on all four of the office walls. They were cross-section drawings, so the women's organs were visible inside their torsos, along with the fetus in each respective stage of development, from conception to birth. I found the eight-week poster, the one that ostensibly matched the appearance of my own body on the inside. The woman in the drawing wore her hair in waist-length, dark curls like mine. The fetus depicted inside her uterus was the shape and size of a magenta lima bean.

I imagined the poor mother as a real person, transformed into a cross section for the benefit of patients like me, and felt a stab of empathy for her. She couldn't have done that to herself. Someone would have had to take a chain saw and methodically bisect her from the crown of her head, straight down between her shoulder blades, slicing cleanly through her torso and the eight-week-old lima bean fetus, until the two sides fell away from each other like moist slices of bread. I imagined my own body cleaving apart like that. Lying on the frozen grass of the Dolans' backyard for someone to notice the two halves while they were taking the trash out to the bins.

In the closet-sized lavatory attached to the exam room, I sat with my jeans around my ankles and rested my elbows on my bare knees. Shivering, I positioned the plastic cup between my thighs. The idea of a doctor examining my vagina—of anyone prodding it with a finger or a tool or anything else—made all the muscles in my pelvis clench with fear. Finally, I peed. Washing my hands, I avoided my reflection in the mirror above the pedestal sink.

Dr. Syed knocked gently before entering the exam room. He was a slim man with kind, olive-shaped eyes and skin the shade of terra cotta.

"It's good to meet you, Julie," he said, taking a seat on the rolling stool across from the exam table. "I've had a chance to look over the questionnaire you filled out in the waiting room." I didn't answer, and he continued, "I'm so sorry about what happened to you." In contrast to the off-putting cheeriness of his staff, he spoke humbly and with reverence, as if every word to leave his lips were a meticulous decision. In another life, he could have been a children's librarian. "This pregnancy wasn't something you chose," he said.

"No. I'm still not . . . I haven't chosen it yet, for sure."

"There's still plenty of time," he said. "That trauma, that experience, would deeply affect anyone. And from your answers here, it seems like you've been struggling with your feelings surrounding all this."

"Yeah." *Nearly every day.*

"Have you been in touch with a mental health professional yet?" he asked. "Someone who specializes in sexual trauma?"

"Not yet," I said. "This was the first appointment I made. I figured a physical exam was the most important—"

Dr. Syed shook his head kindly, interrupting me. "No need for that today," he said. "All we need today is a finger prick to send to the lab so they can confirm your negative result from that at-home STI screen. We'll do an exam when you come in again next month."

Relief hit me like a drug. I'd been too nervous to register that the nurse hadn't instructed me to change into a paper gown.

"For now," Dr. Syed continued, "this folder has answers to all the most frequently asked questions." He handed me a wire-bound packet labeled *Your First Trimester* with a blond-haired, doe-eyed pregnant woman practicing yoga on the front cover. "Is there anything you want to talk about with me in private, before I call your husband in?"

I shook my head.

"Then I'd like to talk to you both about how best to take care of your physical and mental health. Would that be all right?"

"Yes, please."

Dr. Syed left and returned after a moment with Owen, who brought the waiting room copy of the parenting magazine with him, folded open. He'd moved on from the article about Halloween to an equally seasonally irrelevant piece about common back-to-school woes.

"Have a seat," Dr. Syed said to Owen.

"Are you okay?" Owen asked me. "How'd it go?"

I shrugged. "I didn't need an exam."

"I'll plan to see Julie back here in a month," said Dr. Syed. "For now, the most important thing is that you both have mental health support to make the best decision for your family. Julie, I'm going to refer you for an appointment with a psychiatrist I know and respect. I'll tell her it's urgent."

"Maybe they can get you on an SSRI," Owen suggested. "I mean, if it's urgent."

"It's unlikely you'll be able to start on a brand-new antidepressant, as long as you continue to be pregnant," Dr. Syed said to me. "But your trauma history is a strong predictor of perinatal mood disorders." My *trauma history*. It sounded deceptively simple when he put it that way.

"Mood disorders?" Owen asked. "Like postpartum depression?"

"Postpartum depression, postpartum psychosis—" Dr. Syed stopped abruptly as if he wished he hadn't begun the list. "Depression affects up to twenty percent of new mothers, even those without—"

"What does that mean?" I said. "Psychosis. After giving birth?"

Dr. Syed cleared his throat. "That's very, *very* rare. Fewer than one tenth of one percent of new mothers experience those symptoms."

"Symptoms like what?" I asked.

"Delusions, auditory hallucinations, any feelings like you might seriously hurt yourself," said Dr. Syed. "Or hurt the baby."

I'd seen a news segment about a woman who'd drowned her infant when it was a few weeks old. She'd pled insanity at the trial. I tried to imagine what had gone through her mind as she'd watched her own child choking, spasming, then finally going cold and still as porcelain. The clarity of the fantasy frightened me. Even more frightening was the indifference, the absence of feeling conjured in my heart by such an objectively disturbing image.

After I had the baby, if I remained passive and unfazed, I could end up like the mother in the news segment. I could harm my own baby. I could kill it.

Dr. Syed shook his head as if he'd read my thoughts. "It's extremely rare," he said. "And as I said, we'll keep on top of your mental health throughout this whole experience."

We thanked Dr. Syed and left, the wire-bound folder tucked under my arm and my next appointment booked for the following month. On the drive home, we stopped at Dunkin' Donuts to satisfy my sudden craving for chocolate Munchkins. We listened to Dashboard Confessional and laughed about the matching family Halloween costumes Owen had discovered in the waiting room's outdated parenting magazine. He was excited about *The Wizard of Oz* as a theme, especially dressing the baby up like a cherubic Cowardly Lion, but I didn't think Daisy would appreciate being carried around in Toto's basket. Neither of us mentioned postpartum psychosis.

NOW

CHAPTER 12

EMERGING FROM THE woods, I feel safer at first. The kitchen light beckons me home, a beacon across the sea of unkempt grass. As I near our back porch, though, the humid night air seems to go frigid.

The back door stands slightly ajar. I can't remember if I pulled it shut behind me when I followed the Dolans outside, but that must have been at least ten minutes ago by now. My pace slows involuntarily. Owen will have noticed if I've left the door open, especially with the kitchen lights on. We still haven't installed a screen; he'll be annoyed at me for attracting the insects inside.

I pause at the top of the stairs and give the door a gentle tap. I peek into the kitchen. All the lights are on but the room is empty. Stepping over the threshold, I can tell something isn't right. Tension carves through our home like a hunter in the den of a hibernating bear. When a brash voice reaches my ears through the fireplace, I know who the trespasser is. Diana. Where did she come from?

I stop inside the kitchen door on a mat that reads in a stern font, DOGS WELCOME. PEOPLE TOLERATED. Some people tolerated more than others, truth be told, and most people tolerated more than my mother-in-law. The kitchen door clicks into place behind me, closing me inside the house with the two of them.

Three of them. Thomas is here, too, of course.

"It does sound crazy," Diana is saying in the front entryway, "but I'm glad you told me." When did she even get here? And what could Owen possibly have told her that sounds so crazy? It wouldn't take much for her to believe I've gone off the deep end, and from the sound of it, he's already complained to her about the latest way I've let him down. Failing to appear for the Dolans' social visit is exactly the kind of faux pas Diana would find unforgivable.

Climbing the few steps to the landing, I contort myself against the interior wall of the staircase so that I'll be able to spy on their conversation. The front entryway is tiny by modern standards, with hardly enough space for even two adults to stand without jostling each other. If I go in there, it will be too crowded. Besides, I don't feel up for interacting with Diana right now.

Owen stands with his back to the stairwell, blocking my view of his mother. He rests his weight on his heels and bounces side to side gently, almost imperceptibly. Thomas's head is barely visible above the burp cloth draped over Owen's shoulder. Diana's arrival must have woken them from their nap.

Her Boston accent ricochets loudly off the entryway's timber walls. ". . . if you've given any more thought to Thomas's . . . test," she says carefully.

What *test*? Diana wants us to run some kind of test on Thomas? That could mean the doctors suspect there's something wrong with him, some developmental limitation resulting from his arrival at only twenty-seven weeks. It's possible Diana's already talked to me about this test, whatever it is, and I've completely forgotten; I've been so absentminded lately. I rack my brain but for the life of me, I can't remember Diana mentioning any specific test that we're supposed to be deciding about. To ask her about it will only be to provide her with more evidence that I'm a lousy mother who can't remember the most crucial things about her own child's health.

I should be grateful to my mother-in-law for managing the medical screenings and procedures that come along with Thomas having been born extremely premature, especially since I'm having so much trouble staying on top of anything myself. She's been eager to put her experience with newborns to use as a grandmother—all those godchildren have been excellent practice. It stings, though, each time I'm reminded of the responsibilities I can't handle. The role I can't play.

I'll have to ask Owen to explain what his mother is talking about later. He'll be disappointed that I've forgotten; that's one more thing I'm unable to do right. But if we're going to be running any tests on Thomas, we need to make that decision together.

Diana goes on, "It makes sense to do *something*. . ."

"No, it doesn't, not right now." Owen interrupts her, his voice solid. "It won't fix anything. I told you, DNA isn't enough proof anyway."

A DNA test. The revelation drives through me like a hot poker. Diana wants Owen to go behind my back to find out the identity of Thomas's biological father. Here I found myself feeling guilty for not appreciating her help keeping track of Thomas's health records, while she's been plotting to get more information than I want her to know about the conception of my child. More information than even *I* want to know right now.

Running that DNA test is an inevitability, of course. At some point, even if we never press charges, Owen and I will have to learn the truth for the sake of making decisions regarding Thomas's health care. Notably, though, Diana has never mentioned the DNA test to *me*.

"Besides," Owen continues, "I couldn't do that to Julie." The entire room seems to cool with relief. Owen would never betray me at his mother's whim. He understands that I've been putting off testing Thomas's DNA because I'm still recovering from the trauma of the way he was born. That emergency C-section was no vacation.

I think again of *Healing from Trauma* left out on the table beside the davenport. Owen must be growing impatient for me to put my mother's lessons into practice. I dragged myself through the core of that book before giving birth, and its main point is straightforward. Getting over serious trauma, fully healing, requires a process of reconnection with the body. I'm supposed to be practicing breathing exercises when I feel overwhelmed and taking up activities like yoga. I'm supposed to be reestablishing the relationship between my mind and body so that Owen can declare me sufficiently "healed from trauma," and we can finally run that DNA test on Thomas. There are many, many things I'm supposed to be doing.

Instead, I stand completely still in the stairwell, listening. Hiding. Maybe I can get up to the bedroom without Diana seeing me. As I turn to continue toward the second story, her voice comes again from the front entryway, more tentative this time.

"Look," she says to Owen. "Obviously, Julie's not going to tell you herself. But I think she *wants* you to do something about it."

Her insinuation infuriates me. How dare she talk about me this way in my own home, as if she knows me better than my husband? The way she phrased it makes it seem like I'm being secretive about the rapist's identity, like I'm *choosing* not to share that information. She's speaking to Owen as if he's been cuckolded. Of course, I can't tell Owen who raped me, and it has nothing to do with whether I want to tell him or not. I can't tell *anyone* who raped me because, as Diana has been informed more than once by multiple people, I don't remember.

Now would be a good time for me to speak up for myself.

I should confirm that I, too, am in the dark about who raped me, that I'm not ready to run a DNA test on Thomas to find out, and that Diana needs to mind her own goddamn business.

"Don't try to guess what Julie wants," Owen snaps, putting an end to her line of speculation.

As long as Diana's not successfully convincing him that I'm a cheater and a liar, I'm more than willing to let Owen handle his mother. She can believe whatever she wants, as far as I'm concerned. What my husband believes, though, matters to me more than anything. When we eventually run a DNA test on Thomas, sometime in the unforeseen future, it's a decision Owen and I will make together. And we'll make that decision because it's the right time for our family to find out who raped me, not because Diana wants us to.

Owen continues in a softer tone. "I have some work to finish up after dinner. Do you want me to order a pizza?"

When Diana responds, the determination in her voice has given way to exhaustion, or maybe pity. "No, I'll make us something simple," she says. "You go put the baby down." Her heels click across the front entryway, toward the kitchen.

"Thanks, Mom," he says.

The clicking stops. "And Owen?"

"Yeah."

She sighs, as if she's spent time preparing what she's about to say next. "You're doing *so much* right now," she says. "More than any husband should ever be expected to take on." The tenderness in her voice is laced with pride.

Her words must feel to Owen like being wrapped in a warm blanket. To me, they feel like a splash of acid. "Julie—"

"I know." He stops her before she can directly insult my mothering skills. She's ready to launch into a litany of specific ways I've failed so far, and neither Owen nor I can bear to listen. It would be too much to confront, too much to excuse. The implication is enough.

The worst part is that Owen hasn't defended me. On the contrary, he said *I know*. He might have interrupted his mother, but I can tell that he agrees with her. *He knows*.

THEN

CHAPTER 13

"YOU'RE TURNING TWENTY-NINE today?" Dr. Ruth Bridges looked downward toward the bottom of her monitor, referencing my medical record in a separate window from our video chat. A crooked part divided her straight gray pixie cut into uneven halves. Framed degrees from impressive institutions hung on the stenciled wall behind her. "Thanks for meeting with me on your birthday," she said. "Happy birthday."

"Thanks," I said, tilting my screen away from my face to avoid the glare through the windows behind me. For our video chat, I'd set up my laptop on the kitchen table without accounting for the position of the late morning sun. "I was surprised you could meet with me so soon."

"Dr. Syed is a respected former colleague," Dr. Bridges said by way of explanation. She nudged her polychromatic reading glasses up on the bridge of her nose.

A video chat seemed like an impersonal way to meet with a psychiatrist, but that didn't bother me at all. It was a relief to avoid meeting a new therapist face-to-face, to remain safe inside my own house, behind my laptop monitor. It wasn't that I didn't like therapists. I respected them and the important work they did for many people's mental health. But the emotional labels and descriptions they fed me and waited for me to repeat back rarely matched the emotions I was experiencing.

After my parents had died, I'd had a handful of first-time appointments with a variety of mental health professionals, all of whom had claimed never to have heard of the Merritt family or how Charles and Patricia had perished. One of them had prescribed me Zoloft, but I'd never picked up the prescription from the pharmacy. I hadn't felt comfortable taking a pill at the direction of someone who'd spent a total of fifty minutes nodding slowly in my direction, looking vaguely disappointed.

"Do you have a strong support system?" Dr. Bridges asked. "How does your partner . . . Owen, right? . . . how does Owen feel about this pregnancy?"

"He's always wanted to be a parent," I answered, "so his vote is to keep it." Owen had reiterated that vote once again before he'd left for work that morning, in anticipation of this appointment. "Plus, he's Catholic."

"What about you, Julie?" Dr. Bridges's voice was mellow and confident, as if she were certain this fifty-minute video appointment could overcome whatever emotional obstacles I was up against.

"You mean, do I want an abortion?" I picked at the skin around my thumbnail. "I have a while to decide, still."

"Abortion is an option for you, here in Massachusetts, up until twenty-four weeks of gestation," Dr. Bridges confirmed. I heard the *click-click* of rapid typing as she took notes. "It says here that you're eight weeks and three days along, so yes, you do have some time."

I was grateful to her for saying only that and for stopping there. I wasn't sure what I'd been expecting from this video appointment, but so far, her lack of judgment around my decision-making process was a relief.

When I didn't respond, Dr. Bridges asked, "And how have you been feeling? You've been through quite a lot, Julie."

"I can't even imagine being a mother," I said, closing my eyes so I wouldn't have to see her reaction. I knew, in theory, what motherhood entailed: the scheduling of sleep, the changing of diapers and onesies, the obsessing over developmental milestones. But that knowledge existed separately from my personal sense of identity. It would have been easier to envision myself filling in for Liza on the ballet stage than performing the role of Mother.

When I opened my eyes, Dr. Bridges's stoic face hadn't changed. She wasn't scandalized by my confession. "Do you want to have an abortion?" she asked, coming back to her previous question.

"I don't want to be pregnant with this fetus," I said. "I don't want this to be my life. I can't believe any of it is happening. But I'm not sure I can actually have an abortion."

"It's an incredibly safe procedure," she pointed out. "You mentioned that your husband is Catholic. Do you object to it because of religious convictions?"

"No." I shook my head. "I don't think it's morally wrong or anything, and I'm not afraid of the procedure. But what if I have an abortion this time, and then Owen and I can't get pregnant when we want to?" It was one of my worst fears. After an abortion, I'd be temporarily relieved of the pressure of motherhood, but there would still be a long, uphill recovery from the trauma of the rape. By the time I felt ready to try for a baby with Owen, it might not happen. The decision not to have *this* baby, now, might haunt Owen as a missed opportunity for the rest of his childless—and thus miserable—life. If I aborted Owen's only chance at fatherhood, I'd never forgive myself. "We might not be able to have another kid, later," I said. "Giving up that chance feels tragic. And I've had enough tragedy."

Dr. Bridges waited, expressionless, so I rambled on. I told her about the void in my brain where the night I was raped should be, and how I wasn't sure I even wanted the memories back. I told her how Diana had discovered by accident that I was pregnant, how Owen had stood up to her when she'd suggested that I'd cheated on him, and how she'd refused to let us babysit Sadie.

Dr. Bridges listened, typing notes, and only asking a few prodding questions when I stopped to catch my breath.

I told her how my own mother had never shown me what parenting actually *looked* like, in practice; how neither Patricia nor Charles Merritt had ever set an example. How I'd taken their indifference personally, spent my childhood wondering what other children did to earn approval from their parents, what trick I'd never learned that would trigger affection. It wasn't until their sudden death that I'd been able to let go of that perpetually unfilled need, and by then I'd been an adult, about to graduate from RISD.

"For some reason," I finished, "they just couldn't love me."

"That doesn't mean you were an unlovable child," said Dr. Bridges. "None of that is your fault, Julie."

"It was *their* fault," I agreed. "And what if that part of their personalities happens to be genetic? Maybe I inherited it, and no matter what, regardless of where this baby came from, I'd never be able to love it. I can't imagine being a mother," I said. "But I also can't imagine an abortion being part of my life story. I never expected it to be."

"No one ever does," she said. "This isn't your fault, either, Julie, and none of it is fair."

"I want to have a family with Owen," I went on, emboldened by her compassion. "But we were going to do that when I was ready, not like this." I thought of Owen bringing home the cardboard box filled with little strips for testing my levels of luteinizing hormone. "We didn't choose this."

"But you *do* get to choose whether to continue the pregnancy."

Dr. Bridges was right: none of this was fair. But I did get to choose what happened next. I could choose to have an abortion, and then after a certain amount of time had passed, Owen would start fretting about trying to get me pregnant all over again. There would be another cardboard box of little paper strips. The thought of dutifully testing my pee each morning, all that forced anticipation, for the sake of re-creating my current physical state, was repulsive.

Could I choose, instead, to give birth? There were, probably, many loving couples who would seize the opportunity to adopt the baby growing inside me, regardless of the sordid circumstances surrounding its conception. I suspected, though, that if I endured all those months of pregnancy, went through the ordeal of labor, and finally managed to push a watermelon-sized person from the most sensitive part of my body, it would be impossible for me to part with that child at the end of it all. And certainly not with Owen involved, wanting to raise it ourselves.

"With everything you've been through," Dr. Bridges said as we came to the end of the fifty minutes, "and especially since your memory has been affected so drastically, I want to be sure to monitor any changes in your mood. Let's meet again next month."

"Sure," I agreed, feeling substantially lighter than when we'd begun to talk.

"One last thing," she said. "There's a book that was particularly helpful for me after my own pregnancy. You might have read it already." She retrieved a paperback from among the pile on the shelf behind her and held it up in front of her webcam, so I could see the cover. "It's called *Healing from Trauma.*"

My mouth went dry. I was suddenly eager to end the appointment and close my laptop. "That's my mom's book," I managed to say.

"Of course, Patricia Merritt was your mother." Dr. Bridges looked directly into the webcam now, her eyes bashful behind her glasses. "I have to admit something to you, Julie," she said. "When Dr. Syed called to ask if I could squeeze you in for a last-minute appointment, I couldn't help noticing your maiden name. I've always admired your mother's work—"

"And that's why you agreed to see me."

"I should have told you that initially," she said. "I hope it doesn't feel like I misled you. Have you read *Healing from Trauma*?"

"I have a copy of it but I haven't read it," I said. "It won't help. My mom had no personal experience with trauma."

"I see." Dr. Bridges's face settled into an expression of deep comprehension that disturbed me, though at first, I couldn't put my finger on why. Then she said, rather deliberately, "Your mom might have understood more than you think, Julie," and I realized the truth that had dawned on Dr. Bridges, the truth that was no doubt apparent throughout *Healing from Trauma*, and of which I should have already been aware.

My mother had, indeed, been writing about trauma from her own experience. From the moment I'd been born, I realized, the fact of my existence must have affected the direction of her research. She'd been a psychologist searching for her own solution. Despite all the time and energy she'd devoted to her scholarship, though, she'd never discovered how to apply her findings to her life with me. Her trauma had never healed. That trauma, I now understood, had been motherhood.

"You don't have to read the whole thing, cover to cover," Dr. Bridges said. "It's worth giving it a look, though, just to see if it resonates."

"Okay," I said, feeling betrayed. Regardless of the progress I'd made during this appointment, I'd lost faith in Dr. Bridges.

She'd let me ramble on for nearly an hour, asked intimate questions about my relationship with my parents, never revealing that she was already aware of their very public history. I should have known better. For an in-demand trauma specialist to make an opening for a next-day appointment, they'd need to have an ulterior motive. She was, disappointingly, as transactional as so many other adults of my parents' milieu. It wasn't the Merritt family wealth that motivated her in this case, but my mother's work in the field of mental health. No doubt Dr. Bridges was a skilled therapist. Perhaps she might have even been able to help me. But she'd lied to me by omission. She was not someone I could trust.

• • •

It was after dark when Owen found me cross-legged on the davenport, sketchbook open on my lap. After ending the video appointment with Dr. Bridges, I'd collected several items from the kitchen and parlor—a glass carafe, a pomegranate, and Sadie's favorite paintbrush-shaped bookend—and positioned them on the mantel, turning to a practice that always soothed me. I'd experimented with a few different arrangements, changing my perspective with the afternoon light, and was now on my fifth attempt at rendering a still life. I looked over my shoulder toward the front door as Owen stepped inside, carrying a paper shopping bag. I'd made him promise not to surprise me with a birthday celebration. I didn't feel like celebrating.

"There's the birthday girl," he said. "Ah, you're sketching." He greeted Daisy as he put down the shopping bag, pushing her nose away from its contents. "I was worried."

"Worried?" Intricate layers of cardamom, cumin, and turmeric wafted from the bag. My stomach growled as I stood up. "You got Indian!"

"You said you'd been craving it, and when you didn't answer or text back . . ."

"What do you mean?" Retrieving my cell phone from the surface of the secretary, I discovered it had been toggled on Silent since my appointment with Dr. Bridges. The screen displayed a missed call and a series of missed text messages from Owen over the course of the past hour, as well as an unopened response from Miranda in my email inbox. My attempt to distract myself with sketching had been more successful than I'd expected.

"I figured you wouldn't feel like going out," he said. "I can set up a formal dinner table here and we can have a quiet, *Easy Wonderful* night. Sound okay?"

"That sounds perfect," I answered truthfully. "You know me so well."

"You're not disappointed?"

"Disappointed? I'm relieved." I followed him into the kitchen, leaving my sketchbook open on the davenport. "This birthday sucks, no matter what. I've spent the whole afternoon sketching to take my mind off it."

Owen put the paper shopping bag of Indian food on the counter. "We'll make up for it next year," he said, kissing the top of my head. "Alexa, play *Easy Wonderful*." The familiar opening acoustic guitar riff of Guster's 2010 album emerged from the smart speaker on the counter. Owen grabbed a white fabric tablecloth from the cabinet and spread it over the kitchen table. He folded matching napkins and laid them at our places. Then he struck a match and lit a long-stemmed candle in the middle of the table, completing the formal table setting. "Are you going to show me what you've been sketching?"

"It's all garbage," I said, helping him transfer the chicken tikka masala and palak paneer from their cardboard containers onto our dishes. "Miranda responded too."

"What does she say?"

"I just saw the notification," I said. "Here." I handed him my cell phone, Miranda's response pulled up on the screen, and raised my fork to dig in. "Read it to me—I'm starving."

"'Dear Julie,'" Owen began. "'What a nice surprise. I don't know much about your mom's health, but when she was pregnant, she had something called preeclampsia.'" He raised his eyebrows. "What's preeclampsia?"

I shrugged and shoveled a heaping forkful of chicken into my mouth.

"There's more." Owen continued, "'She had to stay in bed to keep her blood pressure down. That's all I know about it. Best, Miranda.'"

"Best?" I repeated. "Not even best *wishes*, just *best*?"

"I wouldn't read into it."

"That poor woman probably thought she'd never have to hear from the Merritt family again."

"I'm looking up preeclampsia," Owen said, still on my phone. "Yikes. Miranda was right about the high blood pressure. It's a life-threatening hypertensive disorder. No wonder they kept your mom on bed rest."

"Does it say if it's genetic?"

"The causes are still unknown, but it says there are high rates in some families." Owen continued to read. "It usually develops after twenty weeks of pregnancy, though. And you're eight weeks, right?"

I swallowed a mouthful of potatoes. "Eight weeks and three days."

"In a few months," he said, "we'll watch out for the symptoms."

"If I'm still pregnant in a few months."

Owen put down the phone. "How did the call with the therapist go today?" he asked.

"Dr. Bridges," I said. "She only took the referral because Dr. Syed dropped my maiden name. Then she recommended that I read my own mother's book."

"Maybe now's the time to finally read it?"

"If my mother had something she wanted to teach me, she had plenty of opportunities to do that when she was alive," I said.

Owen wiped his mouth before responding. "Seems like it couldn't hurt," he said.

I sighed. "I'll read it," I assured him. "Dr. Bridges might not have been totally up front with me, but she definitely knows what she's talking about. If she's confident there's something in that book for me to learn, it's worth giving it a read. I think it has to do with Patricia's personal experience with motherhood."

"The preeclampsia? Was that the trauma in the title of the book?"

"That must have been part of it," I said. "But she never wanted to have a kid in the first place. She probably never wanted to get married, either, even though *that* wasn't something she said out loud."

Owen reached across the tablecloth and covered my hand with his.

I squeezed his hand. "She was always pissed off about it. About *me*. She ended up losing months of her cherished academic productivity to bed rest, all for the sake of a political career Charles never even managed to get off the ground."

"Your dad ran for office?"

"Nope," I said. "Too lazy. But for a while there, my grandparents were actively trying to make it happen. Getting your wife an abortion wasn't an attractive look to voters in 1990. They basically coerced her into having me. They might have even paid her, who knows. Charles was ambivalent, from what I can tell."

"But he never ran for office."

"And she never healed," I said. "Motherhood, for her, was an ongoing trauma. She never stopped regretting it."

"You're afraid that you'll regret it too?" Owen asked gently. To my relief, the understanding in his expression was untainted by pity.

I reached for his other hand. "I would never regret making you a father," I said. "I'm just afraid that even if I didn't inherit a gene for preeclampsia, or anything physical, I might have inherited whatever made my mom regret having me in the first place."

"Don't worry about my feelings," Owen said. "If you want to have an abortion, I'll support you."

"Of course I'm worried about your feelings," I said. "You're the person I'm going to be parenting with, whether we do it now or later. I wish—" I stopped myself before I could wish out loud for a miscarriage. The idea was a monstrous relief, only polluted by the accompanying realization that I would have to pretend to mourn. "Never mind."

There were tears in the corners of Owen's eyes. "Whatever we're doing, we're doing it together," he said.

Diana's words rang in my head: *No, you will not kill this baby.* She'd forbidden me from having an abortion, imperious as a judge scolding an incarcerated teenager. But Owen had defied her. He'd told her she was out of line, that he believed me, that it was my choice from this point onward. *We are not going to live our lives on a rapist's terms*, he'd said. Remembering that afternoon, I felt confident that if we faced parenthood together Owen and I could manage whatever it would demand of us.

"We *can* raise this baby together," I said, realizing as the words left my mouth how true they were. Owen and I had already prepared our house for a family. We knew how to build a solid home. A happy one. We could learn how to come to terms with the origins of our family, over the years. As for my mental health, I would read my mother's book, and maybe I could convince myself not to fear my transformation into a mother. I could remake the violent trauma I'd never asked for, reimagine it as something that was hopeful in the end. I could finally reclaim myself, physically and emotionally, from the person who'd attacked me.

The realization that I wanted to go through with this pregnancy and give birth to this baby rose, bright and unyielding, from within me. I would embrace this burgeoning life. By turning inward, by nurturing myself and my future child, I would leave behind the ghost of my own mother's shortcomings. It was the best way to gain control over my life from now on. It was the best way for me to heal.

NOW

CHAPTER 14

ON MY WAY downstairs, I hear Owen's voice thanking his mother for something in the kitchen. I stop to listen on the landing where the staircase splits. Maybe she's agreed to babysit next weekend so we can have a proper date to celebrate our anniversary. Owen and I will have been married for five years on September 20, and we haven't even begun to talk about how we'll mark the occasion. Neither of us has had the energy to think about celebrating, but I know it will be a relief to finally leave the house together, the two of us, the way it used to be.

"September twentieth is next Friday," Diana says to Owen, as if she's read my mind about our upcoming anniversary. "You're not wearing your wedding band."

I've noticed, too, that Owen has begun leaving his silver

wedding band in the tray on top of the highboy by our bedroom door. I haven't asked him about it yet, but I assume it's because he's gained a few pounds since Thomas was born and some days, the ring won't fit on his finger. My own fingers were too swollen during pregnancy for my engagement ring or wedding band to fit, so I haven't been wearing any consistent outward signs of our marriage bond either.

"It's these sausage fingers," Owen says. "Most days, I wear it."

If that's a good enough explanation for Diana, the stickler for marital traditions, then it has to be good enough for me. I've never been big on symbolism anyway, and Owen knows that. He was the one who offered me a diamond ring when he proposed; I'd have been happy to forgo the exchanging of rings all together. But he insisted on that tradition, even if he was willing to be flexible about having a big, Catholic wedding at St. Catherine's like his mother had always envisioned.

"Are you going to do anything special?" Diana presses.

I should let them know, right now, that I'm standing on the landing. I shouldn't wait to overhear Owen's answer to her question. If he's planning something to surprise me on our anniversary, it's only respectful to let him keep it a secret. Part of me knows it would be a shame to ruin it for him. But another part of me wants to know immediately, and that part is victorious.

"Actually, I've been making something from all that wood we have left over from the back porch," Owen says.

"*Making* something?" Diana sounds incredulous.

"Five years is the wood anniversary, right?"

"Is it?" she asks.

"That's what you told me when you gave Cindy and her husband that wicked nice cribbage set for their five-year."

"That's right, they loved that set," Diana says. "Wood is the traditional gift for the fifth anniversary, of course. I'm sure whatever you're making will turn out beautifully." The lack of excitement in her voice undermines her kind words.

I'm as surprised as Diana to hear that Owen's been trying his hand at woodworking. I'll be impressed if he can teach himself to fashion some kind of gift for me from the leftover cedar planks we used to rebuild the house's back porch. He's not the most naturally gifted craftsman, but that only makes his aspiration to build me something by hand more endearing.

I'll never be able to match the effort, even if I start working on a project right away. I'll have to think of something else. I could buy him a fancy cribbage set like the ones Diana doles out to her godchildren's parents as a reward for making it five years without getting divorced. Owen would think that was hilarious. Marrying him was the best decision I've ever made, and he deserves to be reminded of that on a big anniversary like this one. Especially after everything we've been through this year.

Owen wasn't the first person I dated seriously, but he was the first one with whom I'd ever attempted to imagine a future. He'd offered to wait a while before going on our first date, to give me space to mourn my parents. I hadn't wanted space from him, though. He'd taken me to the New England Aquarium on the waterfront in Boston; the next weekend, we'd checked out a dilapidated miniature golf course right off Route 95. For the next two years we explored our respective cities—Providence, where I lived with Bethany, and Cambridge, where Owen lived alone in a fourth-floor Central Square walk-up—as I processed my complicated grief.

The night he asked me to marry him, we'd been strolling along the greenway in Boston's North End after a sea-food dinner. It was a breezy June night, and the lawn was crowded with picnicking couples enjoying the weather. Children in soaking wet jumpers splashed in the granite fountain. I'd recently finished a commission and was feeling like a student on summer break. Owen and I had been casually discussing the prospect of investing in a renovation property for weeks, and now he returned to the subject.

"This morning on the commute, I was flipping through the real estate section," he began. "I saw this little farm-house, really old, like built in the 1700s. It's for sale."

"Where?" I asked.

Owen sat down on one of the swinging benches overlook-ing the greenway and motioned for me to join him. "It's in this random little town called Lee, out in the western part of the state, the Berkshires," he said. "It's about two hours from here. Here's the listing." He took out his phone and clicked onto a window he'd left open on purpose. The unas-suming, saltbox timber structure had survived centuries of inhabitants already. In the listing photograph, the slate-gray paint was peeling and the front lawn was overgrown with sedges.

"It needs a lot of work," I said eagerly.

"That's where you come in!" He was glowing with anticipation. "What do you think? Want to go check it out next weekend?"

"Sure," I said. "Now let's get some dessert. I saw a whole slew of gelato places back on Hanover Street."

"Actually." Owen rummaged in the front pocket of his jeans. "I *brought* some dessert." He produced a pint-sized plastic bag of red gummy candies. "Juju Bears," he said, offering me the bag.

"Owen! Where did you even get those?" I laughed out loud, puzzled and amused. "I'd rather have gelato."

He shrugged, still holding the bag out for me to take. "Try one." His hand was trembling.

"Owen . . ." I said, as my fingers closed around the bag's contents. I opened the top and looked inside, confirming what I'd already guessed. Among the candies was hidden a modest diamond ring. When I looked up, he was no longer seated beside me on the bench but had dropped to one knee on the flagstones.

"Juju Bear," he said, his amber eyes shining. "You are the most brilliant, beautiful person I've ever known. Since the first night we met, I've never doubted that we're meant to be together—"

"I've never doubted it either!" I interrupted. A sprinkling of delighted laughter erupted from the crowd that had gathered to watch, and I felt a burst of self-conscious pride. This was the kind of scene that was only supposed to happen in romantic comedies, to actors whose roles had been written and whose lines had been rehearsed. Here I was, though, on the receiving end of the kind of proposal that passersby stopped to observe and would later recount to their friends.

"Will you make me the luckiest man in the world?" Owen asked. "Will you marry me?"

"Yes," I shouted, smiling so hard my cheeks quivered. "Yes, of course, I'll marry you, Owen Porter." I threw my arms around his neck as he stood, and he pulled me up with him, lifting my feet from the ground.

"Hooray!" cheered a small girl who'd emerged, dripping, from the fountain where she'd been splashing with her older siblings. Someone whistled loudly as Owen spun me around, and I threw my head back with delight. We were surrounded by applause. Then the crowd dissipated and the children went back to playing in the fountain. Owen lowered us both onto the bench and wrapped one arm around me, so we were swinging side by side.

"My mom will want us to have the ceremony at St. Catherine's," he said, breaking the spell. "That means you'll have to get confirmed, 'cause Father Eagan's pretty strict about that kind of thing." He paused, as if considering the weight of his assumption for the first time. "Is that cool?"

I imagined St. Catherine's with its Gothic nave and its endless rows of pews. The blank, alabaster eyes of the Virgin Mary in the sanctuary. The enormous crucifix suspended over the marble altar. "I'm not getting confirmed as a Catholic, Owen," I said. "And besides, I don't want to get married underneath a huge re-creation of Jesus's dying body."

"Fair enough." He laughed. "Where would you want to get married?"

"Maybe in a courthouse or on the beach," I said. "Just the two of us."

"You mean, you want to elope?" It was clear the idea had never occurred to Owen.

"What do you think?"

After a moment, a broad smile spread across his face. He looked like a child who'd been given the keys to a candy factory. "I like it," he said. "Now let's go find some real dessert."

We'd gotten married the next month, on the grand staircase at Boston City Hall. I'd purchased an eggshell-white cotton sundress for the occasion and Owen had worn his best suit with Converse sneakers. Afterward, we'd returned to the Rose Fitzgerald Kennedy Greenway, where he'd proposed, to share cones of gelato and ride the carousel. It had all been so quick, but it hadn't felt like a rushed decision at all.

I'd never seriously questioned whether marrying Owen was the right choice, or whether I'd have been happier, more satisfied, spending my life with someone else. Now, though, I wouldn't blame him for wondering those things about me. All those years ago, he asked me if I'd make him "the luckiest man in the world," and I'd said yes. I haven't been holding up my end of the bargain.

• • •

The air in the stairwell has gone cold, stale. Diana's voice echoes through the house. "What are you going to do about Thomas?"

A fork clinks against a plate. They've started eating without me.

Owen makes soothing noises to the baby and doesn't answer his mother right away. I listen intently from the landing, waiting for him to request a night of babysitting.

"That's what I wanted to talk to you about," he says. There's more clinking. If Diana agrees to spend a few hours with Thomas on her own, we can go out to a romantic dinner in Lenox or Stockbridge. Maybe we can even see a show.

"I'm doing most of what needs to get done, but it's really tough, Mom," he says. *Clink.* "Could you . . . I know you'll have to figure things out with your schedule, and with Sadie, but would you be able to move in here, for a while? Could you stay with us?"

The stairwell contracts around me.

"Just until I can figure things out," Owen continues.

Stay with us? All the warmth I felt toward Owen a moment ago shrinks and burrows into itself, becoming denser and denser until it is a hardened ball of icy resentment. He's not asking for a night of babysitting so we can celebrate our fifth anniversary. He's inviting his mother to move into our house, and he hasn't even asked me how I feel about it. That's probably because he knows *exactly* how I feel about it.

"Honey, of course I will," Diana answers.

I can't breathe. No fucking way is Diana going to live in our home. She cannot be here, all the time, sleeping down the hall, eating every meal with us, feeding our baby. I'll never have the chance to learn how to take care of Thomas. He'll never get used to having me as his mother.

That's not the part that worries me the most, though. Whenever Diana has come to visit in the past three months, while we were waiting to bring Thomas home from the NICU, she's made a point of starting private conversations with Owen when she thought I was napping upstairs or otherwise out of earshot. But I've heard what she says to him. She doesn't believe my story about what happened on the night I've forgotten. She doesn't believe I've even forgotten it. She wants to turn my husband against me and take my baby in for a DNA test, to find out for herself. She wants to catch me in a lie I haven't even told.

Until now, I've felt positive that Owen would never go behind my back and listen to his mother. He'd never let Diana talk him into betraying my trust or into believing that I would have betrayed his. But now he's asked her to move in with us, and I'm not sure what he's capable of anymore.

Owen's words echo again in my mind, the specific way he phrased his request to Diana. He didn't ask her to stay with us until *we* could figure things out. He asked her to stay until *he* could figure things out. I wonder what kinds of things Owen thinks he needs to figure out on his own.

Amid the tumult of confusion tearing through my mind, a thick strand of anger burns steady and bright. He should have asked me. There is no acceptable reason for him not to have asked me first, before inviting his mother to come live with us. What was he thinking? I should be included in whatever conversation they think they're having. I'm about to barge in to confront them, to demand an explanation for their behavior. They should be ashamed for making plans without me, and they owe me an apology.

But neither Owen nor Diana has seen me or knows that I've overheard their conversation. If I storm into the kitchen, I can't be sure he'll take my side over hers. He might say something out loud that he can't take back and that I can't pretend not to have heard. In the worst-case scenario, I'll only end up making myself look completely unstable. Unfit.

Owen might have asked Diana to move in, but that doesn't mean she's won. He's still making me a gift from scratch for our anniversary, after all, and he wouldn't put in that kind of effort if he was planning to leave me. He seems to be struggling with what to do next. If I try to stand up for myself right now, it might backfire. It might convince him to give up on me. I can't risk pushing him over the edge when his patience is already so close to running out.

Having made this wretched calculation, I decide to bide my time. I'll sneak back upstairs and pretend I never heard Owen and his mother talking in the kitchen. I can fix this. I'll start helping with chores and taking initiative when it comes to caring for Thomas. I can make Owen change his mind about the wisdom of having Diana move in with us.

There's still time to convince him we'd be better off on our own.

As I climb back up the stairs, careful not to let them creak beneath me, I can't shake the fear that's hooked itself into my heart. What if, eventually, the love that compelled my husband to take care of me through an unwanted, unfair pregnancy and raise a stranger's baby—what if that love runs out? I could lose Owen. I might have lost him already.

THEN

CHAPTER 15

Spring was in full bloom by the time I saw Liza. She sent me a text message that she was finally home from New York and suggested a hike in the northern part of the county, near Dunbar Brook. Owen was visiting his mother across the state, having accompanied her to Mass in the morning, and I texted him my plans. It was the first clear day after nearly a week of nonstop rain. The air was thick with the smell of fresh earth as I walked outside to meet Liza at the curb.

"Julie!" She jogged around the front of her Jeep and threw her arms wide. Before wrapping me in an enthusiastic embrace, she glanced down at my barely protruding belly. I'd only gained a few pounds so far, but I must have looked noticeably different to Liza, who hadn't seen me in four months. She looked the same as when I'd last seen her but instead of a party dress, stockings, and curls, she wore cargo shorts, hiking boots, and a Red Sox cap.

She kissed my cheek, then pulled back and grasped my upper arms, examining my face. "How are you feeling?"

"Not great," I said. "How's your mom?"

"Doing better, finally." Liza opened the passenger door for me before climbing into the driver's seat. "It was touch and go there for a while, with the new hip."

"She's so lucky to have you," I said.

"Tell *her* that." Liza typed *Dunbar Brook trailhead* into the Jeep's navigation system. "My mom had certain expectations of a volunteer, live-in nurse-slash-maid-slash-chef, and I did *not* meet those expectations."

"Oh, Liza."

"That's just how she is. I'm going back next weekend to check on her, but at least I don't have to *stay* with her this time."

"You booked a hotel?"

"Donny's letting me crash at his studio while he's traveling," she said, pulling onto Route 20. "It's pretty nearby my mom's, and apparently, he got a gig writing songs for this band he used to tour with."

I half listened to Liza describe Donny's newest musical venture. Out the car window, the verdant hardwood forest flashed by like an impenetrable wall, interrupted by bright-yellow explosions of bellwort and honeysuckle. At least, the blossoms appeared yellow to me. But ever since the night I'd forgotten, I couldn't be sure. One thing I'd lost was the comfort of knowing that my yellow was the same as everyone else's yellow, or my red or my blue, for that matter. Things that used to be one color seemed to have shifted a few shades down on the paint chip. As if my reality had slipped behind a different lens filter, one that darkened everything.

"I need to talk to you about what happened at the party," Liza said, reading my mind. "And what you're going to do."

"I know," I said. "You were already in New York when Owen and I stopped by on our way to the police station. Did Marcus tell you I lost one of the earrings you gave me?"

"Don't worry about the earring, for fuck's sake. Wait a minute." Liza lowered her voice, as if the two of us were no longer alone in her car. "You ended up reporting it to the police?"

"Marcus didn't tell you?"

She blinked, as if Marcus's omission surprised her as much as it surprised me. "I guess not," she said.

"He wasn't too helpful," I said, knowing it was impossible that Marcus had simply forgotten to tell his wife. He must have lied to her. Either that or Liza was lying to me.

"Julie—what happened?"

"We made a report," I said carefully. "We gave the detective a list of all the party guests." I pictured Officer Bose's smirk as he watched me from across the table in the police station conference room. "But unless there's another victim, I didn't get the feeling they're going to pursue it."

"Another victim," she repeated. "Like if it was a serial rapist?"

"Right. And the other victim would have to file a police report too."

Liza sucked air through her teeth. "Who else have you told?" she asked.

"Just you and Marcus, Owen of course, and his mom—"

"You told *Diana*?"

"I didn't mean to," I said. "She was at our house, being her usual nosy self. I called a crisis line, too, the night of your party, after I got home. The Elizabeth Freeman Center?"

"I've heard of it," Liza said. "What'd they say?"

"Nothing," I said. "I didn't give them any details—I couldn't remember. I still can't. Has Marcus said anything else?" I asked. "About what he saw that night?"

"He told me he found you outside, alone. I guess you tried to walk home. I said he should have taken you straight to the police station, right when he found you," she said. "He didn't see a rapist running away into the woods, or anything, if that's what you're asking."

It wasn't what I was asking. Liza seemed to believe the only explanation for my sexual assault was that a stranger had been lurking in the woods, waiting for me to walk home alone.

My voice felt like mud. "What if it wasn't a stranger who raped me, though?"

Beneath the brim of her Red Sox cap, Liza's face darkened. "You mean, you think it might have been someone at the party? Someone we invited?"

I felt like I had to apologize for even suggesting it. "I don't know. But earlier in the night, did you notice anything? Maybe someone who was . . ."

"Targeting you?" Liza shook her head vigorously. "I would have told you. I would have *stopped* them."

"Or was someone else missing from the party at the same time I left?"

"I didn't even notice you were gone until I woke up the next morning," she said. "I wasn't paying enough attention." Her voice was congested with tears. "I'm so sorry."

"It's not your fault, Liza," I said. "Don't be sorry."

"I *am* sorry, Julie," she insisted. "But you're right. It isn't about me. Here we are, anyway." She parked the Jeep beside a grove of American beech trees whose bark was blackened and peeling away. "This is the trailhead."

An hour and a half later, my ankles felt like water balloons and I'd developed a trenchant cramp. The afternoon sun was low in the sky as we reached a line of train tracks, and I was more interested in the amount of time it would take us to get back to the car than in the names of the various wildflowers Liza was pointing out. I reached into my backpack for my water bottle and lowered myself onto one of two boulders beside a pile of lumber.

"You doing okay?" Liza asked with a raised eyebrow.

"I'm fine," I assured her.

"Then stand your ass back up," she said, motioning with a flick of her hand. "That's a memorial for the Hoosac Tunnel. There was an accident here that killed thirteen people." In the distance, the line of train tracks vanished into the pitch-black opening of an old granite tunnel. The year *1877* was mounted in marble numbers above it.

"Thirteen people? Shit." I stood up obligingly and examined the simple memorial, which bore no reference to death. "How?"

"They were building a shaft to connect the sides of the tunnel." Liza moved her fists in front of her body as if dragging two heavy objects toward each other. "They were all standing on a platform above it, and BOOM!" Her hands opened dramatically, fingers splayed to pantomime an explosion.

"Oh, my god."

She nodded gravely. "There were so many fumes the other workers left them all for dead," she said. "The thing is, they *weren't* dead. Not right away, anyway." She shuddered. "They survived long enough to build a ladder, to try to escape."

"Really?" I sensed Liza was nearing supernatural territory, and I played along with her, enjoying the prolonged water break. "But if the other workers just left them there," I asked, "how did anyone know they'd survived the explosion?"

"Because later, *years* later, people heard cries in these woods. Moans." Liza gestured back to the hiking trailhead from which we'd emerged. "Things like, 'Help us!' and 'We're stuck down here!'"

"Let me guess," I said, unable to hide the laughter in my voice. "The workers just wanted their bodies to be buried properly? Safely laid to rest?"

"That's right." Liza nodded, either missing my sarcasm

or choosing to ignore it. "That's what spirits need when they leave the world suddenly, unfairly like that. Some hikers eventually went down to investigate, and they found thirteen skeletons," she said. "And the raft they'd built."

"Are we almost to the car?" I asked, standing and stretching my arms above my head.

"It's right up that way." She pointed down River Road. A moment later, I recognized her red Jeep beside the tight-knit grove of American beeches.

"Poor trees," Liza said, pausing before opening the passenger door for me.

"Why's their bark so gross?"

"Because they're diseased," she said. "With fungus. Insects bring it in when they invade them for their sap. It's destroying their circulatory systems."

"That sounds so painful," I said.

"It must be," she agreed. "They're dying from the inside out."

On the drive home Liza was conspicuously silent for a long while. Then she cleared her throat. "Don't take this the wrong way," she said slowly, "but I didn't expect you to still be pregnant. I'm surprised . . ."

"That I didn't get an abortion?"

"There's a clinic right across the New York border," she said.

"It's not a matter of getting to a clinic, Liza."

"Is it because of Owen?"

"Kind of," I said. "He's obsessed with being a dad."

"But it's *your* decision."

"I know that," I said. "And I've made it." I placed an awkward hand on my belly, then removed it as a gruesome thought occurred to me. "Do you think the Hoosac Tunnel ghost logic applies to abortions too?"

"What do you mean?"

"You said when those workers were killed they needed to have their corpses honored, laid to rest," I said. "What about things that die before they're born?"

"Like a fetus? I never thought about it."

"It would be impossible for anyone else to honor the spirit's discarded body, since there would *be* no body," I said, a bit uneasy. "No bones to bury. That means the spirit would never be able to rest."

"But it never had its own body in the first place," Liza said. "It was only ever dreaming. And it will stay that way, dreaming. Miscarriages happen all the time, don't they? And if all those miscarried pregnancies had to stick around to haunt people?" She shuddered. "Ew. No. I *do* think it works the other way around, though."

"Dead mothers don't haunt their kids," I said. "At least, not mine."

"I meant a *pregnant* mother," she said. "Like if someone died while they were giving birth. *That* spirit would hang around."

"To haunt her own child?"

"You think I'm talking out of my ass," Liza said goodnaturedly. "And I probably am, who knows. But since the baby was a part of her body when she'd been alive, right up to the point when she died, I'd say that the mother's spirit would need to feel satisfied that it—*they*, the child—was safe." She leaned over to turn up the radio volume. "It's just a theory."

"Safe," I repeated.

Are you safe? It was what the operator at the Elizabeth Freeman Center had asked me when I'd called the night of the party, right before I'd hung up on her. The word had lost all meaning for me. If I'd been safe, I wouldn't have been raped. I wouldn't be pregnant. Come to think of it, I couldn't remember the last time I'd felt safe. Nor could I force myself to worry about the safety of this fetus.

• • •

The next morning Owen drove me to my first ultrasound appointment. The stained piles of snow lining the parking lot on our last visit to Dr. Syed's office had melted, and someone had planted tulips along the concrete walkway to the front entrance.

"How're you doing, Juju Bear?" Owen asked before we went inside.

"They're too cheerful in there." I sighed. It wasn't only that this was the first ultrasound appointment, the one where I was going to have to look at all the little fetus parts of the little fetus body. It was also that everyone inside that office expected me to be happy about it.

"You can do this." Owen squeezed my shoulder. "Want to do the breathing exercise?"

"I think I need to."

193

I let him take my hands and we breathed in deeply together. Then we let it out. Again. In together—we waited, held our breath. And out. Together. Then Owen opened the door and followed me through it.

The plump receptionist's permanent smile was waiting for us. It twitched slightly as she glanced down at my belly, then back up to our faces.

"Hello, Mr. and Mrs. Porter! Or should I say, Mom and Dad!"

I mustered a weak, reciprocal smile and leaned on Owen's shoulder as I signed my name on the register. The receptionist's eyes were twinkling at her computer screen. "I see you're here for your twenty-week appointment." She peered up with another perky grin, as if she couldn't help herself. "By the way, you look great!"

Once I had started "showing" a little bit, people I hardly knew felt compelled to comment upon my body. I didn't know how I was supposed to react to being told I looked "great" as a pregnant person. "Great" compared to what, exactly? Did the receptionist come to that judgment after sizing me up based on what she remembered of me from my first appointment, before I'd looked pregnant? Or did I look "great," in her estimation, compared to the other pregnant women who'd come in so far that day?

I thought about replying, *Well, your body looks just about the same as it did the last time I saw it, I think, but it's not something that I'd ever mention.* Instead, I looked back at her with a blank expression until she started pretending to take care of some paperwork on the desk.

Owen and I sat down, and I propped my feet up on top of his outstretched legs. Across the waiting room sat a couple about a decade younger than us, both dressed in black hoodies and hunched over their phones. In a stroller beside them, a chubby toddler smeared his snot across the screen of an iPad.

"Julie Porter?" The ultrasound technician's singsong voice preceded her as she swung open the door to the waiting room. "There's the lovely mother!" She held an empty, sealed plastic cup in one hand and extended the other hand toward me. "I'm Amanda."

Amanda wore lavender scrubs and had a high auburn ponytail. As I shook her hand, I was almost certain I knew her from somewhere.

"The restroom's that way, through the exam room," she said, handing me the sealed plastic cup. "At your last appointment, there was protein detected in your urine, so we'll need to keep an eye out for that."

I walked through the exam room into the attached lavatory. As the door closed behind me, I glimpsed my reflection in the mirror over the sink. The hollowed-out eyes reminded me of an expression I'd seen before, years ago, on the face of a former classmate. And then I recognized the ultrasound technician. Amanda Mallory, an acquaintance who was raped while we were in high school, whose resulting pregnancy and miscarriage had been transformed by the faculty into a cautionary tale about drinking beer on campus. I hadn't seen her since she'd transferred away from Andover, and I'd never had a chance to ask her how any of it had been for her. How she'd survived. I was ashamed of my younger self for having returned to everyday life, for never having bothered to follow up with her. I should have written her an email, at least.

But over a decade had passed since then. She'd been able to move away and start over on the other side of the state, it seemed, even if our classmate who'd raped her had never faced justice. Now here she was, probably enjoying her life out in the Berkshires as an ultrasound technician. That was what I hoped for her, anyway.

Finishing up, I screwed the lid back on the little plastic cup, washed my hands, and returned to the exam room across the corridor.

"Is your full name Amanda Mallory?" I asked, handing over my urine sample. Her eyes widened briefly before she recovered, but I caught the panic there. She probably didn't want to run into anyone from Andover. I didn't blame her.

"Do we know each other?" she asked, trying to sound casual. She stored the little plastic cup and washed her hands at the sink, one by one.

I'd expected her to recognize me, at least once I said her name, and now I wasn't sure how to proceed. I wanted her to know I wasn't one of those people from her past who would judge her harshly.

I pulled together the friendliest smile I could and said, "We went to school together. Back then I was Julie Merritt."

Before I'd finished the sentence, recognition flashed in her eyes and she smiled back at me. I hadn't been the loyalist of friends to her, but I hadn't been cruel like so many of our classmates.

"Julie, of course!" Her smile fell away abruptly. "I'm—oh, I'm so sorry," she said.

"For what?" It occurred to me that somehow, she must already know the reason I was sitting here before her, begrudgingly pregnant. Maybe she had access to the questionnaire I'd filled out at my first appointment. Or maybe Dr. Syed had written a note, somewhere on my medical record, that I'd been the victim of a rape. I felt a burst of relief at the idea that Amanda already had that information. I wouldn't have to say the words out loud myself.

"About your parents," she said. "I heard about what happened to your dad's plane."

"Oh," I said. "It was a long time ago. But thanks."

"I saw it on the news," she continued, "and I knew I recognized the name. Merritt. Then afterward, when I read about how you decided to give away all that money, I finally put it together. And I realized, those people who crashed their plane were *Julie Merritt's* parents! I went to *school* with her!" She finished drying her hands and turned back to face me.

It would be impossible to bring up rape, in any manner, now. I was irritated, not at Amanda, but at my parents for having sabotaged my reunion with her from beyond the grave.

"Congratulations to you and your husband, by the way!" Amanda said, shifting back into professional mode. "I'll go grab him from the waiting room."

"Sounds good," I said as the door shut behind her.

Moments later, she returned with Owen, who took a seat in the chair beside the exam table.

"Hey, Juju Bear," he said. "How are you feeling, so far?"

"This is Amanda," I told him, sparing him the answer to his question. "We went to high school together, believe it or not."

"Small world," Owen said.

I swung my feet up onto the exam table, leaned back, and lifted my frumpy maternity shirt to expose my swollen belly.

Amanda smeared a dollop of clear goo across it. "Okay, here we go," she said dramatically. "Let's take a look at this little angel."

The ultrasound wand pressed against the contents of my uterus from the side, then from the other side, then from below, and so on. On the computer screen, amorphous white shapes bent and wiggled against the fuzzy black background of my insides. Every so often, the shapes blended into the vague form of a fetus; whenever that happened, Owen squeezed my hand.

Amanda paused the image. "Look," she instructed, pointing with her pinky finger at a mark on the screen. "Can you see it, there?"

We strained our necks toward the screen, squinting.

"Is that?" Owen began.

"A penis!" she shrieked, looking at us expectantly. "You're having a boy!"

The news didn't please me, nor did it disappoint me. It *did* nudge the blurry white fetus shape on the computer screen a little closer toward "baby" in my mind.

"It's a boy, Juju Bear!" Owen's grin was completely uninhibited.

A moment ago, he'd entered the exam room ready to be sullen in solidarity with me. He'd understood that the relentless joy in this doctor's office might feel a bit grating to someone with a rapist's child inside them, thriving like a parasite. Now, though, Owen was making up for my lack of enthusiasm about this pregnancy by amplifying his own. He was positively beaming at me, as if desperate to convince me that everything was as it should be, that this was *our* baby, that we had planned this. That we'd chosen it.

His eyes begged me to play along, and suddenly I saw him as the rest of the world must see him. For a moment, he was not the person whose sleepy, sweaty scent mingled with my own every morning. He was a stranger, or an acquaintance—an old classmate like Amanda Mallory, maybe. I saw my husband as he appeared to other people: undeniably and agreeably attractive, like the dad in a riverside camping scene in one of his L.L.Bean catalogs. And there in his eyes was the thing that I couldn't ignore, the thing that I couldn't deny him. Even when I looked at Owen objectively, I saw "dad" as an integral part of his identity. He wanted it so badly.

I watched Owen and willed my heart to soften toward the future. If my husband was committed to being a good father for this fetus—this baby, this *boy*—then maybe I could follow his lead. Maybe we could save our family.

"All done!" Amanda handed me a towel to wipe the goo from my belly. "Dr. Syed is just finishing up with another patient." She retrieved a strip of photos from the printer beneath the ultrasound machine and presented them to Owen. Evidence of a crime we couldn't prove. "Dad, why don't you head back out into the waiting room with these?"

Owen nodded and rose from his chair, clasping the sonograms to his chest. He looked back apologetically as he reached the doorway. "See you in a few minutes," he said.

After Owen left, I was alone in the exam room with Amanda. There was an unsteady silence.

I couldn't stand it, so I blurted, "It's great to see that you're doing well."

"You, too, Julie." Amanda pulled open a drawer beside the sink and began to rearrange its contents. My words must have sounded condescending, as if I hadn't expected her to be doing well at all after surviving an unwanted pregnancy as a teenager.

The last thing I wanted to do was to make Amanda self-conscious. I needed her. She might be the only person in the world, the only person I knew at least, who could understand what this was like for me. Unlike Owen, she'd experienced the peculiar agony of going through the motions, measuring blood pressure, stepping on a scale, and constantly monitoring bodily functions. All for a fetus that I'd never asked for, that a big part of me still wished would stop existing.

"It's been so long," I said. "We never really got to talk about what happened."

She looked up from the drawer, turned to face me. "What do you mean?"

The first phrase that came into my mind was, at best, unsubtle: *I was raped too.* You couldn't just *say* that to someone, though. "How you left school sophomore year," I said. "I never asked what happened, afterward."

Amanda tilted her head to one side, shook it almost imperceptibly. "I'm fine, Julie," she said. "Dr. Syed should be right in."

Of course she didn't want to talk about her past while we waited for Dr. Syed. He was her boss, and this was her place of work.

There was a knock at the door, followed by Dr. Syed's friendly face. As Amanda turned back to the drawer, he took a seat on the stool and rolled the computer monitor so that he was positioned across from me.

"How do you feel, after the ultrasound?" he asked.

Hearing that question from Dr. Syed, I regretted not having heard it from Owen before he ducked out into the waiting room with the sonogram.

I shrugged. "It's a boy."

"Congratulations," Dr. Syed said mildly. "How'd your virtual appointment go with Dr. Bridges?"

"I appreciate the referral," I said. "But I'm not going to have another appointment with her."

"Do you mind if I ask why not?"

"I didn't feel like I could trust her," I told him. Amanda closed the drawer and began organizing a stack of paperwork on the counter.

"Say no more." Dr. Syed typed a few words into the computer. "I'll see if I can find you someone else with availability."

I considered telling him not to name-drop my parents when he made the referral this time but stopped myself. I wasn't positive he was the source of Dr. Bridges's information—she could have simply typed my name into a search engine—and besides, he looked as if he had something important to tell me. He pushed the keyboard away from himself and leaned forward on his stool, resting his elbows on his knees.

"The thing is, Julie," said Dr. Syed, "your blood pressure is elevated. That's a new symptom." He continued, "And in combination with the protein we detected in your urine, and your ongoing nausea, I'm concerned."

"What does that mean?" I asked.

"It's not necessarily a big deal, but given your mother's history with preeclampsia, we do have to be careful." He clasped his hands between his knees. "If you experience visual disturbances, flashes or shadows, streamers of light that won't go away, you must come in to see me right away," he said. "Depending on how you're feeling, it might even make sense to go straight to the emergency room."

Dr. Syed kept talking but I was watching Amanda, feeling more and more desperate. She must be almost finished with the paperwork and I only had a few seconds left to make a connection. I needed to start over, without mentioning the reason she'd had to leave Andover, but I couldn't find the right words. I'd never talked about rape with another woman who'd been through it herself, as far as I knew. There had to be a way to bring it up without upsetting her.

Dr. Syed finished directing me to monitor myself for

worsening symptoms. Amanda handed him a manila folder as he stood up.

"Thanks, Amanda." He opened the door and held it for her. "Be sure to make another appointment before you leave," he said to me before he turned and strode down the hallway.

"Wait, Amanda," I said, and she hung back in the doorway. "Would you ever want to grab a coffee, or something? We could catch up on—"

"I don't think so," she said quickly. "Good luck with everything, Julie."

Then she was gone, and I'd missed my chance. I was even more alone than before.

NOW

CHAPTER 16

FOR THE FEW days she's been living with us, Diana has mostly managed household chores and doted on Thomas. But I'm not oblivious. She's poisoning Owen's opinion of me with every sideways glance and passive-aggressive comment. She's been going out of her way to interrupt my time with Owen and to prevent bonding opportunities between me and Thomas. As if she's stepping in to take my place.

I need to show them that I'm getting the hang of motherhood, that we'll be fine living here on our own as a family unit. If Owen sees that I'm at least trying to do my part, maybe he'll agree to send his mother back to Norwood.

That would create a much more stable situation for Sadie. Her parents are currently on another bender, and she's here for the weekend, maybe longer. I overheard Diana say to Owen that she feared Sadie would grow up to face the same addiction issues as her mother. Perhaps our home is, indeed, a better environment than wherever Sadie might be staying otherwise. Selfishly, I hope the four-year-old's presence will provide some much-needed joy around here.

Father Eagan had to make the drive across the state to drop her off. They arrived early this morning, Sadie with a miniature pink plastic suitcase and Father Eagan with a leather-bound Bible, looking like a goddamn exorcist.

I wonder if Sadie's old enough yet to be coerced into altar service. On Diana's mantel there's a photo of Owen dressed in his cherubic white robe, face solemn and eyes averted from the camera. In the photo, he and another boy of the same age are walking down the carpeted aisle of St. Catherine's, beginning the procession to initiate Mass. A younger Father Eagan looms behind them, swinging an ornate incense thurible. In the foreground, the boys look bored, perhaps frightened. Father Eagan, in contrast, appears positively joyful, ecstatic, blissed out of his mind on the fumes of the Holy Spirit.

Now he's in my house. Diana gives him a thorough tour before serving roast beef sandwiches and lemonade for lunch. Then she puts Thomas down for his nap and takes Sadie outside to play in the backyard. I find myself at the kitchen table with Owen and, unfortunately, Father Eagan.

"The baby's name, Thomas," Father Eagan begins, refilling his glass of lemonade. "Where did that come from?"

"It's from the Bible," I say.

"You know how I've always liked the story of Doubting Thomas?" Owen says. "I guess I relate to him."

The priest nods, satisfied. "Have you been leaning on your faith, now, to help you cope with everything?"

"I'm sorry, Father," Owen says. "But I feel like I don't really have faith. Not anymore." His tone is mournful and resigned, as if in addition to his religious faith, he's lost his faith in all good things, natural and supernatural. Physical and spiritual. I realize it might have been Owen, not Diana, who arranged for the three of us to have this conversation. If he's the one who invited the priest to stay, to counsel us as a couple, then I have to participate. I have to try.

"I see." Father Eagan drums his fingers on the table. They're arthritic and speckled with age. "I'm sorry for what your family's been though," he says, in the voice of a practiced counselor. "Many people find that going through this kind of thing, it shakes their faith in God. That's to be expected."

"I've never been religious," I remind him.

"Many of my parishioners, the very faithful or . . . not, find it helpful to search for a higher meaning in their everyday lives," he continues. "Even if the faith you recognize isn't accessible to you right now, in any familiar way, you might be able to find it elsewhere."

"Like out in nature?" I suggest, thinking of Liza's wild-flower hikes.

"Go for a walk in the woods, visit the beach, give your dog a good scratch behind the ears," Father Eagan agrees, winking at Daisy. "Seek out people and experiences that remind you of God's love. You've got to find and appreciate those moments of awe."

"You mean miracles," Owen says, his voice laced with bitterness. "Right? Anything to prove that there's some higher meaning, some lesson to learn from all this. Some message from God in heaven."

I've heard Owen recite that three-word phrase, *God in heaven*, during his private prayers and sometimes in conversation with his mother, always in the same intonation and rhythm. God in heaven. God-in-heaven. *Godinheaven.* As if saying things over and over could make them real.

"Miracles, sure," says Father Eagan. "We can think of miracles like that, as messages from another place. Another, wiser place."

"It just feels like God really fucked up," Owen blurts. He immediately looks as if he regrets the blasphemy. "I'm sorry, Father, I just . . ."

"It's okay," Father Eagan assures him, to my surprise. He takes a sip of lemonade and replaces a disrupted strand of his comb-over. "In times of trial, it's normal to feel as if God is testing you."

"But for what?" Owen demands. "What kind of a God would stage these . . . these random *tests*?"

"And why do some people get tested but not others?" I ask, finding myself swept up in Owen's pointless line of questioning. I'm curious how Father Eagan will respond, from a philosophical perspective. "How does God choose who has to suffer, anyway?"

Father Eagan sighs and removes his glasses.

"Why did *Julie* have to suffer?" Owen rephrases my question. For him, a lapsed Catholic, this conversation is more urgent. His childhood framework for understanding the meaning of the universe was obliterated when his wife was raped. He lost something that night too.

"You know I can't answer that," Father Eagan says finally. He replaces his glasses on the bridge of his nose. "Through prayer, though, we can find the comfort we seek. It just takes time. Will you pray with me?"

Neither of us answers, but that doesn't stop Father Eagan from raising his right hand in the air, to bless us. "*Hail Mary, full of grace, the Lord is with thee,*" he begins pontifically, eyelids lowered. "*Blessed art thou among women, and blessed is the fruit of thy womb, Jesus.*" I expect Owen to join in but he doesn't. "*Holy Mary, Mother of God, pray for us sinners, now and at the hour of our death,*" the priest finishes. Owen's mouth tightens into a firm line.

"Amen," I say, to be polite.

Later, as Father Eagan prepares to leave, Diana accompanies him into the front entryway.

"Owen's doing his best," I hear her say as I reach the stairwell landing on my way to check on Thomas, "but there's only so much *he* can do. I'm sorry, Father." Her voice is repentant; this visit hasn't gone the way she'd hoped.

"He'll find God again," Father Eagan responds.

"You're right, of course, Father," Diana says slowly. There's a strong possibility she senses I'm here on the stairwell landing and wants me to hear whatever she's about to say next. "Let's pray it's not drugs."

I try to imagine what kind of drug would affect Owen this way, causing him to become romantically distant while still managing to parent Thomas and run our household like a competent adult. Does Diana think he's on cocaine? She must have lost her mind. Unless it's not Owen she's praying for.

It's me. I'm the one she suspects of being on drugs. That explains why she agreed to move in with us until I can start acting like a mother is supposed to; she's treating me exactly the way she treated Sadie's mother, Kristen. It also explains the way she's been ignoring me and, recently, regarding me with unfettered revulsion. If I *was* struggling with addiction, Diana's disparaging attitude sure as hell wouldn't be helping the situation. It's clearly only been harming Kristen.

I'd have to be crazy to mess with recreational drugs right now. I'm not even taking an antidepressant. It feels too risky to mix substances with my prescribed dose of postpartum painkillers.

Part of me is offended and wants to confront the two of them, tell Diana she's barking up the wrong tree. I don't have the energy to face her right now, though, let alone sit through another smug Hail Mary from Father Eagan. As I turn to sneak upstairs before they notice me, Diana speaks again in the front entryway.

"Julie was going to have an abortion, at first," she says. That bitch. "They'll always have to live with that, Father."

"Give it time," Father Eagan says, and I can imagine his tactful smile. "This is all so new, still. So new for everyone."

I'm not surprised that Diana would disclose such an intimate detail about my life to her priest. He's been her revered confidant for decades, and she couldn't care less about my privacy. The depth of her judgment, though, astonishes me—her conviction that I'll continue to suffer, that I'll "always have to live with" the sin of even *considering* terminating my pregnancy.

Even worse is her feigned concern for Owen, as if he'll inevitably be punished, too, for loving a woman who could have gone through with an abortion. Diana clearly didn't expect our marriage to survive the stress of that decision. I wonder if she prayed that it wouldn't. I wonder if her prayers might have worked.

CHAPTER 17

IT STARTED RAINING as soon as Father Eagan left and it hasn't stopped since. Stuck inside for the afternoon, Sadie's kept herself entertained by staging still lifes and sketching them, our favorite activity. She gathers items from around the house, three or four at a time, and arranges them with painstaking care on the hearth in the parlor. Then we sit on the window seat with her enormous box of crayons and diligently render the scene. Hours pass this way.

"What happened to this lady, again?" Sadie finishes the sketch she's working on and retrieves the board book *MumBet* from the hearth, where she'd propped it sideways between an empty formula bottle and one of Diana's rain boots. Owen naps in the red rocking chair, and Diana is upstairs feeding Thomas. "Where did she go, after she got free?"

"After she freed herself, she lived right nearby here," I say, reminding Sadie of the board book's age-appropriate history. "Did you know it was my job to help turn that old house into a museum, not too long ago?"

"That was your *job*?" Sadie's clearly impressed, and pride swells within me. I've never inspired this kind of admiration in a child. It's empowering.

"Yeah, I really enjoyed that project," I say.

"Did she live by herself?" Sadie asks. "Was it safe?"

"No," I say. "And no. Remember, from the book? She lived with the Sedgwicks. Theodore, the judge who helped her get free, his wife, Pamela, and all their kids."

The board book doesn't mention Pamela, but after Liza pretended to channel her spirit on our first visit to the Sedgwick house, I studied up on her story. The loneliness that turned into depression. The violent death after drinking poison.

It's another detail, though, that haunts me, something I read about while I was doing subsequent research for that renovation job. After Pamela died, I learned, the rest of the Sedgwick family refused to speak of it. Their communications avoided any reference to Pamela or to her recent death. In the months following her suicide, her husband, Theodore, and their seven living children exchanged hundreds of letters, covering topics that ranged from marriages to education to travel plans. But never once, in any of those letters, did they comment upon the new and unavoidable fact that their mother was dead.

Pamela had lost her mind toward the end of her life, after

burying three young children. Her husband hadn't been able to stand being at home with her, in the same house. Her pain had been too much for him to bear, and eventually, he'd left her out there—out here, in the Berkshires—to die. If I don't get my shit together, there's nothing stopping Owen from doing the same to me.

"Julie?" Sadie interrupts my thoughts.

"Come back over here, Sadie." I motion for her to join me on the window seat. *Healing from Trauma* is still on the table beside the davenport. I hope Owen knows I've been reading it, that I've been putting in an effort. I hope he knows he shouldn't leave me in our house to die alone.

Sadie snuggles in beside me and we watch the rain. It's slowed enough that I can observe the individual droplets as they splatter, fast and violent, against the bricks of the front walkway. I imagine myself trapped inside one of them, hurtling downward, curled fetal with my face pressed against the wet, transparent wall.

I whisper to Sadie, "Do you know the song about the rain and the old man?"

Her eyes widen as she looks up at me. She shakes her head back and forth.

Keeping my voice low so as not to wake Owen, I say, "It goes like this:

"It's raining, it's pouring,
"The old man is snoring.
"He bumped his head and went to bed
"And couldn't get up in the morning.

"... or something like that. I forget the exact lyrics."

Sadie tilts her head back and looks at me through narrowed eyes, skeptical. "That's the same as A TISKET, A TASKET!"

"Sadie, you're right!" I say, honestly amazed that a four-year-old could recognize the similarity.

She straightens her shoulders, proud of herself.

"But, right now, it makes sense to sing the lyrics about the rain and the old man, don't you think? Because we have rain"—I nod toward the window—"and we have an old man, snoring." I point to Owen in the rocking chair.

As if on cue, a snore catches in his throat. He coughs, sighs, and falls back into a fitful sleep.

Sadie dissolves into giggles. "Okay, sing it again," she whispers eagerly, pantomiming the motion of clapping her hands. "I'll sing it too."

We sing it again, and again, softly, until Sadie knows all the lyrics by heart and can perform the song from beginning to end, all on her own. We sit there together on the window seat, singing and giggling while Owen snores beside us, watching the raindrops merge into rivulets and run down the windowpanes. I feel more like myself than I have in months.

• • •

After dinner Sadie goes to bed for the night and Diana and I commence the endless tasks related to Thomas's laundry. It's only mid-September but the rain has brought with it a foreboding chill. Owen lights the first fire of the season before spreading out his accounting work across the kitchen table; so much for his idea of becoming a stay-at-home dad.

He's been throwing himself into his work even when he's at home. I suspect he's using the distraction in the evenings as a tactic to avoid sex, a conversation about sex, or any intimation of sex. According to my mother's book—as Owen well knows—we're supposed to be approaching sex slowly and gently, literally and figuratively. From my perspective, barely three months after a traumatic emergency C-section delivery, sex is far from a top priority. I haven't wanted to have intercourse, nor have I even felt the slightest pang of desire, come to think of it, but I do miss the feeling of physical closeness with Owen. I long for him to pull my hips down against his and hold me there, the smell of Old Spice mixed with sweat, the pressure of his open palms against the bare skin of my back.

Whenever I've subtly tried to initiate that kind of intimacy, though, he reacts by pulling away from me even more. It would be lovely to believe that he's avoiding the topic of sex entirely out of respect for my current mental and physical limitations. If that were the case, though, I'd expect him to at least bring up the prospect of *oral* sex, or suggest we figure out some satisfying hand play, *something* to remind ourselves that we're still the same two people who used to come together so magnificently, so wildly, that my roommate Bethany once left a Post-it on my bedroom door that read, simply: *Congratulations.* That couple was obnoxiously in love. I miss them.

Now Diana sits between us at the kitchen table, folding

laundry with her easy listening playlist in the background. The smart speaker on the counter has always been an eyesore, an ultramodern anomaly in our 1770s farmhouse, and I've never used it enough to make its convenience worth the aesthetic sacrifice. Diana loves it. It's currently playing a Jason Mraz song softly enough that it won't disturb Thomas, who's napping in the parlor, but loudly enough that it disturbs me.

This song was everywhere a few years back, and I never developed strong feelings for it, one way or the other. Tonight, though, it grates on my last nerve. It's not the lyrics, not the smug lilt in Mraz's voice, not even the nonsense syllables he scats so abundantly. It's something about the repetition, the chord pattern, that makes me want to scream.

"Alexa," I say to the smart speaker on the counter. "Skip." I'm pretty sure that's the right command, the word that will interrupt this mindless string of hey-heys to begin the next song on Diana's playlist.

Mraz continues unabated, though, instructing me to open up my mind and see, like him. If I'd just open up my heart, damn, I'd be free, he insists.

"Alexa," I say again, more loudly this time. "Skip." Nothing happens. Fucking Alexa. She's—it's—acting downright antagonistic. Or maybe she doesn't recognize the word *skip*; it's possible I'm using the wrong command.

Mraz continues to vocalize, having moved on from hey-heys to doot-doots.

"Alexa, NEXT!" I try.

Diana exchanges a disapproving look with Owen across the table.

"Alexa, Skip," Owen says firmly, before I can shout at the speaker again. Alexa obeys him. Immediately, the song switches to an acoustic ballad, one I don't recognize.

"Thanks," I say. "She never listens to me."

A high-pitched whine drifts through the crackling fireplace. Owen stares over the rim of his reading glasses in the direction of the parlor and waits, alert, to determine if the whine will expand into a wail that requires attention. The firelight dances across the contours of his face, casting shadows that make him look alternately beautiful and menacing.

We all strain to listen.

With shame, I realize that I must have woken Thomas up from his evening nap. He must have heard me through the fireplace, shouting at Alexa like an idiot. From their exasperated faces, Diana and Owen are realizing the same thing. But this mistake doesn't have to be a disaster. I can turn it into an opportunity to prove that I'm capable of something related to mothering.

"Let me go check on Thomas," I say.

Neither of them protests, and I excuse myself.

The fire has reached a blazing roar by now. The front window's wavy glass panes reflect a distorted, threatening version of the parlor. A log sizzles and breaks apart. The shadows of the flames lap at the walls like demonic tongues. In the crib, Thomas squirms in his swaddle. He must be uncomfortable, bundled up tightly like that.

Gently, I untuck the swaddling blanket from around his little body. His hands, suddenly free, flail outward for a moment before collapsing again onto his chest in loose fists. I fold the swaddling blanket and place it on top of the quilt that covers the crib's railing. Thomas sighs contentedly.

Pleased with myself, I return to the kitchen, where Owen hunches over his laptop and Diana folds laundry, more aggressively now, at the table. It's warm in here, too, but that's not what makes the atmosphere unbearable. The air is stretched taut as plastic wrap around Owen and his mother, leaving no room for me. It's suffocating.

"He's fallen back asleep," I say.

Diana reacts by snapping her tongue behind her front teeth in a sharp *tsk*. Owen says nothing. I scan the kitchen for something to focus on other than my husband's apathy. Grabbing one of Thomas's onesies from the laundry basket in front of Diana, I fold it and add it to her pile on the table.

Next, I pick up a clean burp cloth; it's that one with the baby elephants dancing alongside their happy mothers. I start to fold the burp cloth but stop when I notice what Diana is doing.

The onesie I folded a moment ago is in her hands now. She's undone my work and, for some unfathomable reason, she's refolding the onesie. She folds it slightly differently than I did, tucking in the little sleeves before creasing it along the waistline.

"I just folded that onesie," I say.

She doesn't answer.

I stare at her, boring my eyes into the top of her head as obviously as I can, but she does not look up to meet my gaze. She simply places the refolded onesie back on top of the pile where I put it a moment ago.

I clench my teeth and tell myself this situation is the definition of *fine*. Diana has had deliberate ways of doing things for as long as I've known her. She's not necessarily picking on me. And she's doing us a huge favor by giving us her time and energy when we need her help around the house. I will fold Thomas's onesies however she wants them to be folded. I pick up another one from the basket of clean laundry and imitate Diana, folding the sleeves inward and laying it neatly on top of the pile.

I glance over at Owen to see if he's picked up on his mother's micromanaging behavior. Maybe we can share an eye roll about how controlling she is, even about something as trivial as the way laundry ought to be folded. But Owen's eyes are focused on his laptop screen. He types rapidly, aware only of whatever email he's currently composing to a work colleague. The laundry drama unfolding between his wife and mother is commanding exactly as much of his attention as it deserves.

Suddenly, he stops typing and looks up at Diana. "You okay, Mom?"

I turn back to the kitchen table and gasp. The pile of laundry is gone. Moving quickly, Diana has gathered it up and stacked it all back in the basket, on top of the unfolded clothes. Hugging the basket to her body, eyes lowered, she scoots her chair backward and stands up in one rapid motion. She doesn't look at either of us as she heads toward the doorway.

Over her shoulder, she says, "Don't mind me; I'm going to take this laundry into the parlor."

"I really think Thomas is fine," Owen calls after her, frowning. "He'll fall back asleep on his own."

"He makes noises like that while he sleeps, sometimes," I agree with Owen.

Diana doesn't respond. When her footsteps come to a stop—she must have taken a seat in the rocking chair—I whisper to Owen, "That was weird, right? I tried to help." I lean away from the fireplace so Diana won't overhear me. "It's like she wants to prove something, like she's the only one who knows how the baby's laundry should be folded."

He closes his laptop and rests his hands on top of it. He's listening. Now that I have his attention, though, my mind feels like a jumbled mess. There's so much I have to tell him but I haven't been able to focus, to rank the items in order of importance. What is the one thing I need to say the most?

"This is all . . . really tough for me. This transition, you know?" I begin clumsily. "I know it's tough for you too. I didn't expect it to be like this. I wish your mom didn't have to move in."

Owen's face darkens slightly when I bring up his mother, so I backpedal. "I'm sorry, okay, no excuses. I'm not doing the best job at motherhood," I say. "I'm doing a pretty shitty job, I guess."

I wait for him to protest, to tell me that of course I'm

not a shitty mother. He must know that I'm leaving this silence deliberately, before I continue, for him to reassure me that he understands I'm doing the best I can. He doesn't reassure me, though. Instead, he removes his glasses and presses the bridge of his nose between his thumb and forefinger. The weight of his silence is suffocating.

"Look." I try again with the meager confidence I have left. "Thank you for asking your mom for help. I guess I was too proud to admit we needed it. I wanted to be able to handle this on our own, and I've been trying, you know?"

I keep talking so he won't have a chance to question whether I have, in fact, been trying. Owen knows what it looks like when I try, after all; he's witnessed me in action. When I put my mind toward a goal, I've usually been able to achieve it, whether it's solving a universal design problem or mastering a new DIY construction skill. If I've been trying my hardest to bond with Thomas, Owen must be wondering, then why the hell hasn't it been working? There must be something wrong with me. There must be something about mothering that I'm incapable of putting into action. If that's the truth, that I'll never be a good mother, no matter the circumstances, I can't let Owen figure that out. So on I ramble.

"I know it's not enough and I can do better," I say. "I *will* do better, and then we can get your mom out of here soon."

"Oh, my god, Julie." Owen squeezes his eyes shut. When he opens them, I know with a dreadful certainty that he's preparing to say something ruinous, something I don't want to hear. I sense it in the pensive way he arranges his glasses back on the bridge of his nose. He doesn't even need to say the words aloud, though I can tell they're perched on the tip of his tongue: *She's not the problem, here, Julie. You are.*

Diana's voice rings out through the flames. "Owen? Can you come in here?"

"Yeah, Mom." Owen stands abruptly and leaves the room. Whatever he was about to say, I don't want to hear it. I trot behind him into the parlor doorway, relieved to have avoided another chance for him to reiterate how little faith he has in me.

"You told me you swaddled him," Diana says accusingly. The muslin swaddling blanket, which I removed from Thomas's body and draped over the crib railing, dangles from her manicured hand.

"I did. He always likes to be swaddled when he's napping." Owen tilts his head, puzzled. "Did he kick it off or something?"

"No, it was me," I explain from the doorway. "I took the swaddle off him. It was way too hot in here."

Their heads swivel to look at me in tandem. They seem surprised that I bothered to come into the parlor; it was Owen whom Diana called for help, not me. My presence is superfluous.

"It was wicked hot in here," I repeat defensively. "Do you want me to wrap him back up in that swaddle, right now?"

"No," Owen whispers immediately, vehemently, before I can cross the threshold.

I back up into the front entryway. His overt frustration scares me, even more than his impatience in the kitchen.

"From now on, then," I say, fumbling, "I'll know to always

keep him swaddled, okay?" It turns into a question as it leaves my mouth, and I can hear how pathetic it sounds. I'm Thomas's mother. Putting him to sleep is the kind of thing that should come naturally to me. Neither of the other two adults here is even biologically related to this child, yet I'm the one tagging along, asking for permission to help.

"No," Owen says again, his voice heavy. He turns and strides past me, across the entryway, and up the stairs. The slam of the bedroom door stops me from following him.

"Sorry about that," I say to Diana, embarrassed.

She readjusts the swaddle around Thomas's sleeping body before straightening her back, radiating disappointment. Another mother-in-law would tell me there's nothing for me to be sorry for; another mother-in-law might even apologize to *me,* for having misunderstood my intent in removing the swaddling blanket.

"That was odd," Diana says, finally. Woven through the reproach in her voice is a thread of confusion. Owen's behavior must be unrecognizable to her too. I'm relieved to know that I haven't been imagining his moodiness.

What Owen and I need is an appointment with a licensed couples' therapist. Talking with Father Eagan again will only make things worse. Medication won't fix us either. But a therapist who specializes in working with couples might be able to help us communicate.

Even Owen's mother recognizes that it was odd for him to storm off like that. How could he be this upset about a *swaddle*? As the question occurs to me, though, I know that it's not about the swaddle. The swaddle is one more thing among many things—everything—that I can't do right. It's one more parenting lesson I'm supposed to have learned by now. One more way I'm failing as a mother.

CHAPTER 18

"COME WITH ME," a familiar voice whispers in my ear, the last fragment of a dream that's slipped away. I turn over in bed, searching for Owen. But I already know it wasn't his voice.

On the opposite side of the portable baby bed, Owen lies splayed with his jaw hanging open, one arm tucked behind his head. A half-empty glass of water stands beside a prescription bottle of Ambien on his bedside table, where the digital clock indicates that it's after midnight.

Suddenly, a narrow beam of light flashes across the far wall of the bedroom, then disappears as quickly as it came. Lightning, I assume. The rain must have mounted into a full-blown storm while we've been asleep. I listen for a clap of thunder, but none comes.

The loudest discernible sound is Daisy snoring in her bed at the foot of the mirror. Owen's breath catches for a moment, then returns to its gentle rhythm.

I'm about to settle back down under the covers when, once again, the intruding light shines through the bedroom window. It's coming from somewhere out in the backyard. This time, the beam sweeps across the bedroom wall, pausing as it illuminates the highboy next to the door. Then it disappears again.

A beam of light doesn't behave that way on its own. There's someone outside the house. It's possible that I wasn't dreaming a moment ago when I heard that voice. Whoever's outside with the flashlight could have stood right here, in my bedroom. Maybe they'd whispered "Come with me" in my ear. Maybe they'd wanted me to follow them.

Getting up, I make my way to the window overlooking the backyard, approaching it from the side. If someone's out there, staring back at me, at least I won't be caught in the flashlight like a deer on the road. But the beam of light isn't trained on the house anymore. It bobs and fades in the woods, then pauses somewhere beyond the hobblebushes.

Out in the hallway, a floorboard creaks. Tentative footsteps approach the door to our bedroom. I turn away from the window and force my vision to finish adjusting to the darkness. The long edge of the bedroom door gradually comes into focus.

The footsteps pause, hesitating in the doorway. As the moon emerges from behind a cloud, the bedroom fills with an otherworldly silver light, and Sadie materializes on the threshold. Her wispy blond hair floats like a halo around her face as she watches me with fearful eyes.

"Sadie, is everything okay?" I whisper, careful not to wake Owen. "Did you have a nightmare?"

She slowly shakes her head back and forth. In a tiny, trembling voice, she sings the tune I taught her in the parlor today. But she doesn't use the lyrics about the rain and the old man.

Instead, she sings, "*Some-thing's wrong with the ba-by . . .*"

I follow her gaze to the portable baby bed, right next to where I lay sleeping moments ago. It's empty. Owen snores softly on the other side of it, oblivious. How is it possible that the baby isn't in his bed? *How is it possible*, a cruel inner voice nags, *that I've woken up and made it all the way over to the window without even noticing he's gone?*

"Sadie, is Thomas in your room, with Diana?"

It's the simplest explanation for the baby's absence. If Diana felt it was necessary to come in here to feed Thomas in the middle of the night, though, she'd know better than to take him out of the room. Wouldn't she? It's possible, I realize with horror, that Diana has been sneaking in here to whisk Thomas away from between mine and Owen's sleeping bodies each night. Taking him back to her own room to feed him. Maybe that's what woke me up.

"Is Thomas in there with Diana, Sadie?" I repeat.

Sadie vigorously shakes her head, no.

I don't believe her.

In the upstairs hallway, the radiator hums and clatters. The door to the second bedroom groans as I tap it open.

There's Diana, sleeping alone in the queen bed. A tendril of her silver hair dangles toward the floor. Her face is vulnerable and relaxed, like I've never seen it in waking life. The quilt is kicked back on the opposite side of the bed, where Sadie has climbed out, but otherwise the room is undisturbed.

Thomas is not here.

"I told you . . ." Sadie's singsong voice follows me as I whirl away from the doorway: *"Some-thing's wrong with the ba-by."*

I run downstairs to check the crib in the parlor. When I reach the landing where the stairs split, though, a flash of light comes from somewhere in the kitchen. I change course, heading down that way instead, without going into the parlor.

From outside, the flashlight beam pierces the window over the sink and the kitchen is oddly, garishly, illuminated. The chair where Owen was working on his laptop after dinner is still pushed away from the table. A nearly empty bottle of formula lies discarded on the counter beside the burp cloth with the dancing elephants.

As the light disappears again, plunging the kitchen back into moonlit stillness, a distant, high-pitched wail comes from the backyard.

That noise is unmistakable. I fly across the kitchen without feeling the floor beneath my feet, unbolt the back door, and rush out into the black night, toward the source of the crying. Thomas is not safe.

Barreling onto the back porch blindly, I crash into

something hidden beneath a black tarp. I recognize the hulking shape of our new, unused grill. We'd been meaning to cook out this summer. But then Thomas came so early and we never got the chance.

Now I lift the heavy fabric of the tarp and reach beneath it, finding the handle of a long, two-pronged grilling fork. I'll need something to defend myself.

"Come with me."

There's no mistaking it this time. It's the same voice that beckoned me awake before Sadie came into the bedroom. It sounds like the gravel that grinds into your palms and mixes with blood when you're suddenly thrown, facedown, from whatever you trusted to carry you. The voice is familiar, somehow, and no louder than when I first heard it, but now it's tinged with urgency. It's not an invitation.

I race across the yard, grateful Sadie's no longer following me. Wielding the grilling fork like a weapon, I choke up on it, imagine what it would feel like to stab it into someone's eye. I'll have to take careful aim to ensure one of the two sharp tips makes its mark. I won't miss.

Another scream pierces the night, and I realize with dread that it's coming from beyond the wall of trees. As I approach the break in the hobblebushes, I strain to focus my vision, to locate the well-trodden path in the darkness. A fallen log blocks my way, and I leap over it. If there is someone between me and Thomas, someone who wants to harm him, I won't need the grilling fork; in this moment, I feel certain I could tear their throat out with my bare hands.

When I look up, the Dolans' shed is before me, revealed at once from the darkness. Its double doors are within arm's reach, ajar. The dead bolt hangs from its chain. Despite the stillness of the night, one of the doors yawns farther open.

There, on the muddy floor among the shadows, I see the naked, squirming form of a pale white baby. He screams.

Across the final stretch of dirt and straight up to the open doors of the shed, I lunge forward and throw myself against the wooden floorboards beside Thomas. It's all I can do not to crush his shivering body against mine as I try to warm him, clutching him to my chest, wrapping him in whatever heat I can muster to the surface of my skin. He's fallen silent, which is somehow much worse than his screams.

There's no time to waste; I need to get him back inside the house. Holding him firmly in my arms, I take a step forward, toward the outside. But with a gust of wind, the shed doors slam shut.

We're sealed in sudden, quiet darkness. The space feels too full around us. It's as if the interior walls of the shed are edging toward each other, closing in on me and Thomas.

I try to take another step in the direction of the doors, but I can't move. My limbs are numb, or maybe nonexistent. I know that I have legs, but for the life of me I cannot feel my weight on them.

The darkness around us grows thicker. And then from somewhere between us and the outside, between us and freedom, comes a low, hostile grunt. Whoever made that noise is in here with us, invisible but very, very close.

The deep, throaty sound comes again, a broken chuckle,

but it's behind us now. It's circling. Then rough, viselike hands grip my upper arms and I'm pulled back forcefully, farther into the shed.

My limbs reignite with feeling as I wrest myself away, fall to the floor, then scramble up and heave my right shoulder against the doors. To my surprise, they give way and I hurl myself out into the night.

"No!" I hear a man's voice shout.

Using my hands to break my fall, I realize with horror that they're empty. Thomas is gone. But he was right here! I *saw* him right here. I held him.

The baby's screams reach my ears again, this time from far, far away, somewhere on the other side of the woods, toward home. I begin to run before I can properly catch my balance, stumbling through the thorny sedges.

My shin flares with pain as I trip over the fallen log and pitch forward onto the packed earth. I land hard with a wet thud.

The prongs of the grilling fork are lodged in my side.

Whoever grabbed me inside the shed is getting away, in the opposite direction. I hear him scramble off the path and crash through the underbrush, into the darkness. He's not going to hurt me. There's no time now, though, to wonder about his motive for lurking around the shed with a flashlight.

I have to get out of the woods and find Thomas, wherever he is. Clutching my wound, I leave the bloodied grilling fork on the forest floor and stagger into the backyard. Sadie comes into view on the back porch, as still as a cemetery statue in her cotton nightgown. She holds a bundle of blankets in her arms, her face obscured in shadow as she watches me approach across the back lawn.

"Julie?" she calls. "Is that you, Julie?"

"Of course it's me!" My progress is painful but I reach the back porch without too much difficulty. The bundle in Sadie's arms is silent. "The baby—where was he?" I demand. My voice is harsher than I intend it to be.

Sadie doesn't answer. In the moonlight, her eyes glow with bewilderment. I take Thomas from her as gently as I can. His eyelids are sealed in a shallow, fitful sleep. He's warm.

"Come inside, Sadie," I say, trying to make my voice level. I motion with my head for her to follow me back into the dark kitchen.

The house is still asleep. After what just happened inside the shed, the quiet, empty kitchen should be comforting to me. Instead, in the stillness, my thoughts rush even more wildly. Whoever was hiding in the shed ran away but he could have circled back again once I left the area. He might still be out there. He could try to get inside the house. I double-check that the kitchen door is locked behind me.

I should call the police. Thomas and I might be in danger. Sadie, Owen, and Diana might be in danger too. In a matter of minutes the police will show up with sirens blaring, lights flashing. But then what? What will happen if whoever was out there has already gotten away?

The police will find the shed empty. They could spend the whole night searching the neighborhood and come up with nothing. It might be Officer Bose who's on duty. No matter which officers show up, they'll have to wake up Owen and Diana to make a report, based on my incoherent story. And I'll have to explain to all of them why the lives of two children were endangered tonight, on my watch. They'll have questions for me about how Thomas got out to the shed in the first place. That is, if he even *was* out there. I won't have the answers, not answers that will satisfy the police, anyway.

At best, they'll think I was sleepwalking and overreacted to a nightmare. At worst, they'll think my depression has devolved into postpartum psychosis, and that I'm trying to harm my baby. They might even call Child Protective Services, I realize with horror. They could take Thomas away from us.

"Where was Thomas?" I whisper to Sadie in the upstairs hallway bathroom, once we've used a towel to dry her feet. "Where did you find him?"

"In the crib," she whines, rubbing her eyes. "Can we talk later? I'm tired, Julie."

"Of course," I say, ashamed of the emotional strain I've put on Sadie tonight. The poor child's mother is an addict, for Christ's sake; the last thing she needs is another mentally unstable adult creating turmoil in her life.

I can sort through the events of the night with Sadie once we've both gotten some sleep. Then I'll have to do my best to explain everything to Owen and Diana and, if it seems warranted, we can go to the police to report whoever kidnapped Thomas and hid with him in the shed.

That is, if any of what I experienced tonight even happened. It's possible that Thomas was safely lying in his crib this whole time, until Sadie picked him up and brought him out to the back porch. I followed the flashlight outside without bothering to check the crib in the parlor. He might never have been out in the shed at all. Could I have imagined the entire event?

That voice woke me up by saying "Come with me," leading me outside. It wasn't clearly gendered, male or female. It couldn't have been the same person as the man hiding in the shed, though, that's for certain. It couldn't have been *any* person, since I heard it clearly at incongruous times. That voice must have originated in my own mind, somehow.

And if I imagined the voice that said "Come with me," then it's possible I also imagined the one that shouted "No!" after I hurled myself from the shed. At the time, I was sure of what I'd heard. The shout didn't last long enough for me to have identified the man, though, even if I'd known him. If there even *was* a man out there. The owls around here make all kinds of bizarre calls, not to mention the foxes. With the blaring insect chorus, on some nights it sounds like a bar brawl in our backyard.

There's no question in my mind, though, that I saw the shape of a person with a flashlight. I heard that revolting grunt of surprise when he realized I was in the shed with him and Thomas. I felt him grab us.

An awful thought confronts me before I can stop it: my rapist, Thomas's biological father, is still tormenting me.

Maybe the point of bringing the baby out to the shed wasn't to hurt Thomas at all. Maybe the baby was meant as bait. But if that was the case, I would have been harmed. When I fell onto the grilling fork, whoever was out there could have used it to finish me off, if he'd wanted to. Instead, he'd run away into the woods.

I can't understand how Thomas came to be inside the shed in the first place. He couldn't have been lying where I found him, naked and screaming, and bundled in Sadie's arms on the back porch, safely sleeping, just a moment later. It's not possible. None of it makes any sense, but I have the wound to prove it happened.

Pressing the damp bath towel against my abdomen where the grilling fork stabbed me, I pledge to wash out the bloodstains by tomorrow morning. Sadie waits for me in the bedroom doorway as I grab a pair of my coziest fleece socks from the highboy for her to wear to bed. It's the same drawer where I keep the painkillers. I decide to pop an extra one, just for tonight. This wound is going to kill in the morning, otherwise.

When I locate the orange plastic bottle, I'm surprised to find that it's full of pills. Owen must have stopped at the pharmacy on his drive home from work to refill my prescription. Noticing little ways he could save me trouble and taking care of them, without having to be asked for a favor, is exactly the kind of consideration Owen used to show me all the time. I'll have to remember to thank him in the morning.

"What are those?" Sadie asks as I replace the bottle of painkillers in the top drawer of the highboy.

"Medicine," I say. "Here. Put these on—they'll warm you up."

Sadie pulls on the fleece socks and lets me lead her by the hand back to her bedroom, where Diana is still sound asleep.

"Sadie," I say as we stop in front of the door. "What woke you up earlier tonight? Did you hear something in my bedroom?"

She doesn't answer. In the windowless hallway it's impossible to read the expression on her face.

"Sadie, was there someone in the house?"

She lifts her chin to the side, as if the question confuses her. Then she simply shakes her head, no, and drops my hand. She leaves me standing in the hallway, leaking blood, the bath towel in a pile at my feet.

CHAPTER 19

New, cold sunlight saturates the air in the parlor as I wake up. Flaky piles of gray powder shiver in the hearth; last night's fire has long been extinguished. I must have spent the night down here on the davenport, alone.

Owen's footsteps come sleepily padding down the staircase into the front entryway. Daisy's toenails scrape the floor as she clamors eagerly behind him. I try to remember why I came down here last night and how I ended up in the parlor. Did I wake up hungry and go down to the kitchen in search of a snack? No. I haven't had an appetite in months. Maybe I was sleepwalking.

Through the fireplace, I hear the coffee machine whir to life in the kitchen. Cabinet doors open and close. Owen always used to make cinnamon rolls on Sundays. This morning, he must be baking them special for Sadie.

Sadie. The events of last night come tumbling back to me all at once. I need to find Sadie, to find out what she saw. There's so much I can't explain, even to myself.

Through the fireplace, her sweet, high-pitched giggle blends into a syncopated rhythm with the drip, drip, drip of percolating coffee, and I realize I've missed my chance to talk with her alone. They're all in the kitchen having breakfast together, without me.

The sky outside darkens and shifts ominously. Tentative raindrops begin their gentle patter against the window's handblown panes. *It's raining, it's pouring.* Sadie will have to play indoors again today.

I must tell Owen and Diana the whole truth about last night. It's possible Sadie has already done the same thing. She might even understand more than I do about what occurred, since the details aren't yet coherent in my mind. Regardless of what Owen and Diana have already heard from Sadie, though, I need to go over the facts to prepare, to get my story straight.

When I track the progression of my experiences from last night, the parts I can describe, there's no way around it: they sound like the ramblings of a madwoman. I imagine the way Owen's face will flatten with disappointment as he listens to me recount the incident with the strange man in the shed. Attacked *again*, by *another* man I couldn't identify. Even if he tries to make himself believe me, his eyes will betray his skepticism. Diana will probably outright accuse me of fabricating lies for the fun of it.

The two of them need to take me seriously, though. If Thomas was kidnapped last night, then his life is likely in danger. I'll need Owen and Diana to trust me if they're going to help me protect him.

"Could you please pass me another kind of brown . . ." Sadie's voice floats into the parlor through the cold hearth. "Diana?"

"Yes, honey?"

"Another brown, please. For the roof." She must be coloring with crayons at the kitchen table.

"Here, try . . . this one." I imagine Diana rifling through the gigantic box of crayons, selecting the perfect shade of brown for her goddaughter. Tipping up her chin, peering down the slope of her nose to read the label aloud. "It's called sienna," she says. "That's a pretty name for a color, isn't it?"

A whine comes from Thomas's crib against the wall. I don't remember drying the baby off or cleaning him up after Sadie and I came inside last night. The thought that I could have neglected those tasks horrifies me. After all, last night he was naked on the shed floor, freezing. Wasn't he? Or had Sadie been holding him in a bundle on the back porch the whole time? It's possible he never left his crib in the first place; that neither he nor Sadie was awake with me at all last night. I could have been dreaming, sleepwalking. It seems far-fetched, but every other explanation makes even less sense.

I grasp the railing of the crib and look down. There's Thomas, dressed in his striped footie pajamas, bearing no evidence of the previous night's tumult. His eyes, bright and alert, dart around the interior of the crib. His knees bend and straighten frantically, but he stops moving when he notices my face above him.

Looking up at me with those dark, bottomless eyes, he holds his body completely still.

"Hi, Thomas," I whisper down to him.

His mouth puckers into the shape of a perfect O.

In the kitchen, plates clatter. "Finish up!" Diana says. "We should already be on our way to Mass." Her chair squeaks across the floor as she pushes it back and rises to clear the table. St. Elizabeth's, the Catholic church affiliated with the hospital where I gave birth to Thomas, has a special kid-friendly Mass every Sunday at nine. Driving will be slow and treacherous in the rain. Diana's right to point out that they should have left already if they want to find a seat.

No wonder they didn't bother waking me up for breakfast. I have no interest in attending Sunday Mass, and everyone in this household is aware of my stance. I'll have to wait until after they get back from Mass to talk to Sadie.

Owen's voice drifts through the fireplace into the parlor. "What's that you're drawing, Sadie?"

"The little house," she answers. I rise from the davenport and stoop down in front of the fireplace, hidden from view. Listening.

"I see," Owen replies. "Is that where the three bears live?"

"No, it's the little house outside," she says. "In the woods." I imagine the trajectory of the sienna-colored crayon as Sadie rubs it back and forth, back and forth, over the page.

"Oh, right. Is that one of our neighbors, next to the shed?" Owen asks. "Did you see someone out there?"

Sadie doesn't respond. I crouch as still as possible on the opposite side of the fireplace, listening with all my might.

"That's enough drawing for now." Diana's voice is impatient. "Time to head over to the church."

Ignoring his mother, Owen tries again. "Who did you draw next to the shed, there, Sadie?"

"That's Julie," she says. "With the baby."

Now would be an appropriate time to go in there and explain my version of events from last night. To provide some context for what Sadie's talking about, what she's drawn.

But I'm curious to hear how Sadie will describe what happened last night. And I'm even more curious to hear how Owen and Diana will respond to what she tells them when they don't know that I'm listening.

"What did you say, Sadie?" Owen's voice wavers.

"It's Julie, with the baby," she repeats. "Last night."

That confirms it, then. I wasn't sleepwalking, nor was I hallucinating when I found Thomas in the shed.

When Owen speaks again from the other side of the fireplace, his voice is a thin croak. "Are you saying that you saw Julie out by the shed last night, Sadie?"

"With the *ba-by*," she sings. "When we came back inside to warm up, she gave me these socks to wear. See?"

"That's what I told you, Mom," Owen says. "I *knew* I heard her last night—"

"Sadie, stop it," Diana interjects sharply. "That's enough. It's time for church."

"*Some-thing's wrong with the ba-by*," Sadie sings.

"Stop it!" Diana shouts. "Stop coloring, Sadie, right this instant."

Sadie lets out a shrill sob.

"Don't worry, Sadie," comes Owen's voice, full of comfort. "We can keep coloring when we get home from Mass. We can even set up a life still, if you want. Here, let's put on your raincoat."

"Still life," Diana says. "I'll get Thomas ready and meet you in the car."

The baby's head turns toward the sound of Diana's heels clicking across the front entryway.

"I think you have to go to Mass too," I whisper down to him.

It would be simpler, more reasonable, for Diana and Owen to leave him here with me.

Diana enters the parlor without turning on the lamp and joins me at Thomas's crib side. I position myself behind the blanket draped over the railing, strategically, so she won't notice the blood from where I landed on the grilling fork last night. I need to clean up that wound as soon as they leave the house.

"I can explain about last night," I say, before Diana can confront me about what Sadie's drawn. "It was the strangest thing—"

"We're going to the children's Mass," she interrupts me,

reaching down to gather up the baby from the crib. "Owen's just helping Sadie with her raincoat."

"Oh." Finding a seat at Mass remains Diana's top priority, which means she has no time for an interrogation. That gives me about an hour, depending on the length of the homily, to figure out what the hell happened last night.

"Maybe I'll grab one of those cinnamon rolls," I say. "They smell delicious." Thomas's soft body curls instinctively against Diana's shoulder. It's difficult to keep the envy from my voice. "I'll be here when you guys get back."

Diana takes the baby into the front entryway and drapes a plastic poncho over her shoulders, to protect them both on the walk to the car. I wonder if she'll mention our conversation to Owen.

He didn't bother to look for me in the parlor when he came downstairs, and he doesn't look for me now. Standing alone, staring down at the empty crib, I listen for the click of the front door as it closes behind my family.

Then I head into the kitchen to see for myself what Sadie's drawn. A plate of leftover cinnamon rolls, drizzled in gooey sugar and covered in plastic wrap, waits for me in the middle of the table. My heart softens. Even though I won't go to church with him, I can still count on Owen to save me a Sunday morning treat.

On the table next to the plate of cinnamon rolls lies a sheet of white construction paper. Sadie's crayon drawing. Toward the right side of the page, outlined in peach crayon, she's drawn a cone-shaped human figure. Another,

Thomas-sized cone hovers over the first figure's hands. Sadie's even used a black crayon to scribble a bunch of messy curls around my cone's head.

Julie with the baby.

I'm startled by the sound of the door slamming open. Owen dashes in from the front entryway to retrieve the keys to the Subaru, which he's forgotten on the hook by the stove. With the hood of his raincoat pulled over his hair, he reminds me of the way he looked on the night we met.

"Have a good time at church, babe," I say pleasantly. "Thanks for leaving out the cinnamon rolls." As I speak, a knifelike spasm radiates from deep in my lower belly. I press my hands against it, and they mash wetly into my open wound. Looking down, I find my fingertips sticking together, coated with reddish-brown gunk.

Owen's lips are forming words, but no sound comes out. Then he stops trying to speak and gawks at me.

"Don't be upset—I'm bleeding, but it's not that bad," I say, harshly aware of how I must appear to him. This is a disaster. "I can just run upstairs and clean this up quick. There was someone looking around in the Dolans' shed last night and I saw a light out there, a flashlight I think, so I grabbed the first thing I saw, the grilling fork, in case I had to defend myself, but what ended up happening . . ."

I'm not sure how to finish. This isn't how it was supposed to come out. This is all wrong. Owen's staring at my bloody abdomen, his expression a mix of fear and disgust. I must look like a raving madwoman. Clutching the keys to the Subaru, he closes his eyes for a moment, as if gathering patience. When he opens them again, they're brimming with angry tears.

"Please, just stop it, " he says. "I have to get to Mass." He leaves before I can stop him.

"Okay, bye," I say foolishly. "We can talk about this when you get home."

Car doors slam in the driveway. The Subaru's engine starts up then gradually fades into the sound of the pounding rain.

My husband thinks I've lost my mind. He might be right. I turn back to Sadie's crayon drawing; it's the only clue I have right now about what happened last night. Next to me and Thomas, sandwiched between two very tall trees, Sadie's drawn the Dolans' shed. *The little house.* I trace the outline of the empty rectangle and the opaque, sienna-colored "roof" on top of it. She's used various other shades of brown and green to render the surrounding dirt and foliage.

If Sadie saw someone out there last night, the person who trapped me in the shed with Thomas, she would have drawn another figure, surely. But the brown rectangle is unmistakably empty.

I tell myself that Sadie might not have noticed whoever brought Thomas out to the shed, since they'd been sneaking around, hiding in the dark. That doesn't necessarily mean I imagined the attack last night. It doesn't confirm I'm losing my mind. It's not that I *want* someone to have crept into my bedroom last night, kidnapped Thomas, brought him out to the shed, and grabbed me when I went to find him. That will be catastrophic if it turns out to be true. Still, if Sadie had drawn someone in the shed, or if she'd mentioned something to Owen and Diana about a strange man outside, then at least my next steps would be clear. I'd tell them both exactly what I remembered about last night, without worrying about sounding crazy. We'd go to the police to report the crime and launch an investigation.

If Sadie's drawing matched my memory, it would make it so much easier to talk about all of this with Owen. We could make a pot of tea, sit down on the davenport together, and sort it out. I wish I could trust him to hold me and listen to me and help me come up with a plan to protect our family.

The truth is, though, I'm not sure how he'll react when I tell him what happened last night. None of it makes any sense, even to me. If it sounds like I'm making up a story, it might be the last straw, the final offense that breaks his confidence in me forever. I can't bring this up with Owen until I can figure out if there really was a stranger outside our house—in our bedroom?—last night and if Thomas really was naked out in the shed. Or if, somehow, my mind invented part of it. Could my mind have invented *all* of it?

No, Sadie saw Thomas out there too. *Julie with the baby*, she told Owen when he asked her about what she'd drawn. *Julie* with the baby. No one else.

I have to consider the possibility, then, that I brought Thomas out to the shed myself. The idea is unspeakable. Incomprehensible. Given the obvious gaps in my recollections from last night, though, anything is possible. If I can't trust my own memory, there's no telling what else could I have imagined. What else I could have forgotten.

THEN

CHAPTER 20

"Drink up," said Liza, toasting me with her glass of freshly pressed juice. "Beets are an excellent source of folic acid." We sat on the Dolans' flagstone patio, facing the woods, our legs extended on matching yoga mats. Liza had rolled them out parallel to each other forty minutes earlier.

I balanced my own glass of beet juice, courtesy of the Dolans' new vegetable mastication apparatus, on my engorged belly. "Wow, it's delicious *and* healthy," I said, taking a sip. The beet juice tasted better than any of Liza's previous food experiments, but I wasn't interested in making small talk about gestational nutrition.

I'd made the walk through the woods that afternoon,

ostensibly, to practice yoga with Liza. Another bit of advice from my mother's book. When yoga had come up in *Healing from Trauma* as one of the best ways for victims of sexual assault to reconnect with their bodies, I'd thought of Liza immediately. Who better to guide me in this psychosomatic aspect of healing than the professional dancer and yoga teacher who lived through the woods and happened to be my best friend? Liza was more connected to her body than anyone else I knew. She taught a few different styles of yoga at local studios during the winter, as well as maintaining her daily personal practice. When I texted her that Saturday morning, though, Jacob's Pillow was kicking off its busy season, and I'd expected her to respond that she was slammed in Becket.

To my surprise, Liza had texted back immediately, as if she'd been waiting to hear from me. She'd invited me over to her place after lunch so she could lead me in some gentle prenatal stretching.

I was grateful for the beet juice break, since even the least intense yoga poses were surprisingly exhausting to me. Ever since I'd decided to keep the baby, I'd been following all Dr. Syed's instructions. Daily walks with Daisy. Prenatal vitamins. No weed or alcohol. Not to mention the various diet restrictions. At first, I'd found it exhausting to keep track of all the rules to follow. But soon I'd come to think of those rules as a chance to exert control over my body and this baby growing inside it.

Since the first ultrasound appointment, when we'd learned the baby was going to be a boy, my position had started to shift regarding the identification of the rapist. The baby's biological father. I'd already decided not to perform an invasive DNA test while I was still pregnant, and until now, I hadn't wanted to even think about testing the baby after I gave birth. To do so would set off a chain of unpredictable events with devastating implications. The police would check the DNA results against their database, and they might find a match. Once we knew who'd raped me, Owen and I would have to press criminal charges against them, or otherwise let them go on existing out in the world, probably raping other people.

Berkshire County had recently elected a new district attorney—the first woman to hold the position—and she'd campaigned on preventing sexual violence, among other issues. Still, even if my case went forward, it might be impossible for her office to prove that I'd been raped, that I hadn't gotten pregnant while cheating on Owen consensually, as Diana seemed to suspect.

I'd need to restate everything I could recall about the events leading up to and following the time I'd blacked out at the party, the same way I'd done for Officer Bose. Then I'd need to do it again, over and over, in exactly the same order and using exactly the same phrasing. Countless times, for countless people. Any forgotten information that happened to come back to me could be construed as a lie. If my case even went to trial, I'd need to come up with airtight evidence. I'd need to force myself, somehow, to remember more details about the night I'd forgotten.

Or I could collect them from other witnesses.

A group of burly men emerged from the garage on the far side of the Dolans' home. Some of them carried shovels over their shoulders; others hefted duffel bags into the back of Marcus's pickup truck. I didn't recognize any of them from the holiday party, but at least some of them must have been in attendance. Marcus waved to us as he hopped up into the truck's bed, where he began to rearrange a tarp over a pile of soil.

"Thank god it stopped raining." Liza sighed, finishing her beet juice. "I've been going insane, coming home to Marcus and Donny cooped up here, crushing Millers all night." She rotated her ankles, flexed and pointed her toes mindlessly, the way dancers do. "And Eddie whenever he feels like it."

As if on cue, Eddie hollered instructions to the crew from the driver's seat of a second truck, which could barely contain his massive shoulders. Impatiently, he reached his arm out the window and slapped the side of the door.

"Haven't you been working a lot?" I asked.

Jacob's Pillow had recently opened its stage to the annual rush of summer dance enthusiasts, consuming every last minute of the time Liza might otherwise spend with me. There was no doubt her responsibilities as a choreographer were demanding, but I suspected she'd been using them as a convenient excuse to avoid another awkward conversation like the one on the drive home from Dunbar Brook.

"Constantly." She sighed. "With the festival starting up, work's been nonstop. That's the problem. I don't even have time to plan *sex*."

"You guys are *planning* sex?" I asked, raising my eyebrows. If she and Marcus were actively trying to conceive, no wonder she'd been avoiding me. I was probably the last person she wanted to spend time with. Her best friend who was pregnant but didn't want to be. What a mood killer.

"We're *planning* it, at least," Liza said. "You know the festival took over my life, the second I got back from the city. Marcus and I . . ." She trailed off.

"When's Donny heading back to New York?" I asked.

"Tomorrow. He offered to check in on my mom, but apparently she's having an absolute blast at the new assisted living home. I just heard from her this morning."

"That's good to hear," I said. "And I'm sure it will be nice to have your husband back."

"What do you mean, *have my husband back*?" Liza repeated my words back to me in a way that made them sound like a warning.

"I just meant Donny's been crashing here for a while. What's it been, almost two months? He and Marcus are attached at the hip."

"I know," she exclaimed, relieved at my confirmation that she deserved to complain. She seemed relieved about something else, too, but I couldn't put my finger on what it was. "Maybe once he gets out of here, we'll make a baby."

An unfamiliar spurt of resentment toward Liza caught me off guard. I understood that the whole process of trying to conceive a baby could be incredibly stressful for couples and, despite my impatience with the direction of this conversation, I wanted to be supportive of Liza while she went through it. At the same time, though, I envied her for getting to make the decision to become pregnant at all. She must know that I would trade places with her in a heartbeat.

I swallowed my discomfort, reached over, and squeezed Liza's shoulder. "I'm sorry you're having such a tough time," I said, infusing my voice with empathy. "But it will happen. And when it does, you are going to be such a great mom." The last word—*mom*—broke in my throat.

Liza looked up with damp eyes, suddenly self-aware. "Oh, my god, Julie, I am so—I'm so sorry," she stammered, using her fingers to blot her eyes. "I can't believe I just brought that up with you again. I'm so stupid!"

"You're not stupid," I told her. Marcus, Eddie, and their crew had pulled out of the driveway and the yard was empty now. "I'm actually glad you brought it up."

"I thought you didn't want to talk about it."

"I didn't," I said. "But since I'm going to have this baby, I need to figure out who raped me, even if the police can't. Or won't."

Liza tilted her head to one side. "Can't you just get some DNA from the baby? That would tell you who it was for sure."

"If their DNA happens to be in the system already. But that wouldn't prove to the court that the conception was nonconsensual, unless the DNA matches a convicted serial rapist or something." I'd been researching my options online and had come across a state-by-state legal guide. "And even then," I told Liza, "in Massachusetts, a prosecutor needs to present 'clear and convincing evidence' to prove a rape happened."

"What counts as 'clear and convincing'?"

I shrugged. "Not the testimony of the victim, that's for sure."

"Like, witnesses?" Liza cringed. "Or else, what? The rapist gets off?"

"Worse," I said. "The rapist who's just been identified by DNA could try to claim parental rights to his biological child."

Liza shook her head, incredulous. "Why would a rapist want to take custody of a baby? Their *victim's* baby?"

"To avoid jail time, I guess." The law made perfect, patriarchal sense, and I wasn't surprised at Liza's indignation.

"Hey, ladies!" Donny Rocket emerged from the family room in a sweatsuit. He pulled the sliding door shut behind him. "Can I ask you a favor?"

I wanted to tell him no, that this was a particularly disruptive time to make his request. Before I could politely decline, though, Liza leaped up from her yoga mat.

"Anything for you, Donny." She adjusted her headband, shaking off the remnants of our conversation with a flick of her hair.

"Can I play something for you two?" Donny asked. His hair hung around his stubbly face in dark, unwashed waves. "Maybe you could tell me what you think?" He shifted his guitar suggestively.

The last thing I wanted to do was listen to Donny Rocket play a song he'd written for some band he used to tour with. I might have enjoyed a performance at another time, if it weren't interrupting a crucial discussion about the most traumatic thing to ever happen in my life. Even then, though, I was confident my musical opinion wouldn't matter to Donny.

His request, I suspected, had more to do with Liza, who delightedly pounded the bottoms of her feet on her yoga mat and squealed, "Yes. Yes!"

Donny lowered himself onto a lounge chair in front of us and made a show of tuning his guitar, taking his time.

"So," he said conspiratorially, "don't tell Marcus, because he wants me to be earning my keep by trimming some hedges, or whatever." He began to finger-pick the guitar strings. "But sometimes, you know, you just have to write what comes to you."

Liza giggled aggressively, rearranging her limbs on the yoga mat. As Donny's broad hands strummed along with his baritone voice, she closed her eyes and bobbed her head, unabashedly enjoying herself. Her attitude had shifted completely when Donny arrived, as if we hadn't been discussing my rape a moment before.

I glared down at my bloated belly, unable to hear Donny's lyrics over the resentment buzzing in my ears. Whatever his song was about, I didn't like it. There was something hopelessly unoriginal about the chord progression, something trite. The more he played, the more it bothered me. When Donny was finished, finally, Liza leaped to her feet and exploded into applause. I stood up as quickly as I could, attempting to match her enthusiasm. Maybe a standing ovation would satisfy Donny's craving for attention, and he'd leave us alone so we could continue our conversation.

I needed more time with Liza.

But as I clapped, a fuzziness started nibbling around the edges of my awareness. Then a colorless haze encroached on my vision, opaque, blinding. I slammed into a wall of panic—suddenly everything wanted to destroy me, including my own brain, blaring inside my skull. My skin sizzled on my bones, and I wanted to squirm out of it, leave this skeleton and this body and this self behind and float away into nothingness.

My mind compressed, then started to sink back into an animate darkness. The darkness became viscous and surrounded me, telling me with a dire certainty that nothing was worth all this, that life had turned out to be just as disappointing as I'd expected it would, that it was time now to let go. My suffering had all been worthless, had been for its own sake. I felt ready to give up. That readiness alarmed the lingering part of me that still harbored concern for my body, still cared how it appeared from the outside. *Outside.* I was outside, I remembered. This darkness wasn't a permanent part of me. Frantic, I tried to blink it away, but it stuck to my eyelids like molasses.

Someone's arms were wrapped around my back. Supporting me.

"Julie?" Liza's frantic voice sounded so far away, as if she were leaning over the edge of a well, yelling down to where I was trapped, drowning, at the bottom. My vision came back to me in hesitant splotches, and I could see that she was using all her strength to keep me from keeling over.

Donny held his guitar by the neck at an awkward angle. "What happened?" he asked, taken aback. "Are you okay?"

I eased myself out of Liza's grasp and took a few steps toward the edge of the patio. The Dolans' backyard came into focus ahead of me now, and the unruly woods beyond that, but a bright magenta aura shimmered around the perimeter of my vision.

"I don't feel well," I said. "Something's not right."

What the hell had just happened to my brain? I was too young to have a stroke, and besides, my power of speech didn't seem to be affected in the aftermath. I wasn't slurring my words and I wasn't paralyzed. It must have been some kind of panic attack.

"You're just going to leave?" Liza called after me. "We were in the middle of yoga—Julie?"

"I feel—I have to go home," I managed to say. "I get really light-headed these days, with the pregnancy and everything." If Liza yelled anything else after me, I was too rattled to hear her. I didn't want to stay on the Dolans' patio a moment longer. I couldn't bear to hang out with Liza and Donny after I'd fainted in front of them like that. Donny hadn't so much as mentioned my pregnancy, and Liza clearly saw me as a fragile rape victim who could hardly perform a simple yoga pose, let alone interact with other people. Whatever happened next would only reinforce her perception of me as damaged.

I slowed my pace when I reached the woods, trying to steady my heart rate. I'd never blacked out before, randomly, when I was completely sober like that. I'd never lost my sense of sight for any period of time, even briefly. But I'd also never been pregnant before, I reminded myself.

Pregnancy involved a whole mess of unfamiliar symptoms that would strike anyone as bizarre the first time they went through it. It was possible that I'd simply stood up too quickly when I tried to applaud for Donny's stupid song. Being pregnant, I'd briefly lost my bearings. My sense of stability. It was no more than a temporary setback, though. I'd stop by the Dolans' house again later that week, after Donny had returned to New York. Without him breathing down our necks, accosting us with songs, I'd finally be able to talk to Liza.

NOW

CHAPTER 21

DIANA MEANDERS ON the footpath a few strides ahead of me. Her hair is tied in a single braid, and she's wearing Thomas on the front of her body in a long piece of fabric that she's fashioned into a sling. It should be me and Thomas, walking alone, together. But Diana has made it impossible to keep the commitment I made to Owen, to be a better mother. She won't even let me try. From behind them, I watch Thomas's tiny head, covered in a warm knit cap, as it bobs up over her shoulder with each step.

The leaves have begun to change from green to gold and crimson, tinged with burnt orange. In a few weeks, leaf-peepers in camper vans will arrive from all over to look at the foliage, tooling along at twenty miles per hour down Route 20. Then tourist season will end and the leaves will fall, crumbling beneath the feet of costumed children and saturating the air with the musk of their decay. Each year a few stragglers hang on too long. The stubborn ones that won't let go. They quiver in the wind on withered stalks, clinging to the otherwise barren branches.

After my family returned from Mass an hour ago, I tried to get Sadie alone, to talk about what happened last night. Before I had the chance, though, she left to spend the afternoon with her mother, Kristen. They're going to see a matinee of the new How to Train Your Dragon film. Then, by court order, Kristen has to bring her back here. Back to Diana.

Immediately after Sadie and her mother left for the movie theater, Owen went out again to get some extra paint from Marcus. Apparently, the Dolans have a few cans of powder blue left over from a recent project, and Owen's going to use it to finally paint the third bedroom upstairs, Thomas's nursery. He just as easily could have gone to the hardware store to buy new paint in exactly the right shade, instead of borrowing whatever the Dolans happen to have lying around. That's what he should have done.

He shouldn't have reached out to Marcus for help with anything. Despite my friendship with Liza, Owen always said he never trusted Marcus as far as he could throw him, even before what happened at the holiday party. And since Thomas was born, they've seen each other even less than usual. To me, at least, Owen hasn't so much as mentioned Marcus after that one time he and Liza stopped by, when I acted like a weirdo and hid from them. I wonder what he's doing over there.

I have so many questions for Owen when he gets back, and I'm relieved to have a little more time to gather my thoughts before facing him. Because he'll certainly have questions for me too. He'll want an explanation for what Sadie drew at breakfast this morning. He'll want to know what the hell I was doing outside in the middle of the night last night with the baby.

It surprised me when he told Diana that he'd heard me get up. I hadn't heard Owen stir; I didn't realize he'd woken up.

Ambien was supposed to be stronger than that.

Diana speaks to Thomas with purpose, instructionally, and her voice travels back to me on the autumn breeze. She's playing an observation game with my son, teaching him about the natural surroundings. I hear her describing the colorful leaves, explaining that the rhythmic tapping in the distance is a woodpecker in pursuit of carpenter ants. She points out a milky band of quartz crystal in a schist outcropping, tells the baby it's a reminder of God's majesty, as if he can comprehend the meaning of her words.

"Look at the trees," she coos. "See them up there, Thomas?" Overhead the aspens bend and flutter their heart-shaped leaves obligingly, but Thomas gives no indication that he notices them. "They've been here forever," she says.

Through a cluster of lofty cathedral oaks, up ahead to our left, the Dolans' shed comes into view. I quickly scan the area for a clue about what happened last night, about who might have been out here with me and Thomas, but nothing is amiss. The structure that trapped me inside, so sinister in the darkness, now appears ordinary. Completely unremarkable, expect that someone has looped the dead bolt back through the wrought iron handles on the double doors.

"The oak trees here are big and old," Diana tells the baby, allowing her voice to take on a singsong, storybook quality. "They've watched every person who has ever walked along this path, over all the generations. They even watched the first people, settlers who came here all the way from England, long, long ago."

"And even before the settlers," I add pointedly, "they watched the Mohicans, the indigenous people who established this trail."

"Lots and lots of people," Diana says, ignoring me. "And now here *we* are." She stops walking suddenly, forcing me to stop, too, so I don't collide with her. She leans forward and whispers in Thomas's ear, loudly enough for me to hear, "Do you think they're watching us? Right now?"

Thomas's eyes lock on mine. They widen. Diana turns to face me and we all stand completely still, listening to the air around us.

We're not alone in the woods.

At first it sounds like a small animal intent on scurrying home. Or burying something. But as it continues, the noise grows rougher. Rhythmic.

It's coming from behind the shed.

Next to me, Diana stands frozen, both hands protectively on Thomas.

The partial outline of a bicycle's inverted front tire is visible through the shed's window below the slope of the roof, identifiable by its brand-new treads. I imagine Liza arranging the bicycle against the shed's back wall, posing its body so as not to block all the light from the small window.

Suddenly, there she is, scampering around the corner of the shed. In the very moment I recognize Liza, unmistakably, I also recognize that she's with a man.

Diana shivers and pulls Thomas closer to her body. She makes a beeline back to the edge of the woods, nearly knocking me over.

"Come on, let's get home," she says under her breath. I watch her hurry with my son back through the hobbleberry shrubs, across our backyard, and into my house. But I don't follow Diana.

Instead, I hide against the peeling bark of a birch tree, a few yards from the corner of the shed. Liza's giggle rings out on the crisp air, lustily at first, then hushed by a male voice, playfully stern. If it sounded like Marcus, I'd assume they were messing around while out raking leaves or something.

But it doesn't sound like Marcus. It couldn't be Marcus, because Marcus is at the Dolans' house with Owen, loaning him powder blue paint for the nursery.

There's silence now. The two of them must have heard me. I want to peek around the birch tree, to see what they're doing, but they might be standing right there on the other side, waiting to confront me. Liza and whatever man she's out here with.

So what, if they are? This anxiety I'm feeling is misplaced. I have nothing to fear from Liza. There's no reason to hide from her. As I lean out from behind the tree, feeling ridiculous, the silence breaks.

Heavy, voiced breathing comes from the other side of the shed. The air throbs, suddenly electric with humidity. There's Liza, wearing only a wool sweater with her hair wild, being thrust against the shed by a fully clothed man of average build. I recognize the dark, disheveled bun in his hair.

Without meaning to, I gasp.

"Shit! Shit." Liza swears and scrambles to pull on her jeans. I quickly move from behind the birch tree to a neighboring pine, which offers wider cover. Liza's too preoccupied with panic to notice me. She knows they've been caught. But I don't think she realizes I'm the one who's caught them.

"Go that way," she hisses.

There's an exasperated grunt, a whispered exchange, followed by the sound of Donny's footsteps tearing through the woods and fading in the direction of the Dolans' house.

"Shit," Liza mutters again. From behind the pine tree, I watch her button the top of her jeans, step into her sneakers, and retie them. She makes a slow circle around the shed, scanning the area cautiously, as if she expects someone—me—to leap out at her. After a few moments, though, she drops her vigilance without spotting me. She lowers herself onto the shed's stoop.

I look longingly in the direction in which Diana hurried off moments ago, wishing I were the one who made it home first, carrying Thomas.

Liza rests her elbows on her knees and leans forward. At first, I think she's hunched over her phone, sending a text message. Then I see that she doesn't have her phone out at all. She's holding her head in her hands. Crying.

I should go to her, to let her confide in me about what the hell she's been doing out here with Donny. If our positions were reversed, Liza would do everything in her power to comfort me. But our positions would never be reversed, I remind myself, since I'd never sneak out to fuck Donny Rocket in the woods. And for some reason, I don't want Liza to know I've seen her. I stay hidden behind the pine tree while she slumps over her knees on the shed's low stoop, weeping quietly.

Questions pile on top of each other in my mind. Was this a onetime sexual encounter between the two of them? Something about the familiarity with which their bodies moved together told me it was not. So how long has this been going on? Was it going on last spring, when Donny dragged his guitar up on the Dolans' patio to interrupt our yoga session with that uninspired song?

I think back to the way Liza giggled and tossed her hair, eager to please him. Before I lost my vision, panicked, and fled, I'd suspected that Donny's performance was a pretense to spend time with Liza. But I'd been so distracted by my own misery that I might have missed something obvious between them.

Their affair could have been going on even longer than that. As far back as the holiday party, come to think of it. I mentioned to Liza, accidentally, that I'd noticed Donny flirting with her. And she pretended to have no idea what I was talking about.

She's been lying to my face, I realize. And for what? Liza doesn't need to cheat if she wants to sleep with someone other than Marcus. Long ago, the two of them told Owen and me about the open relationship they'd maintained while they lived in New York; monogamy has never been their rule. But as Marcus's best friend, Donny would likely be off the table as a condoned extramarital partner. That must be why they're sneaking around.

If Donny is here visiting from New York, that means he's staying with the Dolans in their home. He's crashing with his best friend Marcus, helping him out with landscaping projects during the day, and lying through his teeth. At this very moment, Marcus must be helping Owen load containers of paint into the Subaru, completely unaware that his best friend has been having sex with his wife. It's enough to make me feel sorry for Marcus.

Maybe I've been wrong about the power dynamic in his relationship with Liza. That look he gave her in the kitchen the night they brought over the casserole and gifts for Thomas—I assumed it was dangerous. But maybe it was suspicion that I'd noticed in Marcus's eyes. If Liza and Donny are being this careless, maybe he already knows about their affair.

"What the fuck is this?" Liza says, giving me a start. For a moment, I'm sure she's noticed me behind the pine tree. She doesn't come any closer, though. Instead, she squats down beside the shed, to retrieve something from beneath the stoop.

She stands up and opens her hand to examine what she's found. There in her palm is my missing earring. Its golden sheen is barely visible beneath the layer of reddish mud caked on its body and between the points of its wings. It must have been there for months, hidden from the elements beneath the stoop.

I lost that earring the night of the party. That means, however it got all the way out here, partially buried in the dirt by the shed, it's evidence. I'm about to call out to Liza, to let her know I've seen her. We should get that earring to the police. Something stops me, though, an instinct that tells me I'm right to stay hidden.

If Liza's been lying to me all this time about her affair with Donny, what else might she have been lying to me about? I can't trust her with anything now. She's not who I thought she was; or maybe she's exactly who I thought she was.

Before I can decide, Liza straightens up and looks at the sky, as if to guess what time it is. Then she turns and sprints toward her backyard, taking my missing earring with her.

CHAPTER 22

THE HOUSE FEELS dead when I return. I step through the back door and into the empty kitchen. Three paint tins, powder blue, are stacked in the corner by the stairwell. The laundry from the morning has been folded neatly, placed in its basket, and left on one of the chairs. Afternoon sunlight steals through the window blinds, casting diagonal stripes against the timber wall.

A notecard waits, propped on top of the basket of folded laundry. Creased down the middle, it stands on its edges. A little white tent bearing news I don't want to read.

Time slows down as I reach out and pick up the note. Below it rests Owen's silver wedding band. His distinctive, left-handed printing glares up at me in blue ink from the white cardboard.

I'm sorry to leave you with Thomas. I hope you can
understand.
Love, O

Owen left. I sensed his absence in the house when I
returned, and now it's everywhere. Undeniable. This isn't
the same kind of absence, either, as when he's late coming
home from the office or when he's out running errands for
a couple of hours.

He hasn't left in a way that ends.

The vagueness of his note infuriates me. He wrote that
he hopes I understand, but how can I understand when
he didn't explain his reason for leaving? He couldn't even
bother to sign his full name. It's only four letters long,
O-W-E-N, but he didn't care enough to write more than
the first letter. A circle. An empty fucking circle.

My vision blurs as the rage I've been ignoring since
Thomas's birth overflows. Perhaps even worse than Owen's
succinct, cruel note is the fact that he left today, the day
before our fifth wedding anniversary. No wonder he's been
avoiding a conversation about how we're going to celebrate.
No wonder he hasn't asked his mother to babysit tomorrow
night. We were never *going to* celebrate because there's
nothing to celebrate, not anymore. He's given up on me.

After everything we've been through this past year, Owen
chose to abandon me now, when Thomas is only three
months old, a newborn barely past his due date. It hasn't
even been a year since I was attacked at the Dolans' party.
Owen knows that whatever happened on the night I've

forgotten, it traumatized me. And since that night, things have only gotten worse. The pregnancy. The emergency C-section. I've never needed Owen's support more, but he chose to leave me with a premature baby.

He's not only left me with the baby. He's left me with the baby and *Diana*. Since his mother moved in with us her presence has formed another knot, yanking the tension in the house tighter and tighter. I wonder, now, about the truthfulness behind the reason she moved in with us. According to Owen, she came to support us with childcare and chores, ostensibly to help me adjust to the role of motherhood as I healed. He might have invited Diana to move in for another reason, though—one having nothing to do with my recovery. Maybe he brought her here to model for me how easy it can be to care for an infant, if you're the right kind of mother. To show me how it's done. To replace me.

I'm not the only one Owen's abadoned, though; he's abandoned Diana as well. She's the one who's been bringing Thomas around with her in that fabric sling wherever she goes. Not to mention Sadie. I wonder what they'll do now. It seems impossible that Owen could possibly expect the bunch of us—me, Diana, Thomas, and sometimes Sadie—to go on living here together.

Or does he expect me to leave now too?

Owen told Diana that he heard me get out of bed last night, but he never mentioned it to *me* . He even had a chance to ask me, when he came back inside to grab his keys on the way to Mass. Instead, he stood there and listened to me ramble. After Mass, he headed over to the Dolans' before I had a chance to explain Sadie's drawing. *Julie with the baby*. Does Owen think I snuck out to the shed with Thomas, in the middle of the night, for some demented reason that wouldn't make sense to a sane mind? Sadie's drawing suggested as much, and I didn't do myself any favors by blathering incoherently at him. He should have given me a chance to explain, though. There were plenty of opportunities for him to bring it up before he went over to the Dolans'. Before he left me with his wedding ring and a note.

Maybe the reason he didn't ask me about what happened last night is that he knows I'm unreliable. Neither he nor Diana has been treating me like an adult with fully functioning mental capacities, and I can't blame them. It's not as if I'm exuding positive, balanced energy these days. Whatever *this* is—this bone-deep, sucking darkness that's always lurking at the border of my consciousness—probably looked like laziness from the outside, at first. Now they must assume I've gone completely crazy.

It's one thing if Owen believes the worst about me, that I'm a cheater, a liar, a terrible mother. I'm afraid, though, that he assumes the worst *for* me. He must think I'm psychotic, like Pamela Dwight Sedgwick, a prisoner in my own mind. And he's abandoned me here.

It comes down to Then and Now. Then, even with all the unknown and terrifying circumstances surrounding my pregnancy, Owen was there for me. He listened to me, trusted me, and supported my decision-making the best way he knew how. I did the same for him. The Owen who held me on the davenport while I cried, breathing in together, then out together, again and again until I'd calmed down, never would have left me on the day before our anniversary.

Now, after Thomas's birth, he's been different. He's taken on much more of the childcare than either of us intended, it's true. That's never been fair. But the Owen I know and love, Owen Then, would have risen to the unexpected responsibility. Fatherhood was his only purpose in life, ever since he'd missed out on the other side of that relationship. Instead of embracing our new family, though, Owen has been sulking. Childcare responsibilities, which had been the pinnacle of his hopes and dreams, have turned into a reason to avoid me rather than to bond as a family. He's hardly been speaking to me at all. He's left *Healing from Trauma* on the side table for me to revisit, bookmarks deliberately placed, but now that gesture seems more passive-aggressive than considerate. As if placing my mother's book beside the davenport, unmentioned, even counts as a supportive gesture.

We used to like to sit in silence together, usually on the davenport, reading or working or playing on our phones. Now, if we happen to be in the same room, he leaves as soon as he can find an excuse. Sometimes even without an excuse.

I've been different too. Over the past three months I've been far too distracted to even attempt to understand what this ordeal must be like for Owen. It's not that I haven't been interested in his emotional landscape, necessarily. It's that I haven't been interested in much of anything other than dulling the lingering pain from the surgery. Then there's the fact that before Diana moved in, before Sadie came to visit, I told Owen that I would focus on our relationship. I told him I'd prioritize my mental health, that I'd learn how to care for Thomas. I promised him that I would become a better mother, but I haven't followed through.

I've let him down. The realization settles over me like a shroud of shame. I've let Owen down, and the more I think about it, both of us have been letting each other down for months. We've been drifting past each other through the rooms of our house, lying in bed next to each other some nights but falling asleep and waking up alone. I can't remember the last time we cuddled on the davenport in the parlor.

If I'm being honest with myself, the distance between us has festered so long that it's become almost comfortable, like the familiar pain of a stab wound before yanking out the knife. The fear of what comes next is so intense that the distance hasn't been hurting me as much as it should.

This hurts, though. This feels final.

He left his wedding band behind, so it has to be final. That ring was a symbol he'd insisted on buying; he's the one who cared about tradition. I grab his ring from on top of the laundry pile and slip it on.

The blaring silence in the kitchen is interrupted by the sound of Diana's socked feet coming down the stairs. Reaching the landing. If she's been upstairs this whole time, then she doesn't know Owen's gone. He must have avoided confrontation by leaving while I was outside and Diana was upstairs. I worry, fleetingly, that I'll never see him again.

The light over the kitchen table flickers on.

I slide off Owen's wedding band and place it back where he left it, on top of the folded laundry. For some reason, I don't want to tamper with the scene. It feels important that Diana should witness exactly what her son has done. Owen's note lies unfolded, exposed. There is no hiding it. Diana will know that I've read it and I cannot bear to meet her eyes.

Her plan worked. After all her months of needling, she finally convinced her son that I've been lying to him about the night I can't remember, and now he's left our not-real marriage after all.

Diana isn't gloating, though. She doesn't scoff at me, nor does she comfort me. She stands stoic, her arms limp at her sides and her face unreadable, staring at the piece of paper.

It dawns on me that in his haste, Owen didn't write "Dear Julie" at the top of his note. Diana might assume the message is intended for her.

"He left his wedding band with that note for me," I blurt. I meant it as an explanation, but it comes out sounding pathetic. My husband has abandoned me with a child I never wanted and here I am, searching desperately within his last, callous gesture for a modicum of love. As if the fact that he deigned to leave a note—two measly sentences and an abbreviated salutation—makes his betrayal any easier to forgive.

That coward ran away, while his mom was upstairs and I was outside. He didn't just leave. He fucking absconded.

I hope you can understand, he wrote.

"I understand," Diana answers, still not looking at me. I hate her for what her son has done.

The doorbell rings, and we both jump. Before I can say anything, Diana goes into the front entryway and opens the door for our visitor.

I can't decipher the words from the kitchen, but the voice's melodic timbre is unmistakable. It's Liza. She's driven over, for some reason, instead of walking. She must have turned around and come directly here after she made it home, out of the woods. She and Diana exchange a terse greeting, and the front door closes again. I remain rooted in place beside Owen's note.

Soon, Diana's footsteps pad back upstairs from the front entryway. She's brought Liza into the parlor and left her there to wait for me. Liza must have lied and said I was expecting her. I wasn't.

She knows I saw her and Donny out by the shed. She's come to confront me and demand my silence. Or, I realize with a twinge of humiliation, she might be here to check up on me. It's possible that she already knows Owen's left me, that she found out the news before I did. He was over at her house, wasn't he, right before he dropped off the paint for the nursery? The paint he borrowed but apparently never intended to use.

I wasn't prepared for her to show up here today. I thought there would be more time to figure out what was going on. Without knowing what Liza knows or believes, I can't imagine how to approach her. But I don't have to, because she's standing in the kitchen doorway.

She's wearing the same gray, loose-knit wool sweater and her hair is pulled away from her face witha a plastic headband. Poised on the threshold, she hesitates like a performer unsure of her cue.

"Liza, hi," I say. "Come on in."

"I found your earring," she says too loudly, without moving. "It was out by my shed. I took it home and put it in a Ziploc bag, so it's safe." She pauses, balancing on the threshold. "Were you there too? In the woods today?"

She knows I was.

"Liza—" I say, gathering my thoughts. She must have seen me hiding behind the pine tree, but she doesn't know how much I saw. She doesn't know that I witnessed her cheating on Marcus, that I recognized Donny. If I lie to her, though, she'll lie right back to me. "Yes," I admit. "What the hell are you doing?"

"I don't know what I'm doing," she says, pressing her palms together in front of her body. "The thing is, Donny's the only one who's been there for me, really *there* when I needed him, and I know it would kill Marcus, but I can't help it if I love him—"

"Hold on, you *love* Donny Rocket?"

"—and it's like I don't even *know* Marcus anymore," she continues as if I hadn't interrupted. "He's been so horrible . . ." Her face crumples into tears. "Oh, Julie," she cries. "I've been horrible too. I was the worst friend. I'm so sorry."

"It's all right," I tell her even though it's not all right, not really. I've never experienced loneliness like these past few months. Liza's commitment to her work, even her mother's ongoing health crisis, doesn't excuse the way she's dropped off the face of the earth since Thomas's birth. I've needed her, and she hasn't even bothered to send a text.

I respect this new straightforwardness from her, though, and if I'm being honest with myself, I'm not interested in judging her for having an affair with Donny. There were so many questions I'd wanted to ask her, so many lies with which I'd wanted to confront her, when I saw them in the woods. But now that she's standing before me in my kitchen, all I want to do is give her a hug.

Before I can move, she grabs Owen's note from where Diana left it on the table.

"Oh, yeah, that's from Owen," I say, as if the note was something I'd been about to mention anyway.

Liza's shoulders fall as she reads the note silently. But instead of the shock I expect to see on her face, there's only a mix of sorrow and determination. She's not surprised.

No one else will be either. If Owen believes Diana's story, there's no reason for anyone else to doubt it. They'll see me as an unfaithful basket case. He'll be seen as the victim. My victim.

Liza places the note back on the table, neatly folded, although for a moment it looks like she wants to crush it in her fist.

"He was gone when I got home just now," I say.

"Well, *I'm* still here," she says firmly, and I'm overwhelmed with gratefulness for her friendship.

"Thank you," I say. "I need to prove I was raped."

Liza is nodding as if this has been her idea all along. "Let me help you."

"A DNA test would fill in the details I can't remember," I say, feeling buoyed by her confidence. "It won't prove the sex was nonconsensual, though. Like I told you, the biggest risk is that Thomas's biological father could sue for custody."

"You said you called the Elizabeth Freeman Center hotline the night it happened, right?" she says. "That's not exactly evidence, but it proves you were upset, that you needed help that night. It should count for something."

"Right," I say. "At this point, I've already lost Owen to a lie. He thinks I cheated on him, no matter what the DNA test says." I point at his note. "I have to take the risk. I need to know who raped me."

Liza's face brightens. "Marcus is at home. He's there right now," she says. "After I found your earring out by the shed, I brought it home with me to hide somewhere safe, and his pickup truck was in the driveway."

"Can we go there now?" I ask. "Can we talk to him together?" Marcus has already lied to my face twice, but I'm hopeful that I'll have better luck with Liza there. She's his wife, after all; she might be able to coax the truth from him.

"We can try," Liza says. "Come with me."

THEN

CHAPTER 23

LURID STREAKS OF flickering light danced across my sight. Dozens of them. I blinked at the wiggling, menacing stripes, tried to clear them away. The night before, while I'd been rinsing the shampoo from my hair, similar flashing streamers had encroached upon my peripheral vision. I'd rested my weight against the shower wall for what felt like only a few minutes, until the streamers had dissipated. I was going to tell Owen about it when he woke up this morning. I hadn't gotten the chance.

This time, the sensation wasn't stopping.

The tile floor was cold on my bare shins as I leaned against the edge of the powder room toilet. I used the sleeve of my bathrobe to wipe the vomit from the corners of my mouth. The slight movement reawakened the terrible pain that had bloomed between my eyes in the middle of the night and hadn't gone away. It felt like an ice pick performing a sudden, enthusiastic lobotomy.

"Owen!" I cried. Desperate tears collected in my eyes, further obscuring my already blurred vision. "I'm seeing those lights that Dr. Syed said . . ." It was impossible to form a coherent sentence. The sharp, driving pain burned brightly behind my forehead.

Owen appeared in the doorway within seconds. He flew to my side on the floor by the toilet, which he flushed without mentioning its contents.

"You're having visual disturbances?" Leave it to Owen to remember the technical term. "Are they still there? Do you still see them?"

"Maybe they're fading." I let Owen help me up and onto the closed lid of the toilet. There was no reason for us both to be in a state of panic, I reasoned. When the stabbing headache had started last night, I'd chugged a full glass of water, as Dr. Syed had instructed me to do. But by now I'd vomited it all back up, along with that morning's oatmeal. The visual disturbances were probably the result of dehydration, I told myself. Nothing another glass of water wouldn't cure. "I guess they're gone now," I said.

They weren't gone, though.

"Just to be safe—" I didn't finish my sentence before Owen was helping me up again, grabbing the keys from the hook by the stove, and helping me ease my distended body into the passenger seat of the Subaru. We both knew what this meant. We had to get to Dr. Syed's office. Just to be safe.

We took the same route that we'd driven a little over a month earlier on our way to the ultrasound appointment where we'd found out that Thomas was going to be a boy.

Owen pulled the Subaru into a spot right at the front of Dr. Syed's parking lot. He came around to help me out of the passenger door. The intensity of the visual disturbances had faded but I still had that pounding headache.

I was rushed into the exam room whose walls were covered with cross-section diagrams of pregnant bodies. The one that most closely resembled my own, now, was labeled *Seven Months*, and I studied the fetus drawn inside it. It no longer looked like a lima bean, or even a tadpole. I imagined that frail creature breathing, its lungs expanding and contracting in rapid flutters. I imagined it struggling for air, the translucent throat convulsing, the lipless mouth gasping and choking. Numbly, I wondered whether that kind of death was happening to the would-be baby boy inside me.

The door opened immediately, and Dr. Syed stepped inside, followed by Owen, who pulled the rolling stool up next to the exam table where I was sitting and grabbed my hand. It looked strange in mine, like I had never seen it before. My own hand was clutching his, and it, too, looked foreign to me.

My eyes darted back to the diagrams on the walls but suddenly I couldn't tell what they were even supposed to represent. The words labeling the different parts of the pregnant bodies blurred into gibberish. They weren't even written in English. They didn't make any sense.

I stood up quickly, panicked, but couldn't catch my balance. My swollen, sweaty fingers braced against the linoleum counter. Nothing in the room felt familiar.

Something was wrong and I tried to tell Owen, but before my mouth could form the words, I tipped forward into darkness.

NOW

CHAPTER 24

THE CONVERSATION IS going nowhere. Sitting next to Marcus on the Dolans' sectional couch, I'm careful to maintain enough space between us so that it's clear he and I are on different teams. Liza stares him down from the doorway to the foyer, her hands balled into fists.

"I already told you what happened that night," Marcus says. "Way back when it happened, I told you!"

"You had a neat little story, didn't you?" Liza snaps.

"It wasn't a story." The words land individually, slowly. He's making an effort to cooperate with his wife's interrogation, probably for my sake. "I found Julie behind the house, cleaned her up—you know all this."

"Why were you outside?"

"What do you mean?"

"You said you found her on the back lawn," Liza says. "What were you doing outside?"

"I told you," he says. "I was cleaning up."

Marcus warily relays what he told me and Owen the morning before we reported the rape to the police. Some part of me hopes there will be new information sprinkled in about the night he found me. Something to fill in the details I can't remember.

Instead, though, he tries to punt the conversation over to me. "Julie said she couldn't remember anything."

"I can't," I say.

"But *you* remember," Liza says to Marcus. Her voice drips with bitterness. "You found her out on the back lawn that night, right? And she was missing an earring?"

"What? I don't know," Marcus says.

"It doesn't matter," I say quickly. I shoot Liza a harsh, sideways glance that I hope will shut her up. She seems to be on the verge of telling Marcus about the evidence she discovered out by the shed. If he's lying to us about where he found me on the night I can't remember—if he's lying about anything, which he almost certainly is—Liza would be a fool to show him our cards.

"Whatever," she says, backtracking. "The earring doesn't matter."

"Wait, I remember now," Marcus says. His forehead is creased in concentration. "Julie *told me* she was missing an earring."

I remember now too. I mentioned the earring to him when he drove me home that night.

"I've been looking everywhere for that earring," I say, hoping Liza will play along. But she's not paying attention to me. Her eyes glisten with intensity as she trains them on her husband.

"Whose baby is it, Marcus?" she asks.

He shrugs and doesn't answer.

Liza's voice sparks with rage. "Marcus," she says, "Thomas is yours, isn't he."

The weight of her accusation hits me full force, at the same time as it hits Marcus. "Oh, my god," I say. "Liza, are you serious?"

Marcus stares at her, his mouth hanging open, as if he's forgotten I'm still in the room. "You think . . ." He can't finish the question.

Tears are streaming down Liza's face but her voice doesn't waver. "You lied to the police," she says. "But you can't keep lying to me."

"Oh, *I'm* lying?!" Marcus's face transforms, as if an animator has redrawn it into a mask of fury. The ridge-line of his jaw shifts beneath his skin. His eyes glaze over and harden. "You're the one fucking around with Donny, Liza," he says. "And now you're acting like I did something wrong." He sits back on the couch, crossing one ankle over the other knee and folding his arms in triumph.

Even if I didn't know Liza as well as I do, it would be obvious that she's working hard to make her face unreadable. She needs to find out how much Marcus knows. How much she can still get away with. "Don't change the subject," she says. "And—don't be stupid. You know that's not true. About Donny. We're just friends."

I look over to see if Marcus is buying this. He is not. His eyes narrow to slits.

"We both know what you've been up to," he says. "Because I have proof." He pauses, as if he enjoys torturing his wife. Then he snarls, "I installed cameras over a year ago, all over this property."

Liza blinks a little too casually. "Where did you even . . ."

"I still had them in storage, after we moved back from the city." An arrogant smile creeps across Marcus's face. "You thought I'd sell all my old equipment?"

Liza recovers her composure. "If you installed cameras all over the place, over a year ago, then I guess you must have footage from the night of the holiday party."

Marcus nods again, still smirking.

I'm sure my face looks as horrified as I feel. "You need to give that to the police," I say. "You should have done that already, Marcus."

"Where did you tell the police you found Julie that night?" Liza demands. "Out in our backyard, right?"

"How many times have I told you this?"

"Let's go look at what happened," Liza says.

"What?" Marcus and I ask at the same time.

"Let's go look at the footage your hidden cameras got from the night of the party. Before you 'found' Julie outside." Liza makes dramatic quotation marks with her fingers to underscore that she strongly doubts his version of events.

Marcus stands abruptly and claps his hands. "Fine. Let's

go," he says. He isn't smiling anymore. To no one in particular, he adds, "It wasn't me."

"I guess we'll see on the cameras who it was, then," Liza
snaps as she trails him into the foyer and up the sweeping
staircase. "I guess we'll find out, once and for all."

I follow them. I'm ready.

Muted scenes from different rooms in the Dolans' house
flash across one of the wide computer monitors in Marcus's
office. Liza and I watch over Marcus's shoulder as he takes
us back in time over a year. From the look of it, he's installed
discreet cameras in nearly every room of their mansion.
Somehow, Liza never noticed over the past year that she
was being recorded. The gross violation of privacy makes
me angry on her behalf, but then I remember why he felt
compelled to set up the cameras in the first place.

Candid, security-style footage of the Dolans' everyday
lives plays in fast-forward before our eyes. Marcus playing
beer pong with Eddie and his landscaping crew in the finished basement. An elderly gentleman—Marcus's father,
maybe?—unknowingly coming very close to pressing his
nose right into a hidden camera that must be positioned
over the toilet in their downstairs powder room. Liza preparing an elaborate meal in the kitchen, wandering in and
out of the frame of a camera tucked behind some incon-
spicuous appliance. Marcus and Liza making enthusiastic
love in their giant bed. Before I can look away from that
last scene out of politeness—although at this point, we are
far beyond politeness—Marcus clicks over to a window
displaying a wide view of their backyard.

He freezes the video and says, without looking over his shoulder at either of us, "This is the night of the party."

"Good," Liza says. "Play it."

The mouse clicks again and the screen flickers to life.

Nothing happens at first. The camera seems to be positioned along the railing of the back patio. The staircase down to the yard is visible in the upper-left corner of the frame, and the rest of the screen is gray, an expansive lawn obscured by darkness.

Marcus clicks impatiently along the timeline at the bottom of the screen, speeding up the playback of the recording. We fast-forward through the last minutes I can remember of that night, barreling toward a truth I've been avoiding for nearly a year.

As the milliseconds tick by along the bottom of the screen, I imagine what I must have been doing during the party right then, at 9:56, 9:57, 9:58 p.m., perhaps even being recorded on another camera inside the Dolans' house. Was I accepting someone's seemingly friendly offer to bring me a new drink? Was it already too late for me?

10:35 p.m. We all see it at the same time.

"There," Liza yells, waving her hand at the monitor. "There's a light or something. Pause it!"

Marcus clicks to pause the video.

"Go back," she instructs.

He sighs dramatically, making a show of being put out by the whole exercise. "Fine," he says, trying to make his voice sound exasperated. But I can tell from the look on his face that he's genuinely curious about what we're going to find.

He scrolls in the opposite direction, taking us back, back, back to the time before I was raped. He clicks one more time and we all hold our breath.

The staircase down to the backyard flashes white as the frame washes out with light. Then the picture suddenly comes into clearer, brighter view, illuminated by the wobbling beam of a flashlight. After a few seconds the beam of light widens, dulls, and disappears. The back lawn is empty again.

"That's it?" Liza seems to be thinking the same thing as I am. She's leaning across the keyboard to grab the mouse from Marcus. "Let's get a different angle," she says. "Where's the footage from the camera inside the living room? Did you put one in the butler's pantry?"

Marcus doesn't try to stop her. "Sure did," he says. "But it would take months to find the right file. I haven't gotten around to organizing all the different feeds from the interior cameras." His nonchalance sends a chill creeping down my spine.

"Haven't gotten around to organizing . . . ?" Liza steps away from the computer monitor and stares at Marcus, her face contorted in disbelief. "How could you just be sitting on this evidence?"

"I was trying to—to catch you," Marcus stammers.

"You've been hiding this footage from the police, from everyone, for almost a year," Liza says. "And the whole time, I thought—"

"It doesn't matter." His voice sounds very small and distant.

Suddenly, the floor of his office seems to tilt upward and away from me so that I slide off it. Helpless, I plummet into a void whose edges I can't fathom. A different voice, comforting and terrifying at the same time, emerges from somewhere deep in my memory.

"Come with me," it beckons.

CHAPTER 25

I LAND WITH a heavy thud on a different floor. The floor of the Dolans' storage shed. My right earlobe burns with fresh, searing pain as my earring is ripped out, the metal backing yanked straight through.

At first, the only thing I'm aware of is a man breathing unevenly beside my ear. His hand comes into focus on the floor beside my head. It's chapped and covered in blood. He cut himself on the wing of that little golden sparrow, I realize, before he tore my earring out. His raspy breath merges with the far-off sound of someone screaming and fills the space inside the shed, vibrating with an urgent violence, and now it is everywhere.

I don't feel the dampness from the floorboards soaking through the fabric of my shirt and melting into cold filth against my back. I'm completely separate from the body trapped beneath this man's horrible weight. I'm nothing more than a vibration, like the scream that rattles the shed's walls around us.

Free of my body, I realize something with a comforting certainty. Ever since Thomas's birth, there's a legitimate reason I've been putting off the DNA test. I haven't had any desire to know who his biological father is because I haven't *needed* to know.

I've spent what feels like an eternity searching for some version of bearable truth within this horror. I've gathered the slippery fragments of memory, clutched at half bits of information when they flutter like debris to the forefront of my mind. I've collected them like clues.

But after all, I haven't been receiving intentional messages from "another, wiser place," as Father Eagan put it. No one's guiding me from some invisible, ethereal world that makes infinite sense—what Owen calls "God in heaven." No grand scheme has been orchestrated to lead me to the identity of this rapist.

The rapist isn't important enough for that.

What he did to me will always be wrong, in every sense of the word. It shouldn't have happened, and it doesn't belong here. It doesn't belong in my story. He forced himself into my life, into my narrative. He's loomed there ever since, but he doesn't deserve the space. This story isn't about him.

Letting go isn't about him either. He probably never thinks of me at all, and I could hate him for it. I could hate him for not knowing that I hate him, for not even caring whether I move on from what he did to me. Whoever he is, though, it doesn't matter to *him* whether I choose to hold on to the terror of what he did to me that night or not. He doesn't suffer in the least when I allow the fear to swirl like fumes in my chest, exhausting me, waiting to smother me in my sleep.

The only person who is worse off for not letting go is me. This truth is suddenly a part of who I am, and who I will always be from now on. It vibrates right along with me, in synchrony, as if we are one. As if it's been waiting for me to notice it here and let it match my frequency. The truth is that I can let go of him. He will not be real for me anymore.

As soon as that acceptance settles over me, I come back into my body, below his. My limbs, which had been numb, suddenly course with inexorable strength. With more power than I've ever felt, I press my forearms and knees against his chest and shove. Hard. His body takes the impact, then it disappears, vanishing into the darkness of the shed like a ghost.

I'm alone on the floor of the shed. The screaming fades to a dull ringing in my ears, then evaporates nearly into silence. Whoever raped me is gone but the stench of his breath lingers for a moment in my nostrils. Stale beer mixed with something else, something distinctive that I haven't been able to remember clearly enough to identify until this moment. But now, briefly, the odor is unmistakable. A menthol cough drop.

CHAPTER 26

"YOU *KNEW* IT was Eddie." Liza's incredulous voice drags me back into Marcus's office. She's jumped up from her chair so the two of them are eye to eye.

I can still hear someone screaming, but it's far away. I have no idea how much time has passed while the truth has come flooding back to me. How long I've been sitting here, completely blacked out. It hasn't been long enough, apparently, for Liza or Marcus to notice anything is wrong.

"Obviously," Marcus says. Condescension curdles around the corners of his words. "He's my little brother."

"Why?" Liza shouts at him. "Why would he *do* that?"

"How the fuck should *I* know?" Marcus says. "He was wasted."

"Did you see him rape—"

"I asked him later, the next day, if he'd hooked up at the party, or where he'd disappeared to for like, half the night," Marcus says.

"And that's when he told you?"

Marcus scoffs. "What did you want me to do, call the fucking cops?"

Liza shakes her head back and forth in disbelief. "You've been protecting him," she says. "At the trial, the judge will need clear and convincing evidence to prove—"

"Whoa, whoa, whoa." Marcus holds up a hand. "Eddie's got a prior, remember? The fight outside Bucky's? You can shut the fuck *right* up about a trial, Liza."

"*You* shut the fuck right up," I snap at Marcus. The brutal screaming gets nearer, as if its source is somewhere in the room with us. "Do you guys hear that?"

"Even a DNA match doesn't prove it," Liza continues as if neither of us has spoken. "Because Eddie could just sue for paternity rights if the Porters accuse him. He could take Thomas."

I nod in grim agreement. She was listening that day during yoga on her back patio, after all. I assumed she'd forgotten everything I said after Donny interrupted us. She took my words to heart, though.

"Eddie hates kids," Marcus says.

"I know, but if he got custody of Thomas, then he wouldn't be convicted of the rape," says Liza. "And you know how Eddie would treat that baby."

"Then maybe the Porters should just let it be," Marcus says, clearly impatient with the direction the conversation has taken. He'd been perversely excited, I realize, to catch his wife cheating on him. He wants to get back to the footage from the hidden cameras.

"Fuck you, Marcus," I say. "We're not going to let it *be*. Eddie raped me and Owen's convinced I cheated on him."

"Eddie will tell everyone it was consensual," says Liza. "That Julie actually wanted to have sex with him, or that they were having an affair or something."

The impatience on Marcus's face has been replaced by something darker. "Maybe it *was* consensual," he says, and each word is like a hammer to my sternum: Maybe. It. Was. Consensual. That's how he plans to testify, then. He'll say that he witnessed me having consensual sex with Eddie the night I got pregnant. If we push this to a trial, Marcus is willing to lie under oath to protect his little brother.

Liza's eyes widen in horror. "You would . . ." She shakes her head without finishing. Then she snaps into action, heading for the doorway. "We have to tell Owen it was Eddie," she says as she passes my chair. "Let's go."

"Liza." I'm about to stop her but I change my mind. Maybe she has the right idea.

Now that my memory has partially returned, there might be a way to save my marriage. I remember that Eddie cut his hand on my earring, badly; it will be covered in his DNA. I'll tell Owen that I'm ready to test Thomas's DNA and we can do so immediately. Once we get the results, that earring will be the evidence we need to prove it was Eddie who raped me. Liza will happily testify as a witness, if she needs to, that I never would have had consensual sex with him.

I need to get in touch with Owen and tell him that I remember now. I need to tell him that Marcus has known it was Eddie all along. That he hid the video evidence. Maybe once he knows the truth, Owen will come home and fight for our family.

Liza's already on her way down the hall.

"Owen was over here earlier today," Marcus says, as if I'm not standing right there. He rises and crosses the room in one stride, following Liza. "They tested the DNA last week, before the kid even left the hospital," he calls after her. "Owen already knows."

The screaming blares louder, until it drowns my awareness.

Owen already knows.

If that's the truth—could that be the truth?—Diana must have convinced Owen to discreetly test Thomas's DNA at St. Elizabeth's before he was discharged on the thirteenth. I try to imagine how something that important could have happened without my authorization. It's possible they handed me a stack of paperwork and lied to me about what I was signing. Owen should know better than that, but I wouldn't put it past Diana.

Over the past week, when I've overheard the two of them discussing Thomas's DNA test behind my back, I've assumed they were deciding whether to do it without my permission or not. But they'd already gone ahead and done it. Owen has known who raped me for almost a week now.

He's known that the lab found a DNA match, and that it was Eddie, and he's been hiding it from me.

Owen never keeps secrets from me. He should have told me as soon as he found out. There's only one explanation, one reason he would lie. It's the same reason he told Diana not to bother pressing charges against Eddie with the results of the DNA test. "It isn't going to fix anything," I'd overheard him say, back when I believed they hadn't yet done the test.

He said it wouldn't fix anything because Owen believes I cheated on him with Eddie. He believes I lied to him, and to his mother, and that I tricked him into making a false report to Officer Bose, all for the sake of concealing a decision to have consensual sex with Eddie *fucking* Dolan. He believes I coerced him into raising the child of the person with whom I betrayed him. No wonder Owen hates me. That's the person he thinks I am.

It explains his heartless note. I thought he wanted to work on our marriage, to coax me out of my depression, to help me remember how to feel like a person again. I thought he wanted to build a family together with Thomas. But he left me today without even mentioning the results of the DNA test. Without giving me a chance to convince him to stay. He must have been planning to leave me ever since I gave birth to Thomas. It would have been too cruel to bail on me while I was pregnant, regardless of the circumstances. Even Diana wouldn't have condoned it. Now, though, Owen believes I've carried on a charade, *pretending* to have been raped, for months after giving birth. If that's the extent to which he mistrusts me, no wonder he's been biding his time with one foot out the door. I wonder if he ever trusted me.

The sound of screaming is everywhere now. High-pitched and hopeless, it ricochets off the far corners of the room and charges back at me, cramming itself down my throat and into my lungs. It fills my body, triggering a burst of pain in my abdomen. It's been days since I tripped over the fallen log and landed on the prongs of the grilling fork. It should be healing, but it's getting worse instead. The pain billows outward, throbbing angrily.

Instinctively, I bring my hands to the wound. The skin presses away from my fingertips like loose earth along the edge of an open grave. My flesh caves inward, damp, rotten.

It's started to decay.

As I feel my body collapse into itself, I finally understand the source of the noise that fills every particle of space inside the room. It's been me, all along. I've been the one screaming.

CHAPTER 27

"SOMETHING'S WRONG WITH the baby."

I manage to choke out those five words before I lose my power of speech.

No; it's not the baby. Something's wrong with *me*. Thomas's body is still a physical component of my own, still buried in my uterus. I'm watching myself from the outside, witnessing Dr. Syed's office from a perspective completely removed from my physical form. If this is an out-of-body experience, it's also out-of-time. I immediately recognize Owen's Guster T-shirt from that day months ago, back in the middle of June, when my "visual disturbances" wouldn't go away. He's sitting between the exam table and the counter, still holding my limp hand. My body is slumped over his lap, motionless.

Everything looked so strange to me before I lost consciousness in Dr. Syed's office, but now I experience the scene as vividly as the one I just remembered in the shed, which simultaneously occurred three months later than where I am right now—in mid-June, at Dr. Syed's office, with visual disturbances—and somehow, at the same time, moments ago.

What happens next feels more like déjà vu than like remembering.

Dr. Syed snaps into action and administers aid to my unconscious body. Amanda jogs into the room pushing a stretcher ahead of her. She's already on the phone with the team at St. Elizabeth's, the hospital where I'm supposed to give birth—but not until twelve weeks and four days from now.

They move swiftly to get my body onto the stretcher, with one hip propped on a pillow to support the weight of my pregnant belly. Amanda rushes me past the no-longer-smiling receptionist out to a waiting ambulance.

In the operating room at St. Elizabeth's, the loudest sound is the conflicting rhythm of two desperate heartbeats. They emanate from monitors attached at various nodes to the torso pinned open on the surgery table. Hushed instructions and questions buzz among the assistants, the nurses, and the obstetrician.

A blue privacy curtain blocks the gore from Owen's view. He looks much too pale. I recognize the anger on his face, and suddenly, it makes sense to me. From above, I see everything clearly, for the first time.

Thomas is delivered from my open abdomen, born extremely early at only twenty-seven weeks of gestation. He's cleaned, measured, and whisked away to the neonatal intensive care unit, where the nurses will coax him to vitality. He will be incubated and fed from a tube. He will learn how to live.

One of the assistants does her best to sew up the wound where my uterus has been sliced open but her hands won't stop trembling, and the obstetrician doesn't correct her work because it doesn't matter. They let Owen stay by my side for as long as he wants to. He holds my hand until it's over.

When it comes down to it, there was a split-second choice between two lives, between two stories, and the choice was made. The tiny creature that would become Thomas had existed, dreaming, for twenty-seven weeks. That was too long for the doctors at St. Elizabeth's to risk losing it.

Thomas would get to live but he would never get to have a mother. The full truth has never been obscured from me, only unnoticed: I haven't really been here at all, and I will never belong here again.

I'm overcome with a sedative sense of comprehension. Scenes from the past three months unfold before me anew, but through a different, focused lens.

I see Owen recoil from my touch, ignoring me—mostly— when I tried to engage him. I see him feeding, changing, and bathing Thomas, desperate for his mother's help. He sits across from Father Eagan at our kitchen table, struggling to make sense of how he could have ended up in this situation, raising the child of the man who'd raped his wife. Alone. *Why did Julie have to suffer?* I haven't been speaking to Owen, haven't been touching him, haven't been sitting beside him on the davenport at all. I've been haunting him.

I see Liza, clairvoyant, standing alone in my kitchen after I caught her with Donny in the woods. *Let me help you.* She listened to me the same way I'd watched her listen to a different ghost in the Sedgwick house, years earlier.

I see Diana redoing all the chores whenever I attempted to help her, mistakenly thanking Owen for completing the tasks I was sure I'd done around the house. Refolding the laundry. Swaddling and unswaddling the baby. I see her whispering to Father Eagan in the entryway, confessing to him that I'd initially considered having an abortion. *They'll have to live with that, Father.* She was concerned for Owen and Thomas, coping with that knowledge.

I see Sadie drawing a crayon picture of the shed for Owen and Diana. *Julie with the baby.* I've needed Sadie, and she's needed me to play a role in her story these past few months too.

I see poor Thomas belonging in my arms, and also belonging at home with Owen. Existing at once as a living, breathing, human child, and simultaneously as a ghost, with me—if only when we were together in the shed, where this all started. It's only in the shed that I've been aware of my body, at all, since Thomas's birth.

I assumed the painkillers were steadily numbing me to the physical world. But now I see the orange plastic bottle again, as it looked when I found it in the top drawer of the highboy. Full, unopened. It wasn't my prescription, though.

Owen didn't leave the house because he thinks I was unfaithful or because he hates me. He left because I couldn't see that I was the one who was meant to go.

When Diana saw his note in the kitchen—the note he left for her to find there—she said "I understand" aloud to an empty room.

Finally, I understand too.

CHAPTER 28

On the other side of the woods, in the home Owen and I built together, Diana stands at the kitchen sink. She holds one of Sadie's plastic dishes beneath the faucet and absentmindedly moves a soapy sponge across its surface. At the kitchen table, Sadie is coloring a field of wild-flowers with a brand-new box of crayons, a gift from her mother. Kristen was sober when she brought Sadie back from the movie theater this afternoon, and she promised to return in the morning for another outing.

The whole room aches with the weight of Diana's sorrow. I can't believe I didn't notice it before. Distracted by my conviction that she was trying to turn Owen against me, I couldn't see how hard she is working to provide stability for him, for Sadie, and for Thomas.

I don't know how to approach Diana or what I can do to make any of this bearable for her. All I can think of is to stand directly behind her and try to absorb some of the melancholy emanating from her body.

Almost immediately, she stops washing the dish and catches her breath. For a moment, she doesn't move. I focus on imparting the room with the gratitude I feel, and she exhales slowly. Her shoulders relax.

I know she understands what I want her to understand: her presence in our house has saved Thomas. It's saved Owen too. She's been wallowing in regret for treating me unkindly while I was alive, but she doesn't have to do that anymore. I'm deeply thankful for what she's doing, for what she will continue to do for the rest of her life. She is taking care of the people who needed me.

Now I understand the struggle she and Owen have been facing over what to do with Thomas's DNA test. All their tense conversations make sense. They've had the results since they brought him home, as Marcus said. They weren't debating the test; they were debating what to do with the information they already had.

Diana's been trying to convince Owen to go to the new district attorney and formally accuse Eddie of rape, but she has more faith in the justice system than Owen does. She wasn't in the conference room with Officer Bose. Owen must have done some research and discovered the same thing I did, that if he presses charges, Eddie could demand parental rights as a strategy to avoid a rape conviction. If that strategy succeeds, Owen will lose Thomas. He can't bear the risk of having to hand his son over to Eddie's custody.

Obviously, Julie's not going to tell you herself, I remember overhearing Diana say to Owen in the front entryway. *But maybe she wants you to do something about it.* She'd sensed the truth, or perhaps I'd somehow conveyed it to her from where I was lurking in the stairwell. I did, indeed, want Owen to do something about it. Desperately. He'd been right to tell her, though, that DNA wasn't going to be enough to prove that Eddie had raped me.

Something stirs on the other side of the fireplace. I leave Diana and move into the parlor to investigate the noise. Owen is there, hunched forward in the red rocking chair with his forearms resting on his knees and his head lowered.

He came back.

His eyes are clenched shut, his brow furrowed. In his hands he holds a small, rectangular cedar box, its surface unfinished. His lips move around familiar words. "*Thy kingdom come. Thy will be done in earth as it is in heaven . . .*" His voice cracks around the word *heaven*.

He's trying to pray.

Curled up beside the fire, Daisy breathes a sleepy little lament. I recognize it as the sound that brought me into the parlor just a moment before. I lean down to stroke her forehead.

In the crib, Thomas, squirms contentedly in his swaddle. His eyes glisten and I know he recognizes me. He will never know his mother. But this period of three months, this time we've stolen together, has been just long enough for him to feel the weight of my hand resting on his chest before waking. To hear my voice in his soft, seashell ear. His eyes flutter closed again and he sighs, falling back into sleep.

None of this is fair or right. I shouldn't have to say good-bye to any of them. The only comfort I find is in knowing that they felt me near them during this time, in between, before I could let go. They've let me comfort them. I've let my own mother comfort me, too, through *Healing from Trauma,* her life's work.

I want for Owen and Thomas and Diana what neither my mother nor I had: a long life free of any further tragedies. I want Owen to have the option to find closure around what happened to me, to take the case to trial if he wants, to learn the whole truth. What I want, though, has nothing to do with how Thomas's life began or how any of their lives will turn out in the end. That will be up to them.

"... *as we forgive those who trespass against us . . .*" Owen recites.

With horror, I recall the last time Owen saw me, when he'd come inside to grab his car keys before Mass. I was standing in the kitchen, bleeding from the wound in my abdomen that I'd just discovered. It didn't make sense to me yet, so I convinced myself I'd fallen on a grilling fork. Owen must have been terrified to see my ghost, rambling about a strange man hiding in the shed, clutching at the place where they'd removed Thomas from my body.

I must have appeared that way to Eddie, too, when I found him snooping around the shed with his flashlight. Returning to the scene of the crime. The thought of how I terrified him out there—without even meaning to—provides a fleeting, vengeful thrill.

Owen, though, I feel compelled to leave with something better than that gruesome image of his wife. Now that I'm closer to the rocking chair, I can see the box he's holding in more detail. Across its surface, he's engraved my name. This must be what he made from the cedar planks that were left over after we rebuilt the deck. It's the anniversary gift I overheard him telling his mother about, right before he asked her to move in. Below my name, he's etched *February 5, 1990–June 16, 2019*.

My birthday. And Thomas's.

I watch Owen for a moment longer and an idea comes to me. I'll do this now, while he's praying, so he'll always have something to hold on to. I sit down on the ottoman facing my husband and gently wrap my hands around his, so that we're both holding the cedar box he made for me. The box that holds my ashes.

Owen's lips stop moving, but otherwise he doesn't react. Breathe in together. And out together. I wait.

"There you are, Juju Bear," he finally whispers, as if it's a year ago and he's simply caught me daydreaming. But he doesn't look up. His gaze is focused on our hands, which are clasped together over his lap.

"We should have had more time," I say. "I thought we'd have more time."

I lean toward him so he can feel my face pressed against his. His tears dampen my cheek and remind me, for the last time, what it feels like to cry. I tell him that he will be a wonderful father to Thomas, that he already is, and that my life was made more beautiful because I spent so much of it with him.

As for my death, Owen doesn't know what it's been like for me since we rushed to the hospital that day in the middle of June, and he cannot know. I recognize an opportunity for solace, though, a way to help him heal. I tell him: "After the car accident, I've always been afraid, since I knew what that moment would feel like, just before, when there would be nothing left to do but wait for death to come. And, babe, I never had to experience that." I stop and wait for him to look up at me, to show me he understands. "I never knew that I was dying."

Everything I've ever known to be true about love looks back at me from his face.

"So, you see?" I tell him. "There was nothing to be afraid of." I wrap him in the warmth of my voice and hold him there, so that he'll never forget what this feels like. Whatever else Owen comes to believe in, if he ever remembers how to pray, now he knows that he can believe in this, right now, and now, and now.

"There's nothing to be afraid of," he repeats.

"Owen?" Sadie's standing on the parlor threshold. "There's a stranger at the back door, here to see you. She says she's your neighbor."

Liza appears in the front entryway behind Sadie, holding two Ziploc bags. One of them holds my missing earring. The other holds a thumb drive. "I have evidence," she says, simply.

Owen's eyes spark with understanding. This could be enough. It has to be enough. Thomas will be safe.

"Thank you," Owen says.

I remain in the parlor for a final moment, sending all the comfort I can summon into their broken hearts.

And in the next moment, when I will be nowhere to be found, they will still have my story to believe in. I leave it behind when I go. It becomes one of the hundreds of stories that whisper throughout that old home and all others, pressing against the floorboards and rustling across the open hearths, reminding the living of what you are and everything there is to lose.

ACKNOWLEDGMENTS

Thank you to my Wattpad readers, whose generous feedback in 2017 and 2019 helped shape this final version of *Night, Forgotten*. Your words of encouragement have meant everything over the past five years. Thank you to the folks at W by Wattpad Books, especially Deanna McFadden, Monica Pacheco, Rebecca Mills, Delaney Anderson, Amanda Gosio, and Crystal McCoy. Thank you to Katie Joyce, Dr. Mary Joyce, Joan Tozer, Erin Putnam, Kara Guthrie Bleday, Dr. Robynn Stilwell, and Jessica Caimi for your time, open-mindedness, and loving guidance as this novel has evolved, and to Drs. Nadia Mohamedi and Saloni Malik for sharing your expertise and endless enthusiasm as early readers. For believing in my writing and activism since 2013, thank you to everyone on the team at Wattpad (past and present), especially Ashleigh Gardner, Caitlin O'Hanlon, Nazia Khan, Alysha D'Souza, I-Yana Tucker, Aron Levitz, and Nick Jones. Thank you also to Crissy Calhoun and Adrian Van Young for your early developmental editing passes.

For your spotless hospitality during the COVID-19 pandemic, thank you to Raine and Emberlie at Om Oasis in Aptos, California; Tanya and Calder at Creekside Commons in Freshwater, California; and Jared and the ghosts of the Granary at House on Golden Hill in Lenox, Massachusetts. Thank you to Erin Hunt for teaching me about historical renovation for universal accessibility at the Bidwell House, Jennifer Goewey and all the folks responsible for the crucial work at the Elizabeth Freeman Center, and Robin Spooner for sharing your vast knowledge of the area surrounding the Hoosac Tunnel. Thank you to the redwood trees, especially the six growing in my backyard, the Frank and Bess Smithe Grove, and the McKay Community Forest.

Thank you to Norka Saavedra, Gloria Martínez, Laura Daniela Villa Méndez, and the Kids World staff at the Bay Club in Walnut Creek for providing enriching entertainment for my young children while I worked on this project. Thank you, especially, to Joan Tozer, David Leader, and Isaac Tozer for helping look after our family's needs so I could take solo writing retreats.

I am forever indebted to the teachers and professors who encouraged me as a writer and scholar of music, especially Dr. Stefanie Tcharos, Wayne Chatterton, Stephanie Kelsch, Neil Kulick, Jim Kelly, Dr. Daniel Albright, and Dr. Carolyn Abbate.

To my parents and siblings, Dr. Mary Joyce and John Joyce, Katie Joyce, Brian Joyce, and now Ali Joyce: thank you for always believing in my abilities as a writer while wholeheartedly supporting my goals related to the performing arts, music scholarship, and feminist activism.

Finally, to my chosen family, David: thank you for my writing room and for working so hard every day to make this dream life possible. Home is wherever I'm with you.

ABOUT THE AUTHOR

MEGHAN JOYCE TOZER was raised outside Boston, Massachusetts, and graduated from Harvard University. In 2013, Meghan founded The UnSlut Project, an online community for survivors of sexual abuse, and she is both the author of *UnSlut: A Diary and a Memoir* and the director of *UnSlut: A Documentary Film*. After earning a PhD in Musicology from the University of California, she moved to San Francisco's East Bay where she now lives with her husband, their two young children, and their dog. *Night, Forgotten* is her first novel.

RESOURCES

Rape, Abuse & Incest National Network (RAINN): www.rainn.org
*Anti-sexual violence organization; operates the National Sexual Assault
Hotline (800-656-4673) and an online chat hotline (online.rainn.org)
in partnership with local sexual assault service providers in the United
States.*

Canadian Association of Sexual Assault Centres (CASAC):
www.casac.ca
*Network of sexual assault crisis and prevention centers; includes a direc-
tory of rape crisis centers and transition houses throughout all provinces
of Canada.*

Guttmacher Institute: www.guttmacher.org
*Research and policy organization advancing an evidence-based
definition of sexual and reproductive health and rights worldwide;
includes an online tracking tool for abortion policy.*

Center for Reproductive Rights: www.reproductiverights.org
*Global human rights organization of lawyers and legal advocates;
includes a map of the legal status of abortion in countries around the
world, updated in real time.*

National Network of Abortion Funds: www.abortionfunds.org
*Network of independent abortion funds connecting patients to financial
and logistical support for abortion care, inside and outside the United
States.*

DISCUSSION QUESTIONS

1. What feelings does this book evoke for you? What stands out to you most in its exploration of trauma, motherhood, and fatherhood?

2. Several people exert control over Julie's reproductive choices. Owen buys her pregnancy tests before she's ready. Her mother-in-law orders, "You will not kill this baby." The climax in the hospital concerns a "split-second choice." How does choice impact Julie's story and fate?

3. How do the "THEN" and "NOW" timelines impact you as a reader? What's different about Owen and Julie's characters before and after Thomas's birth?

4. Julie struggles to say out loud to her husband that she was raped, as it seems to make the assault all the more real to her. What role does spoken language, or

lack thereof, play in Julie's family life, "THEN" and "NOW"?

5. The main insight in *Healing from Trauma* is for sur-vivors to "reconnect with their bodies in order to feel like themselves again." When and how does that moment happen for Julie? For Owen? By the end of the book, has either of them healed? Why or why not?

6. What do we gain, as readers, by the physical setting in a refurbished 1770s farmhouse?

7. Owen and Julie first met shortly after a traumatic experience for Julie. How did that set the stage for their relationship throughout the book?

8. Julie realizes that her mother was traumatized from giving birth to her. How does the book explore the effects of intergenerational trauma? Consider dynamics between Julie and her mother, Owen and his mother, as well as Sadie and her mother.

9. Sadie loves creating "still life" art, depicting objects before her in real life. What should we infer about her drawing of the shed and "Julie with the baby" inside it?

10. Consider the title, *Night, Forgotten*. Why do you think it includes a comma?